GREEGS

Mitchell Mendlow

CreateSpace Edition

Cover Art By: Ian Adams
donecreative.ca

Short Stories by Mitchell Mendlow available at
http://wattpad.com/mitchellmendlow

Free Ebook @ http://mitchellmendlow.wordpress.com

THE BEGINNING:

of Greegs and Things... but mostly of Greegs

CHAPTER 1

the First Chapter

Hmmm, where to start?

Not on Earth, that's for sure! It is true I am writing this book for publication on the planet Earth in an Earthling language. But all I really have to say about the planet Earth is this:

Not a great place to pop by and fuel up your space ship.

The ship I first came to Earth on was fuelled by investment bankers. Generally agreed upon as the most useless organisms ever to exist in the vast history of time and space, it's common knowledge the only thing they are good for is fuelling space ships.

Common knowledge isn't very common on Earth.

You would think this abundance of investment bankers and lack of common sense would make Earth a damned fine place to pop by and fuel up your space ship.

If you had the same experience I had, then you would not think of it as a great place to pop by and fuel up your space ship.

If you had a space ship.

Which you don't.

Now, many millennia of Earth stories have trained your brain to believe that for a story to truly be a story, it must start with one character (a protagonist), and that person must be followed on a journey in which they will encounter various obstacles in order to arrive at their destination. Without meeting this singular character early on in a story, you may be curious if this is even a story at all, rather than just a random assortment of descriptions of silly creatures on silly planets.

Don't worry. There is a story to be told here, but there's no point in telling it until you understand the setting in which the story takes place. Since you know absolutely nothing about this place, it's going to take a little bit of time. Imagine how little you know about the hair follicles in Julius Caesar's left nostril. Double it, dip it in chocolate sauce and then multiply it by a quintillion or two. That's how little you know about this place. This is how we tell stories in the rest of the universe. Time to catch up.

The main trouble I will have trying to describe the world in which this story takes place is one of tense. To me, from my perspective, all of these events have happened in *my* past. But I am acutely aware that much of it does not occur in *your* past. There is a tense in many alien tongues for this exact literary dilemma. Alas, no such luck with English. Please bear with me in the opening chapters, as I appear to jump between the present and past tense. On the simple, linear time-line of your average human, all of these events have actually happened in what you would call 'the future.' But from the perspective of me, it is the past, and from the perspective of the actual story it is the present. So whatever it is, whenever it is... just be happy knowing that it is. Or was. Or will be. Kind of.

This story begins (began, will begin some day) on a planet you've never heard of. This isn't saying much, considering most of you can only name nine on a good day. A fairly pathetic feat, when you imagine the mind-blowingly infinite sea of planets there are out there, but every species has to start somewhere I suppose. (Pluto is a planet by the way, not sure what it did to your astronomers to deserve being demoted.)

This planet exists (existed, will exist) in a solar system quite unlike your own. There are fifty-nine suns in this one solar system. (Or at least there will be some day, and definitely was when I was there). There are as many as forty-seven planets revolving around each of these suns. Four suns have no planets at all doing anything around them. Near the middle of this vast network of gaseous orbs and rocks there is one sun about five times the size of your own. This sun has thirty-eight planets performing gravitational hula-hoops around it. Eleven of these planets support 'life' as you would define it. In truth, everything is 'alive' (and dead for that matter) but I won't try and persuade you otherwise. You seem fairly set in your ways. Fairly certain of your definitions. Fairly resilient in your steadfast determination to continue believing in your institutions, your corporations, your religions, your political leaders, and most astonishingly... your investment bankers. So I shan't attempt to convince you otherwise. Instead, I will just tell you this little story.

Once upon one of these eleven planets there existed a population of Greegs.

Greegs are a mutation, much like yourself. Not a rare group by any means, you'll find them many places in the vastness of space... unlike yourself.

However, it *is* extremely rare that Greegs will actually find themselves the most intellectually evolved creatures on a thriving planet. In most scenarios Greeg populations would be kept under tight control for fear of wreaking havoc on their planet and the other species on it. They are used primarily as carnival attractions. In small numbers they are harmless and amusing. Sound familiar?

Completely oblivious to this universal normality, The Greegs on this planet found themselves to be dominant and unchecked. They were indeed running the show. Without a multitude of other species keeping their population under control and letting them know how inferior they were, these particular Greegs found themselves blissfully suffering from delusions of grandeur and overdosing on self-importance.

Imagine this!

Even though they were sharing a solar system with 59 other suns and could plainly see several, habitable planets with the naked eye... they were quite certain that their planet was the only one that ever did, ever would, and did currently contain life.

To really make things almost sad, The Greegs believed something else: That all of the other suns and planets and galaxies and universes; all the big things, all the small things, and everything in between that ever did exist in the whole entirety of everything and anywhere... were put there just for them. A kind of mobile for The Greegs to look at and go 'Well, isn't that nice and pretty... thanks for that.'

To make things infuriatingly, impossibly, really just plain difficult to comprehend even a little bit, The Greegs also held another collective opinion. They actually, genuinely believed (with a straight face nonetheless) that they were the smartest and cleverest creatures to ever exist. What a laugh!

Above all though. Above all of their beliefs and primitive understandings of their place in the grand scheme of things, The Greegs suffered from one delusion greater than any others.

Everything The Greegs did, every action they took, every decision they made, was fuelled by one insatiable desire. They desired to obtain and retain large amounts of schmold. Schmold was a green, glowing, sticky, gooey substance that was found deep in the core of the planet. Schmold mining and preservation was the number one priority of all Greegs. They couldn't possibly even consider doing anything without first thinking how much schmold it would cost or what effects it might have on the schmold trade.

Schmold served no actual purpose whatsoever, except that Greegs thought it looked really neat. The ultimate sign of wealth and status and accomplishment was to take a schmold bath. The poorest Greegs would never have, nor could they ever logically hope to obtain, even a little bit of schmold. But they would dream.

"One day, I'm going to make it so big. I'm going to be so successful that I will take a schmold bath every week," they would say.

Clearly no one could ever be so lucky.

CHAPTER 2

the Rebel Groolfh and the Planet Garbotron

Only once was there a Greeg who did not dream of taking a schmold bath. His name was Groolfh, and he had the shockingly original revelation that one was much luckier for *not* taking a schmold bath, as to bathe in schmold is to make oneself filthier than the bottommost layers of Garbotron, an uninhabitable planet used only as a dump for countless millennia. Garbotron was well-known as the worst smelling place in existence. I can attest to this fact, having seen Garbotron with my own eyes; that is to say, having seen the noxious green vapours surrounding Garbotron from 8 light years away. The planet itself is only visible while actually standing on the surface, yet to stand on the surface is to die within seconds. No mortal creature is exempt from this rule. Even if you're a life-form that is biologically incapable of the sense of smell, your mind will instinctively know that you are standing in a place that smells too awful to comprehend, and not wanting to take the chance that through a miracle you suddenly acquire the ability to smell, will shut itself down in a manner best suited to the occasion.

Another important fact about Garbotron is that one doesn't even need to go remotely near it to experience its danger. A dark day in Galactic history was the time an interstellar wind had the unfortunate timing to pass directly through Garbotron's Diaper Mountain. The name Diaper Mountain is slightly deceiving. It isn't really a mountain. More a sort of hemisphere. Defying the logic of space with its unstoppable stench, the forgotten memories of Diaper Mountain casually drifted across several light years before settling down on a peaceful, reddish planet. Sadly, this reddish planet was inhabited. All 9.7 billion resident creatures promptly suffered death when the logic-defying stench arrived. It is a good thing sound does not travel through space as well as aroma, for the screams of the dying creatures were so shrill they would have devastated beyond repair the nearby planet Glassvexx, thus sending millions of shards of apparently unbreakable Jardian mega-prisms hurtling through the cosmos for most of infinity.

Groolfh, justifiably believing he'd made a discovery that would forever transform the history of the Greeg, went forth to one of the highest-up committees in charge of schmold distribution and attempted to explain the futility of bathing in schmold. He passionately argued that bathing in schmold makes you infinitely less clean. He was met with a unanimous vote of disdain and bewilderment. 'Something as ridiculously expensive as schmold is clearly worth taking a bath in' was all the committee said before sentencing Groolfh to death for daring to think otherwise. Groolfh was fired out of a cannon aimed directly at Garbotron VI. Luckily he was vaporized in the atmosphere, however the wind of the cannon fire had the unfortunate timing of passing directly through Diaper Mountain on its way to a peaceful reddish planet.

If these particular Greegs were aware of life on other planets, and were able to notice the interconnectedness of life in the universe as well as I am, they might have adopted a motivational motto that went something like this: 'To deny the usefulness of bathing in schmold is to cause 9.7 billion creatures to die horribly of Garbotron suffocation.'

Such a revelation was not had.

CHAPTER 3

Greeg Career-Paths

Greeg children often fantasized about their future adult career. The only difference with Earthling children, who dream of being any random thing like an actor or a scientist, is that Greegs' career choices were entirely limited to one of the many sub-categories of schmold production. However, Greeg children were still free to dream about which exact area of schmold production they would like to be a part of. Schmold Tunneler? Schmold Taster? Schmold Bathroom Attendant? Some children had high hopes, announcing to proud parents they would one day be the owner of their very own schmold Dealership. Some children aimed their sights low, announcing to embarrassed parents they wished to be a lowly schmold Bottler.

"No son of mine is going to settle for working as a Bottler!" was a phrase commonly heard screamed by the father of the Djoog household. "We won't be able to afford a drop of schmold on the pension of a bottler! What is it? You think you aren't important enough for upper management? I suppose you also think the suns and planets weren't just put there for your own enjoyment?"

"Don't be harsh," the logical Djoog mother might have said. "We don't want him to start pouring water into a schmold pit like the Glurj boy."

"The Glurj boy tainted our schmold pits out of jealousy, because those useless Glurjs never owned a drop of schmold in their whole schmold-less life! Do you want to wind up like a Glurj? Unable to walk down the street without people pointing at you and laughing?"

I later checked in on the Djoog household. Their son fulfilled his dream of being a bottler. With his paltry salary the family were able to afford no schmold at all. In a fit of shame the father leaped into a schmold pit. Although dead, the Djoog father was henceforth thought about with great reverence and jealousy by all Greegs, as it was widely believed that leaping into a schmold pit was the greatest bath one could take.

CHAPTER 4

Further Arrogance and Schlepschen Pools

There are many questions I'm certain you have swirling around your head already regarding the culture, behaviours, beliefs, activities, government and history of The Greegs. One thing you should be asking is "What is the name of the planet these silly creatures live on?" To be truthful though, these particular Greegs have not found it necessary to name their home planet, as astounding a concept as that may be to you. Space mapping space mappers once labelled it "one of 11 planets containing wriggly, walky, breathy things in the hopeless, undeveloped but reasonably entertaining to look at from a safe distance sun system of the 38 planets in the 59 sunned district of Herb," and with that dismissive but wholly accurate generalization, they went on to map, in much more detail, several of the more illustrious and glorious areas of the many universes they happened to be mapping at the time.

The Greegs simply called it 'our planet.' Despite measuring only 597 cm tall on average, (well done with the metric system earthlings, at least you did get something right) the Greegs still had the audacity to believe that their entire planet (measuring an astounding 87, 000 km in diameter, on average) *belonged* to them. As if they had any say in the matter. As if they had any idea how they even got there in the first place. They genuinely believed its only reason for existing was to offer them a steady supply of schmold and to act as their planetary shelter. Not that they knew or cared about what it was sheltering them from. Then again, these were creatures that believed all plains of existence were merely inconsequential pretty things for them to look at. What an arrogant, self-absorbed bunch of jackasses, wouldn't you say?

Another question you may be asking yourself is why The Greegs would be so keen to take a bath in a sticky, wet, green goo. How could they possibly think this was a splendid idea, no less a sign of wealth and status? To be true, if you took aside an individual Greeg and tried to get them to explain to you the rationality behind worshipping a glowing, greenish slime they would not be able to give you a satisfactory or remotely logical explanation. They would look at you in disbelief and say things like "It is the most precious substance that exists, you fool! Why wouldn't we want to obtain loads of it and bathe in it?" You would be hard pressed to shake them from this line of thinking. Even if you did shake them from this line of thinking, the best case scenario would involve them telling other Greegs involved in high up committees and eventually being blasted out of a cannon towards a garbage planet.

You might also be wondering what it is that Greegs do should they be so fortunate as to have a bath of Schmold. Surely they don't just wash it all off afterwards or put their clothes on?! No, they do neither, because Greegs do not wear clothes. They are a naked creature. Hairy, smelly, naked and filthy. Filth is a sign of prestige and honour in the Greeg society. Nakedness, doubly so. To understand why this is the case, you must first understand a bit more about the unnamed planet these filthy, wretched, naked things live on.

One of the 11 planets containing wriggly, walky, breathy things in the hopeless, undeveloped but reasonably entertaining to look at from a safe distance sun system of the 38 planets in the 59 sunned district of Herb is arguably the cleanest, most spotless floating orb within forty seven trillion parsecs of the 11 planets containing wriggly, walky, breathy things in the hopeless, undeveloped but reasonably entertaining to look at from a safe distance sun system of the 38 planets in the 59 sunned district of Herb. The planet is stunningly, immaculately, and amazingly clean. Spotless surfaces that look like varnished marble, shiny glass windows and freshly bleached tile floors abound. All of the things that live on the planet are clean and tidy. They all work cohesively in a truly mind blowing balance, each playing their role in keeping the place absolutely spotless. Gorgeous. Clean. Fresh. Beautiful.

All... except The Greegs. The Greegs look at the cleanliness of the planet in disdain. They may go out on a field trip to view the clean parts of the planet, but just to take a look at. It gives them an icky feeling if they stay out there too long. They much prefer to stay in their filthy mud camps, bogs, marshes and Schlepschen pools. The places where The Greegs reside in great numbers look like big piles of garbage dumped on the otherwise pristine landscape. No one can be sure, but this is most likely because the places where The Greegs reside in great numbers ARE big piles of garbage dumped on the otherwise pristine landscape. Greegs treat their planet as if they were a pack of unruly teenagers, anti-establishment punk rockers and street people whose distant relatives died and left them a ridiculously fancy home. They've done nothing to earn such a nice place, and have no appreciation for its value or how to keep a house like this in order. In fact, they view the house as a sign of snootiness they want no part of. As far as they're concerned, about the only good thing about the house is it has one hell of a liquor supply in the basement. The liquor supply is schmold.

CHAPTER 5

Coverings

To be caught wearing clothes is a most heinous crime. There is no need to inflict punishment, merely the embarrassment of being publicly seen 'all covered up' is enough to send any Greeg into self-inflicted exile. No Greeg has ever been seen 'all covered up' in public without banishing themselves into "the cleanliness," as they call the savagely clean lands outside their "civilization."

It should be noted that despite the fact that no Greegs wear clothing, there are many clothing stores full of coverings for all parts of the Greeg body. It is silently agreed that no respectable Greeg would ever be caught dead in one of these filthy smut shops. Astoundingly, if one was to do the math, they would find that nearly every individual Greeg must have stashed away hoards of cover magazines, coverings, and other cover related paraphernalia. The only industry on par with the lucrative schmold trade was covering.

To be sure, there are Greeg 'Cover Bars' where adult Greegs can go and watch lower class daughters of schmold bottlers cover up their fingers and toes, or maybe even arms, legs and torsos depending on just how skeezy the establishment and how badly the coverers need the schmold. To cover up the genitals would never happen, even in these scummy outposts. Covering the genitals only occurred during the act of procreation. The Greeg equivalent to what you humans would call "Sex" involves an ornamental and intimate genital covering for both male and female. The male covering is a tube that sucks ejaculate out of the male Greeg, funnelling it into a seal-able and sterile tube, where it can be kept for over forty hours. To complete the act, the sterile tube is placed in a receptacle attached to the side of a covering that looks similar to an earthling gas mask. The gas mask forms a suction around the female genitals with a tube leading inside her, directly to the womb. The male ejaculate is pumped into the elaborate female covering and transported right to the biological doorstep to complete an "Attempt."

The Greegs have the highest fertility success rate of any creature on record in any universe.

In their daily lives Greegs are a filthy and disgusting and vulgar creature in every imaginable way. They go out of their way to show off just how slovenly and insensitive they can be. In the private act of procreation however, they are clean, sterile, sensitive, caring and humble. It could be said this is the real Greeg, the one they keep suppressed.   In this act of procreation alone, they become one with the planet on which they reside.

CHAPTER 6

Quiggs

The grimy condition of your average Greeg colony was not always easy to maintain.   The Greegs' desire to live in disastrous mud camps was once put under great threat by an indigenous life form known as the Quigg. Quiggs are (or more appropriately, were) the cleanest creatures living on one of 11 planets containing wriggly, walky, breathy things in the hopeless, undeveloped but reasonably entertaining to look at from a safe distance sun system of the 38 planets in the 59 sunned district of Herb. Whether randomly or because the planet was trying to save itself from obliteration, the Quigg seemed to have evolved with a single purpose in life. To clean. Every bodily function they have (or had... well, you get the idea, or will in a moment) in some way results in something, somewhere being cleaned. The very movement of their feet acted as a natural waxing agent against any surface. Rather than having sweat glands they secreted an antibacterial gelatin from their skin. Instead of hands and fingers they had elaborate scrubbers and brushes protruding from their arms. They also wished for nothing more in life than to be rid of filthy Greegs. In a valiant yet futile attempt to return their planet to its once immaculate state of varnished marble, shiny glass windows and freshly bleached tile floors, the Quiggs offered their impeccable cleaning service to the Greegs, free of charge. All the arrangements had been made to blast anything unclean onto Garbotron. The Greegs would have to do no work at all. Rather than dignify this gracious offer with an answer, the Greegs simply hurled globs of lesser-quality schmold at them from a distance. The blindingly acidic and parasite-ridden properties of schmold indeed make a formidable weapon, however the attack did not deter the Quiggs. Instead of fleeing back to their various homes in The Cleanliness as they should have, the Quiggs in their steadfast manner set about collecting schmold and cleaning it. Only they didn't just clean it. They reinvented it. A stunningly impressive chemistry set was designed specifically for analyzing and purifying schmold, with the intent to remove from it all traces of bacteria and filth. Filtering screens visible from space were built and hung up between the largest of old-growth blue-leaf trees. Quiggs could be seen tirelessly running schmold through the filters day and night. They even successfully removed schmold's unique glow, which was considered distracting and superfluous to the high art of cleaning. They laboured for many suns and moons, perfecting their experiments with a meticulous attention to detail that has only been matched once in the universe (by a strange being we will arrive at much later in the story). They even went so far as to spend 3 wintry years crafting a collection of very fine flasks made out of Jardian mega-prisms. The flasks were never required in any of the experiments, but they looked very clean and pretty nonetheless. A shelf of great honour was set aside for displaying the beauty of the useless flasks, and 4 respectable Quiggs were given the job of dusting them every 7.33 minutes. Oh how the Greegs loathed them. They could barely wait to fill the flasks with all sorts of disgusting things (namely schmold) and then break them. The Quiggs slaved away until they'd acquired a hefty supply of schmold so clean it would have made trillions of dollars throughout the galaxy if properly marketed as an unparalleled kitchen counter-top cleaner. The Greegs saw this as the grossest possible violation of all things that are Greeg. Fear took over the community. The total collapse of localized schmold trade seemed imminent. Numerous Greegs fell into despair and were never seen or smelled again. Many wandered into The Cleanliness in a suicidal fashion not at all dissimilar to the way so many of your humans leaped from skyscraper windows during the 1930s collapse of your fake stock market.

The remaining Greegs came up with what they considered in their stupidity to be a rather brilliant scheme. They stole the purified schmold and mixed it with regular schmold to make it dirty again. The now-filthy schmold was then angrily hurled at the Quiggs, who set forth purifying it all over again. This cycle went unchanged for generations, even outlasting the ridiculously long lifespan of the metallic tetra-turtle. It was finally decided the total extinction of the Quigg species would be the only way to keep schmold in its naturally polluted state. Thus was born the event in Greeg history commonly referred to as 'The day all Quiggs were thrown into a schmold pit.'

It is my fervent opinion that far worse events would have transpired had the Quiggs' plan to send all the trash to Garbotron succeeded. We have already learned about the disastrous results of Garbotron pollution caused by a single cannon blast, so it can be assumed the phenomenal number of cannon blasts required to rid the planet of the Greegs' mess would have caused the destruction of countless other (and better) civilizations. Because the plan failed, one species died off on a planet that had no use for it anyway. That is, how you say, taking one for the team.

Over and over again, great minds have hypothesized and

sometimes successfully proved that time does not exist. Nevertheless, time is always relevant. And short. Especially if you are thrown into a schmold pit, as no creature can tread schmold for longer than an Earth hour (unless of course you're a metallic tetra-turtle or weigh less than helium while on the 7th moon of Grebular). In their final hour, the Quiggs frantically purified as much schmold as they could before sinking below the surface and drowning. Foolish as it was, one cannot help but admire their dedication to cleanliness. Unless of course one is a Greeg.

Quigg skeletons were henceforth sometimes found in the schmold reserves. The Greegs never knew it but the bone marrow of the Quigg contained a powerfully sterile cleansing agent which diffused in the schmold for years after the extinction, thus making all the latter-day schmold slightly less filthy. It's nice to know that even after their complete annihilation, the great Quigg species continued to inadvertently clean up the universe.

CHAPTER 7

TV and Pets for Greegs

You might be wondering what a Greeg did for entertainment when not fishing Quigg skeletons out of schmold reserves, mining for schmold, or taking in the guilty pleasures of a particularly skeezy Cover Bar while intoxicated on mass quantities of schmold. Television is popular with Greegs, but the only show is 'watching schmold,' as all Greeg televisions are merely hollowed out glass cubes filled with schmold. This does not stop them from wholeheartedly believing they are seeing something different when they change the channel (an act that is supposedly done telepathically). A typical Greeg conversation in front of the TV is as follows:

"Turn on the TV." (An act done by removing a blanket placed on top of a hollowed out glass cube filled with schmold).

"What channel?"

"5."

"Ok."

"Actually not channel 5. I've seen this episode of schmold before. Look at that familiar cluster of bubbles in the bottom left hand quadrant."

"But the schmold-guide says it's brand new."

"It's a re-run."

"I'll put on channel 8 instead."

"Good choice. The sheen of schmold is brighter on channel 8."

"I don't like it. Let's watch channel 3."

"The schmold movement is too frenetic on channel 3."

"What channel do you want to watch then?"

"Channel 8."

"But I don't like channel 8!"

These sorts of arguments are known to carry on for hours until someone solves the problem by smashing the television.

A favourite household pet is a school of shimmer-fish. The fish are kept in tanks filled with, you guessed it, schmold. Viewing the fish is an impossible task, being that schmold is the antithesis of clear, but this problem is quickly averted when the fish die and float belly-up to the surface. The underbelly is what shimmers the most anyway, so a floating upside-down dead shimmer-fish is actually the most entertaining type of shimmer-fish a Greeg can own. If you were hosting a party you would be most embarrassed to learn your shimmer-fish had not died before the guests arrived.

CHAPTER 8

The Unbearable Lightness of Being a Greeg

While our Greegs freely romp about their own planet trashing the place whilst drawing blueprints for the next schmold museum, many faraway Greegs languish miserably in cramped carnival cells. As stated, on most planets Greegs are a small-numbered population put on display by creatures of greater intelligence and power. These imprisoned Greegs have never even heard of schmold, much less seen a drop of it, yet buried somewhere in their collective consciousness is the memory of schmold and how wonderful it might be if they had some. Carnival Greegs dream every night of a tantalizingly unattainable green substance. They always wake up just before the moment of acquisition, left with feelings of disorientation and disappointment. When they're unable to sleep they gaze at whatever moons are in the sky of wherever they are and imagine the moons are green and made of schmold. If the moons happen to already be green, well, they especially enjoy looking at those ones because there's a good chance they might actually be made of schmold.

Carnival Greegs do very little while performing, as the mere sight of these silly creatures is enough to send even the most freakishly bizarre alien into a fit of laughter. The most popular carnival attraction is the viewing of sexual intercourse. Every mid-afternoon the Greegs are separated into groups of two (or more if you can afford the tickets) and left to perform for the paying crowd. Most aliens are fascinated with the process of Greeg intercourse. How and why do such brutish slobs perform procreation in such a dignified and sterile manner? The mystery was best discussed by the famous Dr. Kipple in his psychological think-piece *Purified Procreation: Greeg Sex and What it Says About Their True Nature.*

CHAPTER 9

Klaxworms and Flying Grimbat Messengers

As previously mentioned, Greegs are the most intellectually evolved creatures on this planet. That does not say much for everyone else. We have witnessed the folly of the Quigg, but that is nothing compared to the pure lunacy that are Klaxworms.

A Klaxworm is a medium-sized slithery type creature with thorns and barbs and other dangerous things adorning its skin. Klaxworms exist solely on one of 11 planets containing wriggly, walky, breathy things in the hopeless, undeveloped but reasonably entertaining to look at from a safe distance sun system of the 38 planets in the 59 sunned district of Herb. The Klaxworms' estimated 3.2 trillion populace lives entirely in a single cave system. It is crowded and unpleasant to say the least. During the day there's a stifling heat so intense it can boil the organs of unfortunately thinner-skinned Klaxworms, while the sub-zero temperatures of the evening results in all Klaxworms being frozen to the ground like the tongue of a foolish human who licked metal in the wintertime. For about 9 Earth hours every night the Klaxworms are stuck in mid-stride. Once things warm up in the morning they continue their daily routine of hoping their organs don't boil while deciding where they'd like to end up frozen for the night.

Klaxworms do not want to live in this wretched cave. But they don't leave. They are perfectly aware (through aid of flying Grimbat messengers) that right outside their cave exists all sorts of remarkable things like varnished marble, shiny glass windows and freshly bleached tile floors; in short, the entire surface of a planet for their roaming purposes. No one is stopping them, yet they cannot leave. Why is this? A Klaxworm has no great enemy to fear in the world (except the odd Greeg has been known to wander in the cave and eat a few of them for a late snack, apparently forgetting they're deadly poisonous to everything). A Klaxworm will talk your ear off about leaving the cave, how in just a moment they'll slither right out into the vast fields of polished marble, only they never quite make it to the exit. Along the way there's always a distraction, such as a good discussion about leaving the cave, the boiling of one's organs, or the finding of an excellent spot to be frozen in for the evening.

The squalor of the cave has no actual relevance with their desire to leave, for even if Klaxworms had evolved in an oasis paradise they still would have wanted to be elsewhere. To be displeased with the surroundings while at the same time attempting no change whatsoever is the unwavering state of the Klaxworm's consciousness. It is a very disagreeable purpose to have in life, one that usually results in not doing anything other than stewing about in a cave waiting for ones organs to boil.

Are Klaxworms really this stupid? Not quite. They are merely one of the universe's laziest creatures.

Another mysterious creature on this planet is the briefly aforementioned Flying Grimbat messenger. The Flying Grimbat messenger looks like a triplet of tie-dyed Perusian vampire bats mashed up in a quality vice grip with 3 sets of pterodactyl wings frantically flapping to keep its monstrous body afloat. They feed on a strict diet of watered down schmold, making them somewhat of an enemy to Greegs (who fear the notion of sharing schmold). Luckily the fact that Grimbats water down their schmold means they don't use very much of it. If a Grimbat consumed pure schmold the Greegs would have wiped them out ages ago. It is also true that for some reason the Greegs feel a compelling affinity with the Grimbats, as if they are one of them. Flying Grimbats have appointed themselves messengers of the planet, like a spontaneous organic media. The only problem with this flying epidemic of mass media is that nobody wants to hear their mind-numbingly boring messages, making Grimbats possibly the most useless creature on the planet. Certainly more useless than Klaxworms, who at least mind their own business and don't drop excrement on the recently varnished marble. Grimbats are confounding blabbermouths. They are heedless busybodies swooping around the skies, eavesdropping from behind shrubs and sheepishly claiming it's for the good of public knowledge when they get caught doing it. The parallels between Flying Grimbat Messengers and human paparazzi are staggering. In my eyes, the only blatant difference is that a paparazzi looks like a triplet of tie-dyed Perusian vampire bats mashed up in a quality vice grip with 2 sets of pterodactyl wings frantically flapping to keep it's monstrous body afloat, as opposed to having the regular 3 sets of pterodactyl wings commonly found on the Flying Grimbat Messenger.

Like I said, they are a mysterious creature

CHAPTER 10

The Scam of Religious Holidays for Greegs

A Greeg calendar is an interesting collectible to come across in your space travels. Just the fact that Greegs have invented a calendar is mystifying, but matters are made more baffling when you discover there is no semblance of logic or pattern in any of the 473 pages, all of which are constantly being rearranged and rewritten due to squabbles about which holidays should be celebrated and which should never be spoken of again. Random holidays (some enthralling, some downright shameful) are perpetually coming and going, but the celebration of one in particular has always been agreed upon. It is marked on the calendar by every 4.3 rotations of the small moon Dromos, and it is a day in which all respectable Greegs must pay reverence to their deity, known by the name 'Whatever It Is That Created Everything For the Sole Entertainment of the Greeg.' On the day of reverence a Greeg says thank you to Whatever It Is That Created Everything For the Sole Entertainment of the Greeg, and prays the supply of schmold be plentiful for at least the next thousand revolutions round the sun. The centrepiece of the event is the great tradition known as *The Offering of Schmold.* Each Greeg family is expected (nay, commanded by law) to place a worthy offering in front of a stone altar, where slaves of the congregation collect the offerings and take them to a secret volcano that is the living heart of Whatever It Is That Created Everything For the Sole Entertainment of the Greeg. This was once a pure act of sacrifice, but over time the Offering of Schmold became nothing more than an egotistical competition to see who could offer the most intricately expensive display. Much of a Greeg's time between days of reverence is spent planning out and constructing their next offering. Commendable offerings in recent years have included: a 2-dozen set of schmold candles (a truly rare item considering the near impossibility of solidifying schmold short of owning a bottle of Ice-Nine), a flat-screen schmold television (with all the channels of course), a schmold-multiplier (a remarkable machine that can increase your schmold supply at a rate of .03% per rotation of Dromos, assuming you're able to afford the astronomically bankrupting task of plugging it in), and the ever popular schmold-cake (acceptable only when baked to a crispy charcoal texture and stomped on a little bit).

Long ago it was made public to the Greeg community that the congregation had not been taking the offerings of schmold to any secret volcano that is the living heart of Whatever It Is That Created Everything For the Sole Entertainment of the Greeg. They were merely putting the schmold in their own houses. The entire celebration of the Greegian deity is a scam perpetrated by an elite group of maniacal Greegs, who for some unknown reason must own more schmold than anyone else. Was the public upset? Not really. Their desire to compete over who has the most expensive schmold offering quickly trumped the anger of being ripped off.

Greegs love showing off how much schmold they have, even if it results in no longer having the schmold.

THE MIDDLE:
of Carnivals and Things... but mostly of Things

CHAPTER 11

Zook and Naddy

He sat upright in his cage as the sounds of jeering and screaming jarred him from his sleep.

"Come on now, these people paid good money to see you three get it on."

Moments before he was swimming in an ocean of schmold. He didn't know it was called schmold of course. Just knew it felt oh so good. Much better than being poked at with a pointed stick. Which he was at the moment. He farted and sneezed at the same time, sending globules of greenish, yellowish goo cascading down his hairy face. Momentarily sure that it must be schmold, he grabbed the snot and rubbed it all over himself. He got some in his eye which stung and burned. He decided to try and remedy this by jamming his fingers in his eyeballs to stop the pain. It didn't work. It only made him yelp out with more pain. This woke up the other male in the cage. The other male in the cage flew into a rage, furious at being awoken from a fabulous dream. His dream involved having just decided what combination of rotations, spins and poses he would employ after running and jumping off of a 100 meter high dive springy board right into his own, brand new schmold pool.

The other male picked up a pile of Greeg feces and rubbed it all over the first male's face. To make things easier, we will henceforth call these two males Zook and Naddy. There is absolutely no reason to suspect these names have any significance, they are completely random.

Zook, the first male, did not understand why his friend would share such nice stinky feces all over his face like that.

"What a lucky break!" Thought Zook.

Clearly, this terrific new stench and nauseating outward,

physical appearance would guarantee that Zook would get to attempt first, third, and probably eighth as well today. His inability to comprehend Naddy's reasoning infuriated Zook, leading him to grip Naddy by the back of the head and clang clang clang his good friend's face into the bars of the cage until it was all bloody. Just for good measure, Zook pissed all over Naddy's bloody face.

By this time the female had seen about enough. She was completely and utterly turned on. She revealed the sterility covers and the two males rushed over to see which one was to be chosen first, third, and most importantly, eighth.

11 minutes had passed since Zook had first awoken from his nap.

This was why Greegs were such a damned fine carnival attraction!

CHAPTER 12

Specters and Greeg-keepers

Viewing this skeezy carnival show was a gathering of Algreenian fog-specters. They were in dire need of some high quality entertainment, having just finished a legendarily bad cruise of some of the more boring outer dimensions, including a tour of the famous invisible dimension. Life is much worse when everything is invisible, despite what was boasted about on travel posters. Carnival Greegs are highly recommended as a pick-me-up for anyone who has recently visited the invisible dimension, and so here were these Algreenian spectres drifting around waiting for the show.

An impatient spectre tried to pick up a rock and throw it at Naddy but his spectral, non-existent hand merely passed right through the solid object. The spectre then asked the nearest living creature if they would do him the favour of throwing a rock at the Greegs. The creature obliged, throwing a rock at Naddy, further worsening his mangled appearance. While this was going on, Zook thrashed his arms about wildly. It was a ridiculously pointless thing to do.

"We paid for a show!" yelled the rock-throwing instigator.

"Yeah! A show! We want to see something!" chimed in the rest of the crowd.

"Don't you know we've just been through the invisible dimension?" screeched a belligerent specter. "Not a whole lot to see there! In fact, nothing at all."

The Greeg-keeper continued rapping on the cage bars with his electro-club. Greegs usually became obedient once the electro-club appeared. This particular Greeg-keeper was a tall goblin-like creature. He had fangs and claws and red eyes. His name was Reg. He was more frightening than his casually friendly name would suggest, being a tall goblin-like creature with fangs and claws and red eyes.

"These specter-folk haven't got all day," growled Reg. "Or do they?" he added, turning to face the specters. "Are you lot dead? What's the deal with all the floating and the translucence?"

"No, we're not dead," replied one of the specters. "We are living creatures born in a ghostly form. When we die we become bodies of flesh and blood."

"That's stupid. A bit backwards, don't you think?" asked Reg.

"I say the only thing that is backwards is the fact that we have paid you for a non-existent show, when in fact you should be paying us for the wasting of our time."

"I'm not sure you've even paid me," said Reg. "All I've got is this invisible money. Can't even see it to know if it's there."

"We told you, that money is perfectly transferable from within the invisible dimension. Once you're there you can trade the invisible money for any sort of bejewelled holograph-coins or whatever other foolish currency you're trading in nowadays."

"Right," said Reg. "I understand that part. Just not sure when I'll ever bother to go to the invisible dimension, that's all. This money will probably just end up sitting around taking up invisible space on my visible dresser."

"Not go to the invisible dimension? You *must* go to the

invisible dimension," said a specter in a manner snooty enough to suggest that anyone who doesn't go to the invisible dimension is leading a wasted life.

"I don't get it, you've all been going off about how boring the invisible dimension is," said Reg.

"Yeah, but we're specters. We're practically invisible ourselves. We prefer to see solid objects to counterbalance our spectral state. The invisible dimension might be a nice change-up for you though. I hear one of flesh and blood feels thinner while there."

Reg grew annoyed. "Look, I'm never going to visit the invisible dimension. The cost of travelling there is way more than what I'll make trading in the money. Plus I think it's all a scam."

Caught up in their heated discussion, Reg and the specters failed to notice the Greeg show starting in a tremendous way. There was a great battle over who would make the coveted eighth attempt, with Zook prevailing because of his aforementioned newly acquired stench. The show was over by the time the specters focused their attention back on the cage. Because they didn't see anything Reg was forced to refund their invisible money. Unbeknownst to Reg, specters are not great liars. The pouch of invisible money was indeed real, and would have fetched several islands worth of bejewelled holograph-coins, granted Reg could handle the mind-shattering experience of crossing the invisible dimension's psychic threshold, which of course he couldn't, being an imbecilic goblin. After the specters drifted away, Reg approached the cage.

"Those are good customers we lost because of you!" he yelled at Zook and Naddy.

Naddy tried to explain how well the show had gone, and that it was the audience's fault for missing out.

"Never mind," said Reg as he walked away from the cage. "Useless Greegs. Just go back to dreaming about your green pools or whatever it is I hear you muttering about in your sleep."

Zook thrashed his arms about wildly.

CHAPTER 13

Dr. Rip T. Brash Makes a Wager

Dr. Rip T. Brash The Third was neither a doctor nor was he royalty. He wasn't the third of anything, he'd never been to school and he wasn't really so much of a 'he' either. It's just weird calling him an 'it' but he had no discernible sexual orientation. Not because he lacked sexual organs. Rip had no discernible sexual orientation precisely because he had so *many* sexual organs. He had an absolutely ridiculous assortment of penises, vaginas, coil rods, flipper flaps, egg baskets, cram rams, biddle twocks, horm guffles, abble taters, phrish kerrings, wodder musks, mickle shoots, marrinvioles, and all sorts of other exotic pieces of procreation and pleasure. At this point, Rip couldn't really remember which ones he was born with, and which he'd had surgically implanted or removed. He was a hulky thing. A clunky, yet carefully put together specimen. He had many eyes, some of which were capable of site. He had a few brains, some of which were capable of thought. He had four arms, three legs, nine tentacles, eight nipples, three beards (but only one chin)... in general he had a lot of extraneous parts. He was like a car with too many accessories, many of which served no practical purpose. Practicality was not what Dr. Rip T. Brash The Third was all about. Rip was brash though, especially when wildly intoxicated at a carnival, which he most certainly was. He was prone to making outrageous and outlandish claims when drunk. Unfortunately for him, his friends were prone to taking him up on these claims and bets then collecting when he failed miserably to achieve them. This is likely the explanation for most, if not all, of his sexual organs. They weren't really friends as much as they were leeches. This was so true that it was common for intergalactic debt counsellors to suggest to cash strapped clients "Perhaps you should try going drinking with Dr. Rip T. Brash The Third at a carnival." Nobody knew how he had so much money to lose on outlandish bets. It's true every once in awhile he would actually succeed in the task laid out for himself in a loud mouthed, drunken stupor the night before, but not nearly enough times to be breaking even. On this day Rip was more drunk than usual, and so his primary mouth was flapping more than usual. Sensing a real chance to not only cover his debts, but perhaps wind up owning a few thousand civilizations as well, Rip's drinking partner, Jim, wasn't taking Rip up on any of his bets early on in the night. He instead downplayed them as effeminate and pathetic in the hopes that Rip would continue one-upping himself until the bet was so outlandish and impossible to achieve that Jim could never lose.

This is, of course, exactly what Rip did. Beginning with a paltry claim that he could stick his whole head up the anus of a Graffling Wocker Frit, spin around three times, return to the bar and still go home with the prettiest four headed being in the building, Rip eventually got so drunk and ran his mouth to such a degree that he made the most preposterous drunken wager ever made in the long and glorious history of preposterous drunken wagers.

This was it.

Dr. Rip T. Brash The Third opened his drunken face and guzzled back his eleventh Crammington Krish Fortini (about ten and a half more than one should engulf in a lifetime). He slammed the Jardian glass bottle on the top of the bar and shouted out "I got it!"

At this point the entire bar had given up whatever false conversations they'd been having and were all just focusing on Rip's self imposed escalating stakes, waiting to see what ridiculous final challenge Jim would pull the trigger on.

Rip grabbed Jim by the hairy tube dangling from the back of his neck and dragged him to the Greeg cage. A crowd of about 200 visible beings, the odd specter and several recording devices followed the pair out to what had surely become the most interesting thing to happen at the carnival in days. Rip, always a showman, clambered on to the side of the Greeg cage, barely held on to the bars with one hand and held up his twelfth CKF with the other.

"I, Dr. Rip T. Brash The Third, do solemnly declare in the

name of all things..."

Several shouts of 'get on with it' and other such encouragements were volleyed in his general direction, along with several pounds of half eaten food, severed limbs and hunks of hard granite.

"Fine, fine, no sense of tact and ceremony but fine, here it is. I bet you, Graham..."

"Jim!" Corrected the mob.

"Gerry, right, I bet you my priceless fleet of Obotron 7 Space Ships, er, Jill, that I, me, yes, can take a lowly, stupid, useless carnival Greeg, and have them smarter than enough to pass as a decent, semi intelligent creature, person, thing... in two years. Smarter than all of you even!"

The mob went silent. Then a laugh broke out from the back and collectively rolled on up to the front. Jim, rolling around on the ground, unable to believe his luck, screamed out "Yes, yes! Hahahaha YES!"

CHAPTER 14

a Wager with Extraordinarily Off-Kilter Odds Elicits Enough Attention as to Shatter the Planetary Record for Most Teleportations in a Nanosecond

The crowd buzzed over the absurd wager. While trying to imagine the scenario of an intelligent Greeg, the circuit boards of many fine robots were forever liquefied. Things got way out of control when a random spectator phoned his debt counsellor to announce that Dr. Rip just made his most foolish bet ever. After that, word quickly spread that if you could make it to the Greeg cage on the 5th planet from Tralfar in the next half hour then you might also be retiring in the next two years. Cash-strapped clients swamped in debt (hoping to make a bet of their own) immediately flew into a frenzy of action. Many sought out the nearest teleportation booth. On particularly crime-ridden planets you could see line-ups extending miles into the horizon. The fugitives patiently waited in line for days. It is not difficult to muster such patience when you're a guilty tax-evader scheduled for dismemberment.

Debt clients began to materialize all around the Greeg cage. They appeared in random locations, causing certain spectres to suffer the embarrassing act of Bodily Displacement Syndrome.

Rip let go of the Greeg cage and turned to face the ever-multiplying mob. He relished their attention, and was for once happy that a debt counsellor had been phoned. To add a layer of theatricality he paced back and forth in front of the cage. He tripped over a ledge and decided sitting down was the best thing for him to do at the moment.

"I see by the sudden appearance of so many desperately poor people that I have made a good wager."

"I'll bet you can't teach a Greeg how to make a jug of frozen orange juice in six months!" screamed a desperately poor Snail-oid from the back of the crowd.

"Everyone listen here," spoke Rip, "you hopelessly debt-ridden lot might as well teleport back to your places of hiding and await your inevitable dismemberment, because this particular bet is for my old friend Joe, and for Joey alone."

Jim laughed at the thought of being Rip's friend.

"What's so funny?" asked Rip. "Is the bet too good for just you?"

"No, no," said Jim. "You were right before. The bet was made to me alone. All these other leeches... I mean, all these leeches should just teleport out of here."

Some of the leeches vanished. The ones scheduled for an earlier dismemberment stuck around, clinging to the hope of a life-saving bet.

"What say you, Johnny?" asked Rip. "Do you take the bet?"

Jim paused for effect. "I humbly accept your wager."

"Ha ha!" laughed Rip, clapping his hands. "All we need now is a witness."

"WITNESS!" shouted four thousand random members of the mob.

"I guess that's enough witnesses," said Jim. "It's an official challenge. You will acquire a Greeg, and within two years you will make it more intelligent and presentable than anyone here. If you do not, you will give me your priceless fleet of Obotron 7 space ships. I want all the windows scrubbed. And full tanks of gas too. I loathe hunting for investment bankers."

"You know," whispered Rip, "I think this might be my greatest wager ever."

Jim thought he saw tears welling up in a few of Rip's eyes. Suddenly a severed hand that had been momentarily caught up in a time-pocket flew through the air and smacked Rip in the face.

"I'll leave you to the business of finding a Greeg," said Jim as he walked off in the nearest direction away from Rip.

Once the autograph session ended and the crowd dispersed, Rip approached the Greeg-keeper's tent.

"Ahem... hello?" he said as he parted the tent flaps. A rank stench emerged from within. Evidently Greeg-keepers don't live much better than Greegs.

"What do you want?" snarled Reg.

"Haven't you been watching any of the events going on outside?"

"No... I've been in here watching my show."

Rip looked around the tent and saw nothing on which a show could be watched. Not even an imaginary show like schmold TV. All that lay inside the tent were a few tables with dead things placed on top of them. Reg did very little in his spare time aside from eating the nearby population of Crabbits into extinction. Of their skulls he made tables on which to place dead Crabbits.

"You didn't see the chaotic mob right outside your tent? I think we even shattered the planetary record for most teleportations in a nanosecond. You must have felt some of the land-quakes?"

"No, I've been in here watching my show, like I said."

"I'll fill you in," said Rip.

He went on to tell a long rendition of everything that just happened. Being that it just happened, I'll skip ahead. But know that Rip told the story with his usual eloquence and exciting flair for showmanship.

"That's the stupidest thing I've ever heard!" laughed Reg. He banged his hands against the table. Bone fragments were scattered across the mud floor. "You can't teach a Greeg anything! You can't get them to be clean! You've surely lost your fleet of ships to this Elizabeth guy."

"I disagree," said Rip. "It *can* be done. I *will* transform a Greeg within two years!"

"What's all this got to do with me anyway?" asked Reg.

"I need one of your Greegs. How else am I going to win the bet?"

"One of *my* Greegs?" asked Reg. His red eyes glowed darker crimson, as they were prone to do when he grew upset. "Not a chance can you have one of my Greegs! I'm barely getting by with the low number I have right now. I don't even have enough for a double-digit orgy, and the tourists are only paying lots for the big group scenes. There's no way you can have one of my Greegs."

"Think of it like an investment. I'll give you the Greeg back after two years, regardless of whether I win the bet or not," lied Rip. "But imagine I do win the bet... you'll suddenly find yourself in the ownership of an intelligent, clean and presentable Greeg. Never in their history have Greegs garnered those adjectives. Think of the rare attraction you'd have on your hands if you owned such a specimen. Tourists would flock from the farthest dimensions, even the invisible one, just to have a look at this Greeg. You could charge whatever you wanted for admission."

Reg grew interested. "And if you don't win the bet?"

"You'll still have your Greeg back, after only a short two year rental period. And even if I don't entirely transform the Greeg, I'm sure that in a couple years I can at least teach it enough tricks to greatly enhance your outdated show."

"Hmm... I suppose the show is a bit outdated."

"A bit? Are you kidding me?" said Rip, reaching the climax of his suave hustle. "The Greeg show is done. It needs something new. Everyone's seen Greegs having sex, it's just not that crazy any longer." He couldn't have been lying any more. Greeg carnivals were more popular than ever throughout the universe. Just not on the rundown, out-of-the-way planet Reg had chosen to live on.

The painfully slow cogs of Reg's rotted brain began to turn. You could almost hear his thoughts creaking, like the sound of a thousand fingernails scratching The Floating Chalkboard of Elbereth (something that has actually been done, much to the chagrin of those now-deaf folk who forgot to wear earplugs while doing it).

"If I introduced something new to the Greeg show... I could get rich?" he asked.

"That's right!"

Reg lingered over this incredulous thought. "I'll do it!" he finally shouted. "You can have one of my Greegs!"

"You won't regret it," said Rip. "When can I take the beast?"

"Right away!"

"Good. There is only two years after all. But that's still enough time."

"I suddenly believe in you," said Reg, feeling the stoned-like effects of Rip's powerful methods of deception. "You seem like a creature of great intellect."

Dr. Rip T. Brash the Third was indeed a creature of great intellect, however this assumption would not have been made if Reg were a creature capable of the sense of smell, as ordinarily no creature of great intellect would have on their breath the scent of 12 Crammington Krish Fortinis.

Reg led Dr. Brash to the Greeg cage.

"You can have that one," he said, pointing at Zook. "I have suspected he is slightly more intelligent then the other Greegs."

"Why do you suspect that?"

"He bangs his face against the bars slightly less often than the others."

CHAPTER 15

a Pair of Old Friends Take in a Show

The crowd laughed and howled and rolled around on the ground. This would never get old. Nothing made them feel better about themselves than seeing a Greeg be a Greeg, and knowing for certain that they were not a Greeg.

Naddy had, in no particular order, and in the last hour:

- Attempted to eat his left arm
- Realized it was futile considering his lack of teeth
- Strained his neck muscles trying to look at his own asshole
- Tried to pop his neck back into place
- Considering his neck hadn't been popped out of place, suffered severe damage to his spine.

For a brief moment of self-awareness, Naddy actually realized that he was a source of mockery. He felt the disdain and condescension from the carnival goers. He paused for a second and looked out pathetically. His eyes asked the carnival goers if this was really the way things should be. He questioned why they were so much better than him, and if so, why did they simply point and laugh instead of helping him be like them? He hadn't chosen to be a Greeg, he was simply born one. The carnivalites hadn't actually accomplished anything more than him, other than not being born a Greeg. For a nanosecond, he was acutely aware of all of this and he begged with his eyes to be taken out of the cage and to be one of them. His plea faintly registered with no one and was instantly forgotten when he shook off the silly thought at the sight of the female waking from a nap. With no competition from Zook, Naddy had her all to himself. He barely even tried any more. He bumbled over to her side and farted directly in her face. Then he punched himself a few times in the mouth and kneed an inanimate object. Lacking any semblance of self-esteem, the female shrugged & pulled out the procreational paraphernalia.

As the act of sex began it should be noted that I lied a little bit in the previous paragraph. The plea did not *entirely* fail to register with *all* of the carnival gawkers. There was one creature who felt a connection and shared a moment of understanding with Naddy. This same creature was now feeling very strong emotions stirring up inside him as the first attempt went down. While it is true that he was hooting and hollering with the rest of the crowd, he couldn't help but feel a gut wrenching volcano of bubbling anger, longing, jealousy and resentment churning around in his stomach. He tried to dismiss it at first, but he could not deny the fierce reality of the feelings. He surely, undeniably wished more than anything that he could tear off his clothing, go into the cage and challenge the lowly Greeg. He found the disgusting female inexplicably attractive beyond his wildest fantasies. All he wished to do was to rub feces and dirt and bodily fluids all over himself and engage in acts of psychotic and nonsensical physical violence towards the other male. Somehow he knew this would ensure he would get to be the one making the first attempt right now. He didn't know why or how he knew this was important, but he did.

"Savages, hey?" a familiar voice came from beside him, more prodding him than genuinely asking the question.

"Yes, yes, savages."

"Everything about them is savage, primitive and borderline retarded... except when they do this. Look at that, look at how they do it. More elegant and caring than a barrel full of Vibrulant Oolorians."

"Still doesn't make them any less savage or dumb though."

"Not at all. Just a bizarre and random fluke. No real logical explanation for it."

A brief pause, and then the familiar voice continued.

"You're right though, every Greeg is an idiot, a moron, a complete and total twit."

"You can say that again... every, single, one. Good for a laugh, and nothing more. Crammington Krish?"

"You bet," said Dr. Rip T. Brash The Third.

"My treat," said the former Greeg formerly known as Zook.

CHAPTER 16

Planetary Relativity, Astrospeciology
and Fleeing in Haste

It was now 1.7 years after Rip had made his outlandish bet that he was about to win. It should be noted that Rip, being the clever bloke he was, had actually duped the audience considerably. As any seasoned traveller of time and space can tell you, a year is a very relative term. On the planet Schmick for example, a year is about the time it takes you to read:

This.

There you go, another Schmickian year gone by. By the time you next see a period a whole decade will have gone by. The planet Schmick is about four inches away from the sun it revolves around. Well, it doesn't actually revolve around it so much. Not all planets revolve around their suns. Not all go in circles, or ellipses, or ovals. Some make boxes, zig-zags, figure 8's, loop-dee-loops, jittery slaloms, loping spirals, corkscrews and spastic shuffles. Some planets interact with one another as they go about their sun; performing doe-see-does or bumping and jostling as they go. Others go directly at their sun, these are called "suicidal planets." Some don't move at all. They are referred to as "Lazy Planets." Some super intelligent, lazy planets have risen up against their sun, banded together and made the sun revolve around them. These are called "Union Planets." Others, like Schmick, disappear and reappear in multiple places around their sun at a dizzying speed. This makes it appear as if they are actually occupying every single space around the sun at all times. They are doing exactly this. Schmick is not really a planet and its sun isn't technically a sun. But there's no point in trying to explain that to you.

Other planets crawl at a pace that would make Grovulant Sloggerz look like Riptulating Froppers. These planets never use the year as a standard of time. Instead they prefer to time things out in general, ball-park phrases like "When that thing happens later on." These planets are absolutely useless to anyone looking to fuel up their space ship, as clearly no investment banker could ever thrive in such a lackadaisical environment.

So, being that the only sort of creatures who would travel to a remote planet to watch Carnival Greegs with a notorious, gambling drunkard are not the sort of creatures who know an awful lot about the relativity of time and space, and being that Dr. Rip T. Brash was acutely aware of this fact, and that 2 years on this particular planet was longer than the lifespan of most of the witnesses at the Carnival... he was right on schedule to keep his priceless fleet of Obotron 7 Space Ships. That is, had he not already lost them in a much wilder and exotic bet to an Astrospeciologist 'friend' of his the next night... which he most certainly had.

It was all in good fun for Rip. He obtained and lost priceless items at such a staggering pace it barely even registered. What did register was that he was now sitting at the bar with his Astrospeciologist 'friend' and a former Greeg. The Greeg had no memory or recollection that he was once a lowly, degenerate Greeg. The Astrospeciologist was a specialist in Greegs. He was fascinated by them. As was Dr. Rip T. Brash The Third. The Astrospeciologist was telling Rip his latest theory on The Greegs. Through his constant reading and research of seemingly infinite sources of information, he had come to the conclusion that there was a planet buried deep in the 59 sunned district of Herb where Greegs were the dominant species. Through absolutely no knowledge whatsoever, and a desire to contradict anything for the sake of a good drunken wager, Rip proclaimed this was both ridiculous and impossible. Rip immediately and loudly bet all of the possessions of a fellow named Jim he was about to own that such a place did not exist. The Astrospeciologist, whose life's work and lavish lifestyle had been entirely funded by being a 'friend' of Dr. Rip T. Brash The Third, agreed wholeheartedly to the wager. They would leave in the morning in a shiny fleet of Obotron 7 space ships in search of the mystical All Greeg Planet. Or as Rip put it "To search for yet more proof that you're an idiot, and I am right."

The planet they were currently drinking on being the

planet that it was, the morning was quite a bloody long time away. The former Greg formerly known as Zook being the former Greg formerly known as Zook that he was, reacted strangely to the news of possibly going to a possibly existing All Greg Planet. He picked up the bartender with one hand and hurled his body across the bar into a group of very surprised Meditating Mockriffs. This unprovoked outburst of violence was unheard of outside of a Greg cage, and so the reaction from the other creatures in the bar was a combination of shock and anger.

"Hey, how about we leave right now instead?" said the Astrospeciologist.

"Damned fine idea," said Rip, stealing several bottles of Crammington Krish Fortinis from behind the bar for the trip. As they ran away from the angry and hotly pursuant mob, Rip turned to the former Greg formerly known as Zook and asked, "Why'd you do that back there old friend?"

"Must be that last CKF," said the former Greg formerly known as Zook.

Nowadays he was known as Krimshaw, the only real, actual friend of Dr. Rip T. Brash The Third. As the priceless fleet of Obotron 7 Space Ships took off in haste, Krimshaw took a peek out of the window and saw Naddy making his eighth attempt with the female Greg. For reasons unbeknownst to him, this inspired him to inflict serious and irreparable damage to the ship's guidance system, sending it rocketing through space and time blindly. Generally, this is not a good idea.

This time was no exception.

CHAPTER 17

The Finding of a Very Rare Book
Propels our Adventure

Blindly hurtling a fleet of Obotron ships through space is a very expensive thing to do. Each of the 19 ships required to make a proper fleet is a gas-guzzling, top-luxury cruiser with room for hundreds of rich aliens. Why, then, do three measly people require an entire fleet for their mission? They don't. It is an insanely wasteful thing to do.

Investment Banker Preservationists (or IBP, the radicals who perpetually picket outside the homes of people who own very expensive space ships) would be horrified to learn that an entire fleet of Obotrons was being used for the transport of three people. Anyone who cared about following the charts for Investment Banker populations would notice a major dive in the local supply every time the fleet made a pit stop. When Krimshaw mentioned the idea of just bringing along one of the ships, to help out with preservation and all, Dr. Rip and the Astrospeciologist laughed and agreed it wouldn't be right to break up the set. Legions of staff were put aboard each ship, and were happy to learn there was nobody to serve. They were especially pleased to realize the towels would never get used, and could thus remain in their original factory sealed state.

The Astrospeciologist (who shall henceforth be known as Wilx, because that is his name) was busy searching through the ship archives, which included catalogued maps of generally most all of time and space. He attempted to set the ship on some sort of coherent path. It was not an easy thing to do.

Krimshaw continued to gaze out of the epic space-viewing window, wondering about this mysterious planet of Greegs and how he would feel if it really existed, and if they actually found it.

Rip was sitting down, befuddled. He gently cradled the last stolen bottle of Crammington Krish Fortinis. The other two had been smashed in the madness of the getaway. Some might say it is an impressive feat to retain even one unbroken bottle in the process of running from an angry and hotly pursuant mob, but Rip saw the uncharacteristic loss of the other two bottles as a veritable sign that he might be losing his masterful touch in life.

"Can we stop for more?"

"We've just left," replied Wilx.

"You could turn around."

"To the planet with the angry and hotly pursuant mob? We're lucky enough they're not following us. Most of them are too poor to own spaceships."

"I thought Obotron ships were meant to be first class," said Rip. "How can they not have any Crammington Krish Fortinis?"

"There are countless crates of CKF stored in the cargo ship following the rear of the fleet. But it takes a few days for them to catch up to us when we want something."

"What sort of civilized planet do you think we'll land on before then?"

"I don't know," replied Wilx. "Right now the ship is on a distressing course, thanks to Krimshaw's seemingly random destructive behaviour. If I don't correct the trajectories, we might find ourselves drifting into the invisible dimension."

"I hear that place is like an affirmation of life."

"No, it's one of the worst places of all time."

As Wilx pored over the infinite catalogues of star charts and dimensional gateways, Rip leaned over his shoulder and pitifully tried to make sense of the whole thing. Wilx was so adept at flipping rapidly through the charts that all Rip could see was a dizzying array of kaleidoscopic imagery. Rip sneezed violently.

"Hey!" said Wilx. "Cover your mouth! You're getting me drunk."

"Sorry," said Rip, as he took a few steps backwards.

Wilx was well aware the sneeze of someone drunk on Crammington Krish Fortinis is extremely contagious, causing brutal intoxication in otherwise sober people who happen to be standing close enough to inhale said sneeze. Wilx felt his mind go woozy and his eyes go hazy, and he was only slightly aware of his stomach having a near fatal organ-quake.

"I'm going to the study room to work on my language," announced Krimshaw randomly. In actuality he was hoping to find something in one of his books about this supposed Greeg planet.

"No thanks," said Rip, still entranced by the confusion of the charts and thinking drinks had just been offered.

"The brakes don't work on number 3," burbled Wilx, believing Krimshaw had just announced he was going to ride a sonic-shuttle through a Proto-star, one of more dangerous things you can do in life, brakes or not. Sonic-shuttles go so fast you can drive one directly through the centre of a Proto-star while only suffering severe flesh burns on 20% of your body. However if your trajectory is off by even the slightest of increments you'll suffer 100% severe flesh burns.

Wilx had designed a study room at the end of the ship's main corridor. It contained a plethora of strange books which no mortal creature could ever hope to finish reading in one lifetime. No doubt it was one of those collections designed to show off how much reading a person does, or at least how much reading they intend to get around to some day, but probably won't. Krimshaw grabbed an interesting looking book entitled *Very Rare Planets*. He sat down at the desk and flicked on the laser-lamp. The wasteful energy consumption of the outdated laser-lamp was being supplied directly from the ship's tank of liquefied Investment Bankers. Krimshaw had no idea the lives of so many useless organisms had been given up for the purpose of lighting this room. He was fond of the lamp nonetheless.

Krimshaw flipped to the index of *Very Rare Planets*. He skimmed to the 'G' Section. He looked for Greeg. There was a listing for Grebular, the shape-shifting planet, and there was also a listing for Grelk, the planet made of tar pits, but there was no mention of Greegs. Krimshaw thought surely this book would contain the answers he sought. He was frustrated to learn otherwise. He marched back to the main bridge, bringing the book with him.

"Look at this book," he said to Rip and Wilx, who were both

busily enthralled by the sight of a Proto-star encroaching on their ship, or rather, their ship encroaching on a Proto-star, being that the ship was moving and the Proto-star wasn't.

"What's that?" asked Krimshaw.

"Just a Proto-star," said Wilx. "We have to not go through it, or else we'll probably be melted. We're getting dangerously close. Rip and I have been busy discussing which direction would be the best to pass around."

"Just pick any direction," suggested Krimshaw.

"It's not that easy," said Rip. "The total freedom of directional choice while in space is enough to freeze anyone in their tracks."

"Never mind that for now," said Wilx, spinning his chair so that he was no longer facing the impending doom. "What's this book you've discovered?"

"It's called *Very Rare Planets*. I thought it would help us find that Greeg planet, but there seems to be no mention of Greegs in the entire thing."

The eyes of Wilx lit up like the brilliant luminescence of the dangerously close proto-star. "You've found a copy of *Very Rare Planets*?" he asked excitedly.

"Is that a good thing?" asked Krimshaw.

"That book has directions to planets that the ships database has never even heard of. I've been looking for a copy for a long time."

"What, of that book?" asked Rip. "I found that in a gutter somewhere. Only kept it all this time because there's a blurb about me."

"There's a blurb about you?" asked Wilx. "Yeah right."

"It's on page 343."

Krimshaw flipped to page 343. He saw a picture of a rare planet known as Pluto. He read the article about the boring planet.

"What's so rare about Pluto?" asked Krimshaw. "And I don't see anything about you in here."

Rip pointed to the blurb hiding in fine print at the bottom corner of the page. "Read it," he said.

Krimshaw produced a small magnifying glass and

proceeded to read the blurb. "Pluto is considered a rare planet because of all the planets that have been visited by Dr. Rip T. Brash, it is the only one in which during his visitation he did not place an outlandish bet."

"It's true," confirmed Rip.

"What gives? Why no betting on Pluto?" asked Wilx.

"Nothing good to bet on. It's just that boring of a planet. The intelligent species from that star system even stopped calling Pluto a planet. It was removed from the zodiac charts and banned from the school curriculum."

"That's a shame."

"Is it?"

Wilx and Dr. Rip shifted their focus back to the encroaching proto-star and the dilemma involved with not passing through it. Krimshaw continued flipping through *Very Rare Planets*.

"Didn't you say this Greeg planet was supposed to be somewhere in the 59 sunned district of Herb?"

"Yeah," said Wilx, "have you found something?"

"There's a passing reference here of a planet in the 59 sunned district of Herb that has what they call an unexpected creature for its dominant species. That sounds like what we're looking for. The planet is called Hroon. It is water-based and is apparently the fourth most perfect sphere in existence."

"No, that couldn't be right," said Rip. "This Greeg planet is supposed to be an unshapely thing made up of random conglomerations."

"We should check it out anyway," suggested Krimshaw. "It puts us in the sunned district of Herb. Maybe the creatures of Hroon can direct us to the Greeg planet."

"I suppose that isn't a bad plan," agreed Wilx.

Rip pointed at the window. "I must remind everyone of the encroaching proto-star."

"Oh, yeah. Take a left," said Wilx.

A left was taken. The fleet of ships veered away from the deadly proto-star. The movement of the entire fleet was controlled solely by the guidance system of the Obotron 1, the finest ship of the fleet and also the ship on which our characters resided. Wilx set course for the planet Hroon. Being that the guidance system of Obotron 1 was the guidance system that Krimshaw had irreparably damaged, the fleet was only on a vague-level course with Hroon, which meant they would one day probably arrive, but only after experiencing an unforeseeable number of ill-fated shortcuts.

CHAPTER 18

Aimlessly Bumbling Through Space and Time with an Irreparably Damaged Guidance System

Wilx and Dr. Rip T. Brash The Third, being a pair of well-seasoned space and time travellers, were quite used to unforeseeable numbers of ill-fated shortcuts. In fact, if one were to describe their lives, if they had tombstones or obituaries like you after they died, they would almost certainly read:

"Here lies/R.I.P. Wilx/Dr. Rip T. Brash The Third... his/her/its life was an unforeseeable number of ill-fated shortcuts."

'Shortcuts' is a very misleading term though. Long periods of painfully boring floating would be much more accurate. When aimlessly bumbling through space and time with a guidance system that's been irreparably damaged by a reformed Greeg with violent Greeg tendencies bubbling just below the surface, one will spend the majority of the time doing nothing. Seeing nothing. Feeling nothing. Anticipating nothing. Nothing, after all, is what most of this Universe is. It is what most of everything is. Nothing.

Seasoned space and time travellers have developed multiple ways to cope with this. Dr. Rip T. Brash The Third continued building up his tolerance for exotic intoxicants and losing tremendous bets to Wilx, who passed his time writing and reading about every species that has ever existed in the cosmos.

Krimshaw had no such pastimes to pass the time... or the

space. He chose a different method. He went completely insane. He snapped. He flipped. He destroyed a lot of things. He was detained and locked in a Greeg Cage that Rip used for exotic dancers and space whores he wished to especially degrade. Krimshaw felt comfortable here and smashed his face against the bars.

"Better make sure that Jebidiah fellow never sees this relapse," said Rip.

"Died yesterday," said Wilx, not bothering to look up from the latest issue of *Creepy Crawly Telepathic Worm-like Flying Fish That Start Off Rather Small but Grow to be Over 600 Meters Tall and Several Thousand Kilometers Long, Grow Feathers and Scales in Weird Patchy Clumps all Over Their Body, Sprout Extra Limbs Which Serve No Purpose and then Try to Colonize Nearby Solar Systems With Astoundingly Innovative Technology and Weaponry That's Never Been Seen Anywhere Else and Never Will be Seen Again, Only to Have a Sudden Shift In Consciousness and Nostalgia Late in Life, Leave the Battle Grounds and Return to Mate and Raise Young Then Sit Around Talking About How Easily They Could Have Smashed Whatever Hapless and Peaceful Civilization They Happened to Wage War on This Particular Generation.*

This was a fairly average sized title for an Astrospeciology publication. With infinite physical Universes expanding exponentially larger and smaller in a perpetual never-ending sea of possibilities, one had to be pretty specific when classifying all of the species out there. One could never classify something so impossibly infinite to comprehend of course, but one could try. And several did.

Wilx was reading an interesting story about how all of the surrounding, and once peaceful civilizations now had a massive amount of mind-blowing combat technology that was continuously being abandoned by the Creepy Crawly Telepathic Worm-like Flying Fish in their old age. These once peaceful and simple civilizations had been so savagely and nonsensically brought to the brink of extinction that they now harboured quite a bit of anger and vengeance they otherwise never would have. They also never would have had the ability to communicate with their neighbouring victims, except that all of them now had Telepathic Worm-like Flying Fish Technology, and it was only a matter of time before they all had a chat and realized this wasn't an isolated incident, united in coalition and waged savage retaliatory hostilities against the Flying Fish's home planet. The writer was of the opinion that this was just the natural course of events with these creatures and this would somehow eventually lead to the outlying civilizations becoming peaceful again, all of the weapons being destroyed, the Flying Fish being brought nearly to extinction, the outlying civilizations returning to their respective home planets and things starting all over again in a cyclical fashion. This tended to be the way things played out in most universes; they escalated to fevered and catastrophic levels, and then started all over again with a clean slate.

Wilx somewhat agreed, although he was fairly certain that it was only a matter of time and space before the nearby Solar System Swallowing Swatch he'd read about in the latest issue of *Planet Eaters, Solar System Swallowers and Galactic Gobblers* would simply inhale the whole lot of them.

"Good Riddance," said Wilx aloud, entirely unimpressed with the whole ordeal. He put down his magazine and turned to Rip. "Now, let's talk about this Greeg."

"Former Greeg," corrected Rip.

"Well, we've obviously still got a lot of work to do before we can call him that. But maybe this isn't such a bad thing."

"How so?"

"Well, if he's still prone to Greegian outbursts maybe that could come in handy when we do reach the Greeg planet."

"So you really do think it exists?"

"It couldn't be any more clear to me that not only does it exist, but that once our little friend sees it and understands who he is and what we've done to him, we could very well learn more than anyone has ever learned about Greegs, ever."

"A bold statement."

"Care to wager?"

Dr. Rip T. Brash was faced with a predicament he'd never encountered. He had nothing left to wager. Wilx now owned everything he had, ever did have in the past and ever would have in the future. Confused and shaken, Rip looked desperately for a drink. Not a drop to be found. Rip went to his back-up plan. He fumbled with the remote control to bring up the crate-filled liquor ship and sent it flying towards the Obotron 1. Salivating and panting like a dog, pressed up against the glass and staring out at the ship, Rip saw the most horrifying thing he'd seen in his entire life. IBP radicals somehow had located the fleet and set up one of their signature space blockades. In typical radical fashion, an IBP signature space blockade wasn't a very well thought out endeavour. When you consider these were creatures that have devoted their life to preserving the most useless organism ever to exist, you can't expect top quality results. This IBP space blockade consisted of locating the Obotron liquor supply ship, well known as the lifeblood of Dr. Rip T. Brash The Third, and when it was called up to the Obotron 1, materializing several thousand ships in front of it full of IBP protesters holding up hand drawn signs to the glass windows and spelling a message with the ships.

The message was this:

NO

The liquor supply ship being full of nothing other than liquor, the IBP radical's various futile messages reached precisely no one. Then, and here's the crazy part, then they lit all their ships on fire. The logic being that liquor was flammable and would be destroyed. This is true, and it was destroyed. Mission Accomplished. What else is true is that every single IBP protester was also quite flammable and they too were destroyed. Hundreds of Millions of dead protesters... just to piss off an eccentric alcoholic doofus. What is also true is that the sheer amount of investment bankers required to fuel on stand-by and then materialize the IBP blockade into the 'No' formation at precisely that time, was staggeringly more than the entire Obotron 7 fleet could ever consume... ever. It was a curious universal fact that every protestor was inevitably just as, if not more, guilty than what or whoever it was that they were protesting. This is discussed in detail in Karl Von Marxschenhowzer's infamous *"Hypocrisy Inaction: The Plight of the Pointless Protester."*

Wilx happened to be reading *Hypocrisy Inaction: The Plight of the Pointless Protester,* as Dr. Rip T. Brash the Third saw his precious liquor supply explode and then evaporate. Rip then did something he hadn't done for awhile. He went completely insane.

CHAPTER 19

the Cycle of Insanity Finally Gives Way to a Bustling Solar System

Dr. Rip T. Brash The Third awoke in a Greeg cage. He assumed this meant he'd had a damned fine night of drunken sex with a space whore and treated her miserably. He looked out and saw Krimshaw and Wilx staring at him and chatting and remembered this was not the case. He was painfully sober and not remotely hungover. None of his genitals stung like anything. He shook the bars of the cage in futility and screamed.

"What is the meaning of this? What have I done to deserve this?!"

"Aside from acting like a common Greeg and causing irreparable damage to the ship's already irreparably damaged guidance system and urinating all over the miniscule remaining food supply... nothing," retorted Wilx.

Krimshaw laughed hysterically, thoroughly enjoying mocking Rip and being out of the cage. Seeing how pleasant it was to mock the one in the Greeg cage, and not be the one being mocked in the Greeg cage.

This pattern would continue for a long time, as the trio

floated aimlessly through space. Wilx was next in the Greeg cage after he flipped out on Krimshaw for using his latest issue of *Flappy and Droopy Skinned Blob-like Floating Jelly Monsters* as toilet paper. Krimshaw thought this was a huge step in his development, which it most certainly was, considering his history of feces related slip-ups. They each took turns being confined to the Greeg cage, and causing irreparable damage to the ship and each other. This was fairly standard for any beings confined to a ship for this length of time. Most luxury fleets had a Greeg cage in them, which the owners claimed to be put there for devious sexual encounters. It was much more often used for this sort of rotating, musical chairs-esque confinement of rogue fellow travellers gone wild.

Finally, the pattern was broken. An unexpected, unwarranted and un-requested hyperspacial jump landed the fleet smack dab in the middle of the most bustling solar system within five trillion Universes. The New York City of Solar Systems. The China of Solar Systems.

The Kroonum System.

CHAPTER 20

Kroonum

Kroonum is a blue-spotted Zeta Sun that provides warmth and life for 27 planets. Not one of these planets is mellow or uninhabited. They all suffer major problems of overpopulation and a lack of sleep.

If New York is the city that never sleeps, then Kroonum is the Solar System that has never even *heard* of sleep. There are simply too many exciting things to do to even consider the notion of falling asleep. To sleep for even the shortest amount of time while in Kroonum is to miss at least several unprecedented and historically life-changing events in galactic history. The last time someone stepped out for a nap they ended up missing the resurrection of The Beatles, as well as the 12-hour reunion concert that followed shortly thereafter. The seemingly endless show ended with a complete front-to-back rendition of *Abbey Road*, played against the stirring backdrop of Kroonum's famous Whizzling-Firebeam asteroid shower (an event that is believed will only happen four times, ever). This was the third time it had happened. The person who'd stepped out for a nap was later informed of the excellence of The Beatles, and was also told he would do best not to miss the next Whizzling-Firebeam asteroid shower. He ended up missing it on account of being dead, as the fourth and final asteroid shower did not occur for hundreds of years (or 89,126.3 zillion Schmickian years, if you want to get precise in the matter).

"Where are we?" asked Rip.

Wilx looked around confusedly. "We've just undergone an unrequested hyperspacial jump."

"I know...but where exactly did we jump to?"

"I'm trying to figure that out," said Wilx as he scrambled through the star charts. "Look over there...I see a planet missing its top half. Could that be the legendary Clug Raddo?"

"What's Clug Raddo?" I asked.

"A planet that lost its northern hemisphere due to the climactic event of the Dishwashing Chronicles."

"What happened in the Dishwashing Chronicles?"

"Well tell you about it later. For now I need to focus on the fact that we've jumped many universes in the complete opposite direction from the planet Hroon and the sunned district of Herb."

"Do we have any pomegranates?" asked Rip.

"Uh, what are pomegranates?"

"Did the rest of the fleet make the hyperspacial jump with us?" asked Krimshaw.

"Good question. At least someone is having relevant thoughts around here."

Wilx tracked the fleet.

"Hmm...there are only 16 Obotrons currently following us. It seems a couple of the ships didn't make the jump at all."

"What does that mean?" asked Krimshaw. "Two of the ships are still in another universe? Their crew members are just floating around aimlessly?"

"Oh, no. Nothing like that. They've assuredly perished by now."

"What?"

"Without the guidance system of Obotron 1 they were probably sent crashing into the surface of the nearest planet. Or, if you prefer, careening into the vacuum of the nearest black hole. Or maybe they burned up in the infernos of the nearest Red Giant. One thing is certain, they were destroyed by the nearest object of dangerous proportions."

"I thought our guidance system was irreparably damaged," said Rip. "Shouldn't they actually be better off without us?"

"No. It is better to have an irreparably damaged guidance system than to have no guidance system at all."

"Right."

Krimshaw looked out of the window and saw an epic beam of light funnelling towards a planet.

"Why is that light there?"

"What light?"

"Look, there's a beam of light connecting with a planet. It looks like you can see the light moving."

They both immediately recognized the description of a planet that was reached by a road of light. It was, after all, the most famous planet in the most famous of systems. They raced over to the window and confirmed their suspicion.

"It's the road to Lincra!" shouted Rip happily.

"Indeed!"

"What's the road to Lincra?" I asked.

Wilx was ecstatic. "We're in Kroonum! Lincra is a planet in the excellent Kroonum system!"

"What's so excellent about it?"

"I'll answer that one," said Rip. "It's the most bustling solar system within five trillion universes. Some people spend their whole lives trying to get to Kroonum, on account of how exciting it is here."

"Yes," agreed Wilx, "however life is short once they arrive, on account of how dangerous it is here."

"Why does this planet have a road of light?"

"Because it is the most popular planet to visit in the Kroonum system. The light is coming from the mass amount of constantly arriving ships."

"Why do the ships have so many lights?"

"You ever noticed how dark it is in space? You try finding your way around this black infinity without a set of 4000 watt Hyclerion Blinder-Bulbs. You'd end up crashing into the surface of a nearby planet like the recently lost Obotron ships that we will probably never mention or think of again."

"An interesting fact about the road of light," said Wilx, "was discovered the time Lincra closed for renovations. For a few days no ships were allowed to land anywhere on the planet, yet the road continued to shine as brilliantly as ever."

"How is that possible?" asked Krimshaw.

"It is the strongest case of Persistence of Vision ever known. Ships have been nonstop arriving at Lincra for so long that the beam of light seems to be permanently burned into the ocular fabric of space and time."

"Can we stop?"

"Of course."

Wilx instructed the rest of the fleet to remain motionless in orbit. He then guided Obotron 1 towards Lincra. It is a poor idea to attempt manual flight while on the hectic road, so Wilx set the ship to *Go-With-the-Flow* Mode, allowing the flux of the nearby ships to safely glide them to the surface. Before too long, Obotron 1 arrived at the spectacular main parking lot.

The main parking lot of Lincra is so spectacular that many visitors believe they are seeing the entire surface of the planet. They hang around the station for the weekend taking a few photos, then they leave satisfied, having seen none of the actual world.

Rip, Wilx and Krimshaw boarded the ship's floating elevator. This drew many stares from the crowd below, being that Krimshaw was a Greeg and that Obotron 1 was probably the most expensive spaceship in the whole lot. It was definitely the only spaceship with its own floating elevator.

Rip unnecessarily greeted the crowd.

"Hello!" he shouted to the bewildered aliens. "I am Dr. Rip

T. Brash the Third!"

There were a few mutters of slight recognition followed by an unrelated terrorist explosion.

"Ahem," coughed Krimshaw.

"What is it?"

"Why don't you introduce us too?"

"Because you aren't famous."

"How can we hope to get famous if you don't mention us in front of large groups of people?"

"True," said Rip as he pointed at Wilx and Krimshaw. "And these are some people I happen to know!"

"What did you fly here in?" yelled a random alien.

"I'm glad you asked. Our ship is a very rare Obotron. It is one of the most expensive vessels ever made. Feel free to admire it at will! Gaze your eyes upon its pricey qualities! Feel the stinging pangs of jealousy when you realize your own ship is a piece of junk in comparison! If you don't have eyes, then touch the recently waxed surface with your antennae and know that the wax job is better than yours!"

"Hey, don't tell them to admire the ship too much," whispered Wilx. "I'd like to leave with it still in our possession."

Rip corrected his mistake. "Remember everyone, admire the ship only with your eyes! We have a protective shield designed to immediately set fire to anyone who puts a single finger or antennae on the waxed surface!"

"Is that true?" asked Krimshaw.

"No. But I dare them to risk finding out."

The crowd grew visibly anxious wanting to know if the ship would really set them on fire if they touched it. For some creatures, finding out the worthless answer to this mystery was well worth the risk of death.

The floating elevator (which was merely a sort of round slab that frighteningly lacked handrails) touched down on the surface of the docking station. The trio stepped off. The slab immediately flew back up to the ship.

"How do we get the elevator to come back to us when we want to leave?" asked Krimshaw.

"I don't know," said Wilx. "I forgot the remote control. We'll worry about it later. Let's go look around!"

"Good idea," agreed Rip.

The parking lot existed within a domed structure the size of a small moon. Inside the dome were many bizarre vendors. Some of the vendors were boasting the cheapest rates on stolen bottles of Investment Banker, while most were selling maps of the planet.

"We'd better grab a map," suggested Rip. "It is impossible to make sense of the labyrinthine surface of Lincra without one."

"And a good map, too," added Wilx. "Some of these are poor quality." He picked one up from a nearby table. "Look at this one, it's just a white piece of paper that says '*You are anywhere you want to be.*' How does such existential drivel qualify as a map?"

The unkempt vendor selling this object was of the belief that all reality is artificial, and can therefore shift its appearance according to the mind's desire. He was also heavily tripping out on the boiled juices of psychotropic Lincran-leaves.

"Don't be harsh," said the unkempt vendor as he imagined his own hand transforming into a tentacle. "That map contains valuable advice. You should never forget that all your surroundings are a fantasy, and that you can change where you're at simply by imagining you're somewhere else."

"You know what else is a fantasy?" asked Rip.

"What?"

"Your income. Because nobody will ever buy what you're selling."

"Oh, these maps aren't for sale. I offer everything for free, being that any apparent value of money is imaginary anyway."

Rip grabbed a stack of the maps and tore them up until they were tiny shreds. It took a long time. The trio then continued walking as if nothing happened. The unkempt vendor made up some new maps. It was an easy task considering they were merely a single sentence written on a white piece of paper.

"Look at this one!" said Wilx, pointing to a different and infinitely more exciting map vendor. "I'm gonna get one of these."

Wilx left the group for a minute. When he returned he wasn't really holding a map (defining a map as something that can be folded and placed in a glove-box) but rather carried a multi-volume set of 30 pound hardcover books.

"This should help us find everything."

"Look, here comes one of the parking lot shuttle-sliders," said Rip. "Let's board it while we can."

They got on the shuttle before it whizzed off. Shuttle-sliders are dissimilar to floating elevators in the sense that they only move horizontally, but are similar in the sense that they also frighteningly lack handrails.

Obotron 1 had landed almost directly in the middle of the parking lot, meaning that reaching the edge of the dome by foot would have entailed a horrendous, month-long journey with nothing to eat except for maps and other paper products. By taking the shuttle car they would reach the edge of the dome in a matter of minutes. The fare was offensively expensive, but it had to be paid. Most people who attempt walking across the great parking lot are never heard from again.

The instant the shuttle was out of sight, several dozen curious fingers and antennae placed themselves upon the surface of Obotron 1. The disgusting creatures in ownership of these fingers and antennae were happy to learn there was no protective shield setting them on fire. They celebrated this fact by smashing a few of the windows and entering the ship. The intruders proceeded to devour what little remaining food they could find. This was not a great loss as it was all thoroughly urine-soaked. They then proceeded to syphon nearly all of the ship's fuel. Upon leaving, the creatures didn't even bother to use the same broken windows, but rather found a few new ones to crash through.

The shuttle arrived at the edge of the dome. Rip was the first one to walk through the door and see the surface of Lincra, and was therefore the first one to suffer a mild heart attack. It was instantly clear as to why a map is the most valuable item you can own on this planet. The surface of Lincra is actually a myriad of surfaces stacked on top of each other, a gradual layering upon layering created for the purpose of maximizing spacial problems. A planetary version of a nesting doll, there is the one major outermost planet, and within that planet lay a smaller planet, and within that smaller planet lay another smaller planet, and so forth until all the layers of Lincra together form the equivalent ground space of the combined, remaining 26 planets in the Kroonum system. Each layer is known for having its own distinct climate, terrain, life-forms and atmosphere. Visitors are allowed to freely roam between the layers, all of which are connected by way of the Master Ladder.

"I suggest we read some of these books before we go anywhere," said Wilx as he sat down on a bench. Most of the entrances to Lincra are lined with scores of benches, as needing to sit down is the most typical reaction of the first-time visitor.

"What books?" I asked him.

"The multi-volume map of Lincra, the ones I just bought."

"I know, but for a minute I could have sworn you weren't carrying them anymore. I thought you'd gotten tired and thrown them out, deciding to let blind chance choose our ultimate location."

"No," said Wilx. "That's more something Rip would do."

"Not on this world," said Rip. "Even I don't feel like braving Lincra without a map."

"Where should we go?" asked Wilx as he passed Rip one of the many 30 pound hardcover books that he mysteriously managed to carry out of sight.

"You read it to us," said Rip as he struggled to focus on all the creatures zipping up and down the Master Ladder between the layers of the world. "I'm far too hypnotized by this insanity to be able to make out the sentences."

Wilx flipped to chapter one in the first volume of the *Map to Lincra*. "It says we are right now on Terminal Layer Zero. Below the TLZ are the Subterranean Layers 1-66, the innermost layer of which is an observation deck for viewing the fiery planetary core. Looking directly at the core will fry your optic nerves, so it is suggested that only blind creatures visit Subterranean Layer 66. Any creatures allergic to water or other forms of hydrogen-oxygen combinations are advised to avoid every seventh, even-numbered subterranean layer, all of which are water based.

'Above the TLZ are the Floating Layers 1-79, the topmost layer being the only place on Lincra where you can see sky or space, aside from when inside the parking lot dome. All of the lighting for the Subterranean Layers comes from Terminal Layer Zero, which consists mainly of Investment Banker Corral Farms and Slaughterhouses. Well, where should we go first? A Subterranean or Floating Layer?"

"Are there any places designed for people who like to make outlandish wagers?" asked Rip.

Wilx flipped to the index. "No. It says betting of any kind is prohibited on Lincra."

"No betting? That means this will be another planet in which I didn't place an outlandish wager during my visitation. Pluto will have to be removed from the next edition of *Very Rare Planets.*"

"Too bad. Pluto could use the publicity."

"Maybe I'll find a way to make a bet," said Rip optimistically.

"Even if you did, what would you wager? You don't own anything."

"That's not true. I have many fine superfluous organs."

"You've already lost all your superfluous organs to me, remember?" said Wilx. "I intend to collect them as soon as we find a mildly decent surgeon who will perform surgery for all the wrong reasons. In fact, I think there's an entire layer of Lincra devoted to exactly that."

Wilx again flipped to the index of the *Map to Lincra.* "Aha! I was right. Subterranean Layer 39 is known as the Layer of Mildly Decent Surgeons Who Will Perform Surgery For All the Wrong Reasons. Let's go there first."

"No!" shouted Rip as he clung to his stomach. "You can't have my organs! I need them to wager in future bets!"

"Are there any sort of Carnival attractions on this planet?" asked Krimshaw. "I'd like to see more of those savage Greegs."

Wilx looked up Greegs in the *Map of Lincra*. "We might be in luck... Subterranean Layer 53 is a Carnival Zoo. It says many fine animals have been stolen from their natural environment and locked up in tiny cages just for our viewing enjoyment."

"What sort of creatures do they have?"

"Wailing Hair-Beasts, Crawling Eyes, Horrendous Swamp-Swoons, Gelatinous Cubes, Elemental Stone-Golems, hey...look! They even have some of those Flying Grimbat Messengers I've read about."

"But do they have any Greegs?" asked Krimshaw.

"They boast a decent selection of the most savage Greegs imaginable. Let's head over there now."

Krimshaw sauntered towards the Master Ladder. Rip asked Wilx if he would hang back for a minute and help him tie his non-existent shoelaces.

"Do you think we should take him there?" he whispered. "I'm worried about the stares he's been getting, what being an intelligent Greeg wearing clothing and consorting with non-Greegs and all."

"I'm sure it'll be fine," said Wilx. "Let's go over to the Ladder."

"Hurry up!" yelled Krimshaw.

Once Rip and Wilx caught up, the three of them began descending the Master Ladder. The vibe of the Subterranean Layers was uncomfortable.

"I don't like it down here," said Rip. It was a justifiable opinion to have. They were currently passing by Subterranean 11, a layer used mainly as a storage dump for the unneeded organs flowing in from the Layer of Mildly Decent Surgeons Who Will Perform Surgery For All the Wrong Reasons.

"I agree," cried Wilx as they passed Subterranean 12, the Layer Where Nothing is Done Except For Cutting Onions.

"We should have visited one of the floating thingies. Let's turn around."

"No," said Krimshaw. "We have to see the cages. Besides, where there's Greegs there might be information about the all-

Greeg planet."

"I guess so," said Rip. "How many more of these things do we have to climb through?"

"Just 41."

"Sigh."

Everyone was beginning to feel the exhaustion of descending towards the centre of Planet Lincra.

Krimshaw slipped and nearly plunged into the abyss.

"Why is everything connected by ladders?" he asked, referring not only to the Master Ladder but also to the smaller ladders connecting the many smaller layers and the general placement of ladders in most areas of his vision. "On our ship we've got floating elevators and teleportation rooms, yet the most popular planet in the system can't afford something better than archaic ladders? It is a laughably inconvenient tool."

"Pfft, he doesn't know about the KULMOOG," mocked Rip.

"The what?"

"The Kroonum Union of Ladder Makers and/or Official Overseeing Gods," informed Wilx.

"Who are they?"

As everyone descended, passing such places as the Layer of Governmental Operations Concerning Hypnotic Mind Control, Wilx delved into the long story of the Ladder Makers Union.

"The KULMOOG are the oldest and strongest union in the Kroonum system. They started out as just the KULM, the Kroonum Union of Ladder Makers. Their invention of the ladder revolutionized life as they knew it. Suddenly people were able to reach things on high shelves without climbing on the actual shelves and thus breaking them and having to buy new shelves. Shelf makers lost a considerable amount of money on this aspect of the ladder revolutionizing things. People could also now pick fruit without having to climb trees, thus not falling out of trees, breaking bones and requiring pricey hospital bills. Doctors lost much of their income due to the increased safeness of fruit-picking. It also became easier to break into houses; one simply had to pick a window, prop a ladder and climb their way to crime. Companies that made security bars for windows were one of the few non-ladder related ventures to become richer as a result of the ladder. Everyone was affected by the advent of this tool. With so much money being spent on ladders instead of new shelves and hospital bills, the KULM quickly became the richest entity in the system. They became so powerful the Kroonum politicians began to fear their very presence. Naturally, over time, the Ladder Union usurped the power of the politicians and were made the unquestionable leaders of every facet of life in the system. This is when the 'Official Overseeing Gods' part of their acronym was added on. Every job, income and family evolved to rely upon the ladder. Yet as time passed, the ladder became outdated and impractical. Yet rather than keep up with the times and invent entirely new technology and infrastructure (as such things are highly illegal) everyone in Kroonum was forced to subsidize ridiculous alterations to the ladder, to the point where some 'ladders' are not ladders at all, aside from a few obligatory rungs here and there. The details of what constitutes a ladder has been the spark of many fierce battles and riots. Nervous officials are often forced to appease mobs over the building of tools that are not at all ladders. So here we are, forced to climb this absurd device instead of doing something easy like teleporting or floating, all because of the Ladder Union's throne of power watching over us."

"That explains the cluster of planets we saw on the way here, the one connected by an intricate series of ladders," said Krimshaw.

"That is the central processing factory of Kroonum ladders and ladder-related products such as the Varnishizer, the only varnish on the market guaranteed to dry in open space. The cluster is known simply as Planet KULMOOG. It is probably one of the dullest and yet most frightening places you could visit. How is it both dull and frightening at the same time you ask? It is dull considering the fact that nothing goes on there besides the churning out of more ladders and ladder-related products. It is frightening because all your words and actions are charted by the ever present eyes and ears of KULMOOG Surveillance.

Anyone suspected of being a spy or of being even remotely anti-ladder is tortured for information about the supposed perpetual plot to replace the ladder. KULMOOG has grown so paranoid over losing power that generally most everyone is suspected of being a spy."

"Let's not go to Planet KULMOOG," suggested Rip.

"Another place we shouldn't go is the topmost layer of Lincra. There is nothing but a bunch of ladders going up into the sky, leading nowhere. Endless hoards of tourists climb these ladders, but rather than turn around when the ladder runs out they merely attempt to continue climbing, thus falling to their death. There is never a shortage of new arrivals eager to climb the ladders, despite scattered bones covering the ground as a chilling warning sign. A fine living is made selling maps and provisions at the base of these ladders. It is incredibly easy to make a living there, for when you sell someone a map or a provision you merely wait for them to fall off the ladder, then collect your goods from the body and sell them again to the next hapless wanderer. It is not entirely known why these useless ladders exist, but the fact that people climb them is seen around the universe as a prime example of the height of stupidity. People climb the ladders simply because they are there. Some see it as a side-effect of the intense mental-conditioning that has gone down between the KULMOOG and the residents of Kroonum, as if to say the people of Kroonum have been trained to believe in the necessity of ladders to the point where they are physically incapable of stopping themselves from climbing a ladder when they see one. Other ideas are discussed, some more insane than others, including the usual fanatical religious groups who believe the ladders are God's way of announcing the Resurrection of the Messiah, or He Who Shall Survive the Ladder-Climb. Something like 45% of ladder-deaths are said to be people who think they are some sort of saviour. One thing is known, these dangerous ladders are allowed to remain because of the prodigious bribes being supplied to the KULMOOG by the profiteering merchants who lurk by the bone-riddled ladder's base."

"Let us now descend the ladder in silence," suggested Rip.

"To commemorate the passing of the ladder climbers?" asked Krimshaw.

"No, because I'm sick of hearing about them."

And so the group finished the remainder of the journey in silence. With each passing layer they could feel the intense heat of the fiery core growing stronger. Krimshaw shed some of his clothing. He seemed to do this purely out of survival instinct, as heat stroke is the most common shared experience amongst tourists who visit Subterranean Layers, yet it was likely that he subconsciously knew if he wore less clothing the Carnival Greegs would be less offended by his presence. After what felt like eternity, the group arrived at Subterranean Layer 53, also known as the Royal Lincran Carnival Zoo.

The word 'Royal' could not have been a more inappropriate word to place in front of 'Lincran Carnival Zoo.' The place was a nasty dungeon. Greeg feces caked the stone walls. Whoops of pain emanated from an unknown distance. Chutes descended from the roof into the cages, evidently serving as feeding troughs as they spewed runoff organs from the Layer of Mildly Decent Surgeons Who Will Perform Surgery For All the Wrong Reasons. Dangerous aliens slithered along the edges of the shadowed frames, hoping to make a living by pickpocketing the space-yuppies. The space-yuppies were numerous, dim-witted and slow to the reflex. A fine living was made by the pickpockets.

Many passersby had noticed Krimshaw.

"Why do they keep pointing at me and whispering?" he asked Rip.

"Uh... they're just admiring your jacket. Isn't it made from the pelt of a Pelexor Snow-Demon? Those are impossible to kill, and tougher to skin."

"I'm not wearing my jacket. It's boiling hot down here."

"They can see you carrying the jacket."

"I'm not carrying my jacket, Wilx is."

"No he's not," said Rip.

"Where'd it go?" asked Krimshaw. "You said you'd watch my jacket!"

"Your jacket is safe," said Wilx.

"We can see that you don't have it! Don't even try to say you're carrying all those books right now because I can see all of your hands!"

"I assure you everything is fine," said Wilx. "Exposition is for another time."

"He's right," said Rip, eyeing the sketchy scenery. "Let's just find the Greegs and get out of here."

A largish crowd of shady characters were now following Krimshaw. They looked as if ready to pounce. One of the spider-like creatures spoke to Rip.

"Interesting Greeg you've got there. Wearing clothing, walking upright, speaking full thoughts, not throwing feces. Very interesting indeed. Never seen anything like it."

"Shh!" said Rip. "He doesn't know what he is. I have completely reformed his mind to the point where he doesn't even know he's a Greeg. He has no remembrance that he used to be in one of these cages."

"I wouldn't be so sure of that," said the spider-creature. "Look at how distressed and angry he appears. He remembers these cages, all right. He doesn't like being here at all. Doesn't like seeing his brothers and sisters locked up."

"Keep your voice down."

"None of these savage beasts deserve to be proper members of society," said the spider. "I think he should be put back into a cage right now. But not before it's properly explained to him what he is."

"Don't even think about it!"

The spider-creature started fighting its way through the crowd towards Krimshaw.

"We have to leave now," said Rip to Wilx. "They're gonna ruin everything. It's still too early for Krimshaw to know the truth about his identity."

"How do you plan to get out of here? We're completely surrounded by things that can walk on the roof."

Rip surveyed the area and realized Wilx was right. The space-yuppies had disappeared, having been summoned to a needless seminar regarding how to best hoard money. All that remained was the group of shady creatures bearing down on Krimshaw.

"Do something!" yelled Rip.

Wilx did something.

This was a very characteristic moment for these two well-seasoned travellers of space and time. Rip tended to be the sideline motivation, abstractly yelling for 'something' to be done (while actually doing nothing himself), while Wilx tended to be the one who knew what had to be done and did it.

Wilx looked at the nearest cage. It had a sign reading PECKING GRAPPLER-BIRDS. Below this sign was another sign reading NEVER OPEN. They couldn't have chosen a better cage to stand in front of while defending themselves from yet another angry and hotly pursuant mob. Wilx did the unthinkable. He opened the cage. Pecking Grappler-Birds swarmed out, quickly filling up the space of Subterranean Layer 53. They pecked. They grappled. They flew.

"Run!" yelled Wilx.

Rip and Krimshaw followed Wilx down the corridor towards the Master Ladder.

"I think those bird things have them distracted. But don't slow down."

"Can you believe how fast they peck through to the brains?" asked Krimshaw.

"And how effectively they grapple the spinal cord?" added Rip.

"No time to admire the rapid killing technique of the Pecking Grappler-Bird. Everybody get on this ladder now."

All over again they passed the many Subterranean Layers of Lincra. Despite the urgent rush a break was taken on the Layer of Transcendental Levitation. Everyone agreed some mellowing out was in order. After an hour no one had managed to successfully levitate, but the ambient music was still soothing.

Finally they reached Terminal Layer Zero.

"Should we go straight to the parking lot?" asked Rip. "Or check out some of the Floating Layers?"

"Let's leave. I've had enough of this planet," gasped Wilx.

They arrived at the parking lot.

"I didn't notice before how there isn't a single ladder in here," said Krimshaw.

"That's because the parking lot of Lincra is the one shred of property in all of Kroonum that the KULMOOG do not attempt to claim forceful ownership upon," explained Wilx as they walked down the main strip, attempting to hail one of the many crowded shuttle-sliders.

"Why is that?"

"Hundreds of years before the KULMOOG came into fruition, a small group of rebellious Lincran townsfolk (apparently sick and tired of having to walk into the next county in order to legally tie up their horse/horse-like-antiquated-mammal-transportation-thing while they indulged themselves at the tavern/socialization-through-intoxication-establishment) set in motion plans to acquire an eternally binding clause in which they would control ownership of the parking area of downtown Lincra and thus be free to get as intoxicated as possible without having to worry about the long stumble to the horse/horse-like-antiquated-mammal-transportation-thing. Ownership would be passed down through the bloodline of the original rebels, the Parking Lot Lords, until the end of existence. Over time the Lords maximized their ability to get home during warped states of mind by inventing and developing the shuttle-slider. Everyone liked the shuttle-sliders, so the Lords invested all their time and energy into opening up a taxi service. Not really caring about the goings-on of the parking lot other than the revenue-stream of the taxi service, the Lords have given complete freedom to the thousands of resident merchants, squatters, party-monsters, ravers, rockers, bashers and smashers to do whatever they please within the wild confines of the domed-lot, so long as they spend a little cash on a taxi every once in a while. A general pervasive atmosphere of intoxication and immobility rendered the shuttle-slider an unimaginably lucrative business."

"Why do the KULMOOG care about some old clause?" asked Krimshaw. "Why don't they storm the lot?"

"I couldn't say," said Wilx. "But the story goes the townsfolk had at their disposal the means to place a very real curse on the parking lot. Anyone not a part of the bloodline who attempts to exert control over the goings-on of the parking lot will supposedly have their brain explode after the passing of a fortnight. The KULMOOG seem to believe in the curse enough to stay away from here. It is the only known loophole in the ladder-monopolization of things in Kroonum."

Finally they hopped on a shuttle-slider.

Obotron 1 was right where they left it.

"We can't get in the ship," said Wilx.

"Why not?" asked Krimshaw.

"I just remembered I forgot the remote control for the floating elevator."

"I wondered when that problem would become relevant."

"Don't worry about it," said Rip. "Someone has already foreseen the problem and helped us out by smashing a bunch of windows. We'll just enter the ship that way."

The ship lifted off the surface and flew away from the crowded madness of planet Lincra. The rest of the fleet was waiting motionless in orbit.

Only now did Wilx notice all the fuel gauges of Obotron 1 were reading empty.

"Seems we were the victims of fuel-bandits," he said calmly. "Everybody prepare themselves. The ship is about to crash into the nearest object of dangerous proportions."

"Why don't we just drain the fuel from one of the other fleet ships?" suggested Rip. "Let them crash and burn."

"What a great idea! Bless your heartless heart!"

The fuel from another Obotron was ordered to be switched over to their own ship.

The process didn't take long. Afterwards the ship that had been randomly chosen to have all of its fuel drained was destroyed by the nearest object of dangerous proportions, which in this case was the planet Lincra.

Obotron 1 and the now remaining 15 other fleet ships zoomed off into the vast Kroonum system. The ship was chilly, on account of all the broken windows exposing them to the open vacuum of space. Krimshaw put on his Pelexor Snow-Demon jacket. The one that would have been admired by the angry and hotly and pursuant mob if he had been wearing it at the time.

CHAPTER 21

Bureaucracy

When you go about pompously and recklessly unleashing viciously contained zoo animals on the most populated and famous tourist destination in five trillion universes, you tend to raise alarm bells. This is especially the case when you arrive in a shiny fleet of Obotron 7 space ships and leave 16 of them hovering nonsensically around the planet packed with pointless, idle employees. This is even more the case when you carry with you an inter-universal celebrity like Dr. Rip T. Brash the Third and an upright walking, clothes wearing, intelligent conversation having Greeg.

However, this being the Kroonum system, and this being the planet Lincra... these events were barely the six thousandth, five hundredth and forty seventh most interesting/bizarre/outlandish/casualty inducing incidents of the hour.

Nevertheless, hoards of Kroonumite Special Task Force Ranger Pods were immediately sent forth from the Central Kroonum Enforcement & Coercion Department on Persheron 8. They were sent in waves and from different task forces to deal with each assault our trio of travellers had inflicted on the precious foundations of Kroonum Society: Civility, Order and Peace, or COP. Persheron 8 is one of 9 planets and 47 moons in the Kroonum system whose sole purpose is law enforcement, jailing, detainment, execution, rehabilitation, law writing, law re-writing, finding of outdated laws and updating them, finding of updated laws and outdating them, covert undercover operations, and the seemingly never-ending creation, integration and upkeep of more branches of The Upgrading,

Expansion, Keeping Up of and Maintenance of Kroonum Civility, Order & Peace Agency. Confused? I hope not. This is, as you say, barely the tip of the Iceberg.

This fumbling, inefficient schmorgosborg is merely the Solar Enforcement Branch of Kroonum Law Enforcement. There is also of course The Universal Legal Oversight Committee, The Galactic Territorial and Regional Integrated Intelligence Agencies (there are over 976 of these in this particular galaxy, no one is sure which ones are legitimate and which are fronts at this point. None of them are remotely integrated, several are engaged in full out warfare.) These are a mere nuisance, and a cohesive juggernaut of rationality and efficiency compared to the mind bogglingly complicated, freewheeling and unregulated enforcement agencies on individual planets... and let us not even begin to discuss regional law on various sections of those planets. It is far more often that different splinters of legally sanctioned and government orchestrated law enforcement fights among themselves, rightfully believing the other is involved in criminal activity, which they all most certainly are, to a staggering degree.

All of these corrupt, unchecked, interlocked and mangled factions of law enforcement and bureaucracy has led the hyper oppressed and victimized civilians and visitors of Kroonum to retaliate in violent backlashes in the form of Civilian Organized Militia's For The Restoration of Peace, Order and Civility to the Kroonum System. They have developed the mildly confrontational slogan "A POCKS on the COPs." These militia's are inevitably started by once innocent, indifferent travellers or residents who have been chewed up and spat out by various sanctioned policing groups and courts. There is an entire volume of *Hypocrisy Inaction: The Plight of the Pointless Protester* devoted strictly to the militia's. The true irony here is that there never was, certainly isn't now, and certainly never will be, anything remotely approaching Peace, Order and/or Civility in the Kroonum System. This is exactly why it is such an amazingly popular and exciting place.

This is not to suggest that there isn't any real crime in the

Kroonum system. The overbearing, oppressive and clumsily gummed up together 'legal' conglomerate is entirely justified and necessary, considering the astounding number of swindlers, murderers, psychopaths, rapists, gangs, STD's, daredevils, protostar hoppers, insanely violent religious organizations, and sinister plots to destroy and annihilate every single living thing in the system. Not to mention the rather common occurrence of one species happening upon another that they find delicious, and whose vital organs contain nutrients imperative to their survival. This situation is not helped by the four planets solely devoted to the production and cross-universal distribution of the lucrative Kroonum Zoo genre of hard core entertainment, further perpetuating the image of Kroonum as a non-stop sea of wild and groovy crime and punishment, which it most certainly was. This naturally attracted every wackjob, nutcase and borderline Greeg-like being there was to the place; along with every heroic, bravado seeking adrenaline junkie who wished to seek out and destroy every wackjob, nutcase and borderline Greeg-like being in existence. Of course, neither of these polar opposites could exist without each other, and both thrived in the Kroonum system.

It is curious to note that the 9 planets and 47 moons in the Kroonum system owned and operated by The Upgrading, Expansion, Keeping Up of and Maintenance of Kroonum Civility, Order & Peace Agency were by far the most plagued and violently crime filled planets and moons that had ever existed anywhere... ever. Despite this blatant evidence that more policing merely creates more criminals, there is never a demand for less law enforcement, only more. And so nothing changes here in the Kroonum System, it only gets more confusing, crazier and exponentially more dangerous.

There was only one being who could truly understand all of the intricacies of this ordeal, but he was currently writing *'You are anywhere you want to be'* on blank white pieces of paper and ingesting boiled juices of psychotropic Lincran-leaves in a parking lot. Such is the way of things.

"Pull your space ship and the rest of your fleet over to the slightly darker space to your left, immediately, or I'll shoot out all of your windows," threatened the booming P.A. system from the suddenly menacingly hovering ship belonging to The Big Five Planets Parking Board. "You've illegally parked 16 ships with no permit in restricted space... space."

"Well I think you'll find we don't have any windows left to shoot out, so your threat is idle," retorted Rip.

"That's gonna cost you," said the representative from the Interstellar Luxury Space Fleet Safety and Insurance Department: Broken Window Division.

"This is out of your jurisdiction," blared the overbearing and aggressive Sub-Observatory of Galactic Wranglers & Wobblers... a blatantly made up organization notorious for seizing space ships just to release them in confusing mazes they've designed in order to place bets on who, if any, will find their way out. The Trilateral Commission on Hearings of Importance ruled it an activity that must be permitted, due to Abducted Ship Mazing being the official sport of the entire sector of the galaxy, which means banning or restricting it would be a gross affront to The Treaty of Manderbatt hammered out at the infamous Haurunbistle Tribunal. As any seasoned traveller of space and time will tell you, to undermine The Treaty of Manderbatt is to bring on the wrath of the Council of Eleven and a Half Thousand Different Coloured Robes... and nobody wants that.

"I'll handle this one fellas. You lot are under immediate and severe, extra super double arrest for the release of a dangerous and mutilating Zoo Animal," sternly warned the President of the Lincran Vicious & Dangerous Animal Restraint League through a series of no less than 8 interpreters.

"Let him go, we're dropping the charges," screeched a gang of horribly maimed spider like pickpockets, who were much bigger fans of vigilante justice.

"Can't do that I'm afraid," said the Chancellor of Ensuring Charges Aren't Dropped So Spidery Pickpocket Things That Dwell On the 53rd Subterranean Layer of Lincra Can Take The Law Into Their Own Hands.

"I strongly disagree," belted out a group of powerless

protesters from the Collaboration of Those Who Angrily Disagree With Any Form of Legitimately Sanctioned Policing and/or Law Enforcement in the Kroonum System.

"Do you have a permit for that Greeg?" questioned a genuinely concerned member of the strictly volunteer Rounding Up of Greegs and Quarantining them in Zoos Where They Belong Society.

"What Greeg?" asked Krimshaw, terrified, looking around him for this rogue and permit-less savage.

"Indeed, what Greeg?" faked Wilx and Rip, using the opportunity to smash and pull and twist and pound on any and all of the guidance levers, knobs and buttons they could in order to get the hell out of this mess.

"Right," said one of the ever growing mob of ships surrounding the Obotron 1.

"I'm going to count to three," they all said, miraculously in unison.

"One."

"Two."

"FIRE!"

The night sky exploded in a display of fireworks unrivalled by even the most famous Whizzling-Firebeam asteroid shower. Delighted tourists from the Lincran parking lot and the light beam highway cheered enthusiastically, completely oblivious to the fact that they were not witnessing a planned light show but instead the instant death of many prominent organizations and their representatives. If they had known that, they would have cheered much louder, considering most of them were members of the militia, or surely would be soon.

One Obotron space ship packed full of napping employees was also blown to smithereens. If the tourists and Lincran parking lot dwellers had known that, they would not have cared all that much.

14 other ships and an Obotron 1 with smashed-in windows suddenly materialized far away in what appeared to be some sort of ridiculous maze.

"Who's this loose Greeg they're looking for?" Said Krimshaw, frothing at the mouth.

"Shut up," said Wilx and Rip. "We've got to get through this maze now, that's what's important."

CHAPTER 22

the Maze

In vain Krimshaw searched the floor for crumbs.

Standards had long since been lowered to the eating off the floor of any random morsel that slightly resembled a particle of what was once in another lifetime food.

They had been inside the maze for a long time, and for good reason.

An Abducted-Ship Maze does not exist on the surface of a planet. Mazes are free-floating in space, being the combined size of 3.7 medium quadra-level planets.

Over the many ages since its inception, Abducted-Ship Mazing has risen and fallen in popularity. To ensure the public is still getting fresh entertainment, Mazes are carefully designed to be the definitive representation of danger. Nowadays a maze consists of thousands of deadly, twisting corridors branching out like brain synapses from a spherical centre. There is only one exit, hidden deep in the outer realms. Most ships are unsuccessful, as along the way to the impossible-to-find exit are innumerable traps like time-travelling wormholes, squadrons of well-funded Plutonian nuclear-eels, or the recently invented Dementia-Mirrors (drive through one of those and you're only able to make a right turn for six weeks). It has reached the point where being the victim of a Maze is probably the greatest fear in the galaxy. Every time the average Joe Alien starts up his space-cruiser his brain flashes on the very real possibility that he might suddenly vanish from his proper dimension and reappear inside a Maze surrounded by jeering spectators and Plutonian nuclear-eels.

Miraculously, only one Obotron ship had, as of yet, perished in the Maze. 13 fleet ships followed the main crew down corridor 973L.

Scores of spectators were gathered on viewing platforms scattered around the exciting parts of the maze. Galactic Wranglers & Wobblers were in charge of selling the crazily overpriced tickets. Tickets were especially popular for the area in front of the monstrous minotaur that devours ships in a single bite. The minotaur then regurgitates mechanical shrapnel over top of a cheering crowd that abruptly stops cheering when it begins getting rained on by mechanical shrapnel.

Another prominent platform was the headquarters for The Trilateral Commission on Hearings of Importance. Nothing much occurs here except the repeated hammering out of The Treaty of Manderbatt, followed by hostile disputes over what is meant by the cryptic and vague language it was written in. The arguments are simultaneously resolved and renewed by yet another good hammering out of the Treaty.

Directly beside the platform for The Trilateral Commission on Hearings of Importance is an area sanctioned off for those who wish to protest and boycott everything contained within The Treaty of Manderbatt. This group is better known as the Civilian Organized Militia For The Restoration of Peace, Order and Civility to the Kroonum System. Placing these two platforms beside each other inevitably causes a state of miniature warfare. Members of each side are constantly being bombed into space, all of which is part of the master plan devised by the Kroonum Civility, Order & Peace Agency to have both parties wiped out while avoiding scandalous involvement charges. When things get too heated, the Council of Eleven and a Half Thousand Different Coloured Robes is called in from their sitting perch located at the only exit of the maze. There are only two possible verdicts one can receive while facing trail with the Robes. Execution, or be put inside the maze. So it's really just one possible verdict.

The same exact person who designed the impossible-to-navigate mazes had also designed the legal treatise of the Kroonum System. Each system was more labyrinthine and convoluted than the last. Successful navigation is not meant to be a viable option. These mind-bending, logic-defying structural designs were from the painfully twisted imagination of the Grand KULMOOG Commander Flook. We will hear about him again later in the story.

The corridors of the maze act as a sort of one-way window. The ships inside the maze cannot see outward, yet the spectators can see inside the maze with the aid of x-ray glasses (should you choose to visit a Maze Shop and purchase the glasses at a price so astronomical that you will assuredly have no money left over for the fuel home, effectively stranding you and forcing you to rent your crew and ship out as Maze participants, with the promise of a decent pay cheque that would never arrive even in the rare chance that you escaped anyway).

"How long have we been here?"

"Check the calendar," said Wilx as he hit the brakes, barely avoiding collision with a minefield of boiled proto-stars placed at the end of corridor 973L.

"Looks like corridor 973L is another perilous dead-end," groaned Krimshaw.

The words of the now familiar sounding phrase 'Looks like corridor *blank* is another perilous dead-end' passed into the nearby ears of the languid Dr. Rip. His brain processed the meaning behind these words, yet he didn't understand what was said at all. This type of phrase had been spoken so many times by everyone in the last 19 months (being the approximate amount of earth time they'd spent in the Maze so far) that Rip wouldn't listen to any more of it. He'd gone through all the stages of insanity and mental breakdown one can go through, and was now currently reverting to a state of catatonic silence.

"Were you listening?" said Wilx to Rip. "Add 973L to the list of corridors we've tried."

Rip wrote down some miscellaneous letters and numbers, none of which were 973L. In a moment of poor life decisions, the task of writing down the names of the perilous dead-end corridors was specifically delegated to Rip. It was understood he couldn't handle anything more difficult. Wilx and Krimshaw sat him down in a chair, gave him a clipboard, a few pencils and a stack of blank paper, and told him to merely write down exactly whatever they told him. It was a task he had miserably failed at from the very beginning. Not one of the numbers or the vitally important corresponding letters of the corridor names had been marked down properly, the result of which being that the fleet of Obotrons had needlessly gone through many corridors more than once each. It is likely they would have escaped the maze in a matter of sheer weeks if anyone else had been writing down the numbers. Wilx was completely unaware that he had steered the ship around the same time-travelling wormhole at least 11 times.

Writing down the names of the perilous dead-ends may have been the easiest task on the ship, but it was also the most important. Assigning such an essential job to Rip was a more insane act than anything Rip himself had done, including the time he bolted all the furniture to the roof in an attempt to flip the universe upside down.

Dwellers of Earth may be interested to know that almost every single boat or airplane that has vanished while in the area known as 'The Bermuda Triangle" has in fact been the victim of Abducted-Ship Mazing. Any other reported vanishing from that area is merely a sinking caused by drunken pilots. The Wranglers & Wobblers enjoy seeking out species that haven't invented vehicles qualified to operate in a space-maze, and in an act of mockery transport whatever primitive vehicles they do happen to have into the maze anyway. Spectators love seeing an earthbound vessel appear midair in space, only for the vessel to immediately spin out of control and crash. If you wasted your money and are wearing x-ray glasses, the explosions and the writhing of the victims will be made much more exciting through automatic digital-enhancement. The floors of all the maze corridors are lined with the ancient wreckage of missing WWII bomber-submarines and tourist filled float-planes. Back on earth (in a moment of far too common irony) it is considered ridiculous and ruinous to your reputation to go around saying that aliens are the cause of the Bermuda disappearances, whereas the respected individuals who receive government grants and media coverage are the truly ridiculous lot, being the ones to have foolishly named it "The Bermuda Triangle", when in fact it is blatantly rectangular in shape.

"Hey!" yelled Wilx. "Do you see that up ahead?"

"See what?" asked Krimshaw.

"Those two ships in front of us."

"What about them? Fire a couple bombs at them and get them out of the way."

Krimshaw's idea to blow up the unknown ships did not shock anyone. Competition between fellow ships is a frequent part of life inside the maze. Long ago a rumour had been spread that if you destroyed a ship you would later be granted a clue about the Maze exit. The rumour is completely false. Help is never given to a Maze-goer. Being that ship battles are among the most exciting things to happen inside a Maze, the Trilateral Commission on Hearings of Importance were perfectly happy when the rumour permanently stuck around. After all, they were the ones who started the rumour and continually worked to maintain its upkeep.

"Don't fire any bombs!"

"Why not?" asked Krimshaw. "You know the rules. Anyone who destroys another ship will later be granted a clue. Just think about when all our clues finally arrive... we'll have no problem finding the exit."

"There's no clues."

"You don't know that. Fire the bombs!"

"Look," said Wilx, "those two ships are Obotrons!"

Krimshaw looked out the window and saw he was right.

"How did they get ahead of us? I thought all the fleet ships were programmed never to go faster than Obotron 1?"

"That's correct," said Wilx. "Those two Obotrons were already in the maze without us."

Krimshaw took a moment to add everything up. "You mean those are the two ships that never made the hyper-spacial jump into the Kroonum system?"

"Yes. Two of the slower ships in convoy. They must have fallen behind during hyperspace, allowing them to be picked off by the net-wave of the Wranglers. Nobody seemed to notice, probably because the slower Obotrons have always been considered highly expendable. Then the Wranglers caught up with the rest of us after we left Lincra."

"How have they survived all this time without us?" asked Krimshaw. "I thought you said without our guidance system the rest of the ships would be destroyed by the nearest object of dangerous proportions."

"Normally, yes. These two ships are lucky. It looks like their system went into shock upon the sudden disconnection with the guidance program of Obotron 1. The ships were somehow locked in place the minute they appeared inside the Maze. I don't think they've moved an inch the entire time they've been here."

"Good thing they got stuck in an empty corridor," said Krimshaw aptly.

'Keep Moving' is probably the best survival motto one can have regarding a Maze. 'Never, Ever Remain Motionless For Longer than 3 seconds' would be a more helpful elaboration on the previous vital piece of knowledge. To stop your ship in the maze is to assuredly be chomped by a monstrous minotaur or gravitate into a solar whirlpool.

Obotron 1 accessed the rusty databases of the missing ships and re-programmed them to follow along with the fleet. Soon enough the number of Obotrons was increased from 13 to 15. It wasn't a proper fleet, but it was still a belligerently high-priced set of technological waste. Wilx was delighted at having found the missing ships.

"I feel as if we've already passed that wormhole," said Krimshaw.

"Check the list. We're on corridor 193P."

Krimshaw consulted the list. Corridor 193P was not there, despite this being the 12th time the fleet had passed this particular wormhole.

"It's not on the list. I guess I'm hallucinating."

"Good chance."

Suddenly a broadcast appeared on the telescreen. It was showing a large group of Obotron crew members facing the camera.

Wilx was startled by the appearance of the image, especially considering it now blocked his view of the Maze corridor.

"Who are you?" asked Wilx.

"We are the crew members of the two Obotron ships that have until recently been missing," replied Ralph, one of the night-time janitors who suddenly took it upon himself to be spokesman for the group. It was not known whether Ralph had been voted into leadership, made himself leader because he genuinely felt he deserved the job, or fell into the gig by chance having been conveniently standing both nearest the microphone and best framed in the foreground of the camera.

"We're busy," said Wilx.

Ralph felt the pressure to skip to the point. "We just wanted to express our sincere and heartfelt thanks for the recent rescue of our two vessels, as well to send our regretful apologies that we were ever lost in the first place. We dread to think what would happen to us without the guidance system of Obotron 1. We look forward to sustaining a lifelong career out of following you around on your adventures. We would also like to say---"

Wilx cut off the broadcast. "That's enough."

"About the wormholes in the Maze," said Krimshaw, "aren't they time-travelling wormholes?"

"Of course they are," replied Wilx. "Have you ever known a wormhole not to be a time-traveller? Fly into one of those and you'll be transported to any random time in the past or the future."

"So isn't that our way out?"

"What?"

"This maze tours around the galaxy. It's constantly moving. So if we fly into one of those wormholes we'll reappear outside the maze no matter what, because during any other time it won't be here."

Wilx thought this over for a minute. It seemed like a foolish plan, but they had nothing else.

"It's a brilliant plan!" he said.

It actually was a brilliant plan. Flying into a time-travelling wormhole is the only way to escape the Maze. Even the official outer exit is not at all a means of escape. As mentioned before, the official exit is also the sitting perch for the Council of Eleven and a Half Thousand Different Coloured Robes. Anyone who finds the exit is put under trial by the Robes to decide if they are truly worthy of leaving the Maze. No one is ever deemed worthy. The ships are placed back at the starting point instead of being set free like the usual logical rules of finding the exit of a Maze.

"Time-travel is frightening. Everyone prepare yourself," said Wilx as he set the guidance system for the nearest wormhole. He then roped himself down with unbreakable Tjurdian Rope.

"Hey, where's *our* magically unbreakable rope?" asked Krimshaw.

"There isn't any more. You'll have to prepare yourself for the horrid act of time-travel in some other less logical way."

Krimshaw prepared himself by gnashing his teeth, even breaking some of them. Rip didn't move at all. The fleet of Obotrons flew directly into the center of a time-travelling wormhole. When they re-emerged on the other side of the obligatory mind-bending psychedelic light-show, the Maze and all of its war-faring spectators were nowhere to be seen.

"It worked! We're free!"

"But where did we travel to?" asked Krimshaw. "Or when?"

"I don't know yet," said Wilx. "So far all I know is that two of the Obotron ships are no longer with us. They're either still inside the maze or they're forever trapped in the purgatory of the wormhole. One thing is certain, we'll probably never mention or think of them again."

TIME WARP

*of Things that are neither the Beginning
nor the Middle, nor the End... Sort of*

CHAPTER 23

Emerging from a Wormhole with an Empty Stomach

The thing about hurtling through time is that there are far too many things about hurtling through time to even begin attempting to convey to you in a manner that won't take up several human lifetimes. So I'm just going to try and keep you up to speed on the more important things pertinent to our journey and hope you don't get too lost. You will almost certainly get too lost. Don't worry, this is your fault, not mine nor the fabric of space and time's. But try your best to keep up will you?

The first thing that happens when you emerge from a time travelling wormhole, no matter who or what you are, is that you start evacuating whatever body you happen to have in a rather disgusting manner. It is inevitable that after you have done so, for a ridiculous amount of time, you will pretend as if you have not done so, and go about some sort of mediocre task avoiding eye contact with your fellow time travellers. This is not difficult, as thanks to the obligatory mind-bending psychedelic light-show you've all just experienced, your eyeballs will be twirling about like a pinwheel or one of those lollypops you get at Disneyland. Then (always at the exact same time as your fellow travellers) the guilt, shame and sloppiness is finally outweighed by the tremendous need to eat. When you have no food, the need to eat is a dangerous need indeed. This is discussed in detail in Horaticus Neil Travensenzels classic *Cannibalizing Your Crew After Emerging From a Time Portal: How to End Up Eating Dinner Rather than Becoming It.* Unfortunately all of the members of Obotron 1 had indeed read this book several times by now, and had stealthily thwarted the other two's relentless attempts to eat them. When alas it was realized the stalemate would not be broken, and treaties began to be drawn up rationing out each others smaller limbs and not so vital organs in a timely manner, a simpler solution presented itself.

The telescreen flickered and the crew members from a trailing Obotron stared desperately and hungrily into the screen. They were in fact trying to very rationally explain the situation they were in and help solve the problem of feeding everyone and cleaning up all the evacuated fluids and such; but good luck trying to get Wilx, Rip and Krimshaw to listen to a word of it. All they heard was "Hey, look at us, a whole expendable and not terribly important to anything or anyone ship chock full of tasty morsels that'll stop you from having to ration out each others limbs and not so vital organs in a timely manner."

"Splendid good point," praised Wilx. The crew members beamed with pride.

"Stellar work team," exclaimed Rip. The crew members patted each other on the backs and smiled and laughed, ecstatic to have contributed something to anything for the first time in their existence.

"I'll have the one on the left with all the fat hanging down," salivated Krimshaw. The crew members dismissed this is as nonsense. What did he know, he was just a silly Greeg all dressed up, not a respectable leader of a fleet of Obotrons like Wilx and Rip.

They would have re-examined that last line of thinking if they had any frame of reference to do so. They would have had a frame of reference to do so if they hadn't been savagely devoured in a chaotic and wholly shameful display of spit roasts and improvised marinades made from the evacuated ickiness of other crew members. But sadly, they had. None of them had the good fortune to have brought a copy of *Cannibalizing Your Crew After Emerging From a Time Portal: How to End Up Eating Dinner Rather than Becoming It* on board with them. This was a rather silly move, considering the amount of time they'd spent doing nothing at all after realizing there were no towels to fold. But the kind of folks that are crew members in luxury fleets are not great independent thinkers. They tend to just follow the orders of whatever seemingly intelligent being is at the helm of the main ship and not ask too many questions, no matter how ridiculous or perilous they may be, or how clearly they are being influenced by his gambling drunkard of a co-pilot. After all, if he can afford to fly around a priceless fleet of Obotron 7 space ships and idly fill them up with crew members, clearly he must know a great deal more than the crew members about all sorts of important things. The crew members could never dream of owning even one ship, let alone the whole fleet. Even if they pooled all their salaries together, they could still only fill up a half a tank of investment bankers at best. The way they looked at it, they should feel lucky to be involved in anything as expensive and theoretically important as whatever it was that Rip and Wilx were up to. This knowledge of their own lack of importance and self worth kept most of them going, not just in this job, but in their lives as well. Blissfully thinking they'd scored a sweet gig and not wishing to rock the boat, they'd remain dedicated and content right up until the moment things got a bit dicey for the fleet. When things got a bit dicey for the fleet they were the first expendable pieces of cargo that the trio in charge had no issues with throwing overboard or, in extreme circumstances, eating.

12 fully crewed ships and a very heartily overstuffed crew of three in a shiny Obotron 1 drifted on into the nearest galaxy searching for a place to fuel up on investment bankers and restock their food supply, completely unaware when they were. One ship, devoid of crew, and thus useless, was set on fire and lost forever. Not by the crew of the Obotron 1, but by angry protestors of the recently formed Obotronian Crew Members Who Demand The Right to Not Get Eaten By The Three Nitwits Running This Fleet If There's No Food About and We've Just Emerged From a Time Travelling Worm Hole. They organized their movement from within the ranks of all the Obotron ships and brought their coalition to the scene of the heinous massacre. They decided the most poignant statement

they could make was to set the ship on fire in protest and martyrdom, quickly ending the newly formed movement and annihilating any of the small amounts of crew members in all the remaining ships who could be stirred to fight for themselves and their fellow crew.

Incidentally, this series of events would be the opening chapter of the upcoming Revised, Rapple Skin Bound, Flexy Covered, Extra Limited Edition of *Hypocrisy Inaction: The Plight of the Pointless Protester.*

CHAPTER 24

All About Time-Travel

It is one of an astoundingly large and plentiful number of human misconceptions that time is linear. That is to say, that there was a beginning, then there is a middle, then there is an end. This stems from the human desire to make everything about them, and the ridiculous human trait of being completely unable to see things from a perspective outside their own. Time is so much more infinitely complex than this that it is an insult to time to even suggest it is only capable of going in one direction. Even the idea of time going in one direction at all is disgustingly simplistic. To suggest that you can only go forwards and/or backwards in time may be one of the most ridiculous assertions of all time. Literally. But even getting your average human to accept you can move throughout time at all, is dismissed as science fiction nonsense... much like everything that is true and universally accepted as fact. As such, when a human being on Earth writes up a novel about time travel, they tend to go backwards in time or forwards in time. Never, in the history of Earth stories, has anyone ever truly gone sideways in time. Shocking really, since time-travelling wormholes are the number one source of time travel, and sideways travelling accounts for over 79.43% of all wormhole related travels through time. There is absolutely no point in trying to explain sideways time-travel to you, because your brain simply will not allow you to understand it. Just let it be known that our trio has travelled sideways through time; not backwards, and not forwards. Thanks to blatant propaganda perpetrated by Michael J. Fox, this may lead you to think of parallel universes. There is no such thing as parallel universes. There are lots of universes, none of them are parallel. They are Universes, vast conglomerations of swirling galaxies, not gymnastics bars.

Another human misconception about time travel is that when someone travels through time they do not at all physically move in distance. That is to say, if you plant yourself on a green bridge on fifth street and set your time travel machine (another falsity we will arrive at shortly) for 100 years later, you will appear on the exact same green bridge 100 years later, fully undisturbed from a century's worth of passersby who never wondered about the strangely dressed person frozen in the middle of the bridge. This could not be more false. Real time-travel is not so whimsically perfect. A time-traveller instead appears in an unplanned and random location that will likely turn out to be a dangerous place completely unfit to inhabit. Time-travelling while on the surface of a planet is not so worrisome, as you are limited to reappearing somewhere on the surface of that planet (like if you time-travelled out of Hawaii and ended up bobbing around in the South Atlantic), but if you time-travel while floating around in space then you suddenly have no limitations on where you might reappear. It could be anywhere else in space.

'Machine' is a word that has not much business being applied to the art of time-travel, unless one is a death-craving daredevil. As noted, time-travel is predominantly a naturally occurring event, whether one is simply passing through a wormhole, or leaping through a tear in reality caused by the sharp claws of Eagle Gods, or even looking at the sacred waters of the Seladorian Pools, said to be an act so incredible that it sends one spinning diagonally through time. These are the types of things that cause time-travel. Only about .004% of time-travel is achieved with the invention of a technological device or machine, and it usually turns out badly. Death-craving daredevils who invent faulty time-travel machines usually wind up the victim of a nuclear explosion. Time-travel is simply not meant to be invented. Let it happen in nature to the unfortunately dumb people who can't avoid stumbling through tears in reality, but never try to control its spontaneous power.

CHAPTER 25

In which much is Explained, and much is made more Confusing

"Buuuuuuuuuuuurrrrrrppppppp! So where are we?" belched Krimshaw casually.

"You mean *when* are we?" snooted Rip condescendingly.

"You're both not going to like either of the answers," said Wilx ominously.

"Oh no, why's that?" Krimshaw and Rip exclaimed, lurching forward.

"Nothing."

"What do you mean nothing," yelped Rip, gripping Wilx by his shoulder like things and shaking him violently. "Don't you go about making ominous and cryptic statements and then withholding information from me you bastard!"

"I was joking, I was only kidding, I just don't know where we are, thought I'd lighten the mood after all that cannibalism," lied Wilx through his teeth like things.

"Shall we go for an unrelated stroll into the adjacent and sound proof corridor?" suggested Rip, sensing Wilx was hiding something, which he clearly was.

"Fine."

Oblivious to the deceptive transaction taking place, Krimshaw delved into *Very Rare Planets*, scouring for hidden clues about the Greegs. For some reason he was compelled to flip back to the entry about Pluto and Rip. He looked out the window. Then he looked back at the book.

"Hmm," he thought, but didn't know why.

He peered back out of the window again for three point seven times longer than the first glance. He then studied the entry about Pluto for nine and eleven thirteenths as long as the previous stint.

"Interesting," he mused, sure that he was on to something, but still not aware of what it was.

He picked up the half eaten leg of an Obotron crew member and chewed it thoughtfully, gazing out of the window for enough time that Rip and Wilx finished their top secret conversation and re-entered the room.

"Ahem," coughed Wilx.

"Oh my tit faced cunt muffin sandwich on rye to the power of six!" blurted out Krimshaw. "That's Pluto! Outside! We're at Pluto guys! It's right there! Same as book. Me read!"

"I bet you it isn't," quipped Rip, since there was no point in restraining from betting on Pluto any more.

"We're not technically on Pluto, so it wouldn't count against you Rip... plus you have nothing to bet," said Wilx, casually firing up a holographic digital star map. "Unless one of your long shot wagers comes true and you suddenly re-acquire vast amounts of bettables."

"One of them is bound to come through sooner or later with all this time travelling and visiting of solar systems in which I've been to in the past going on."

"Yeah, we'll see about that," prodded Wilx. "For now, we may just be the luckiest folk to ever emerge from a time travelling wormhole looking to fuel up and get some food."

"Why's that?" asked Rip and Krimshaw, who were getting quite good at synchronizing their questions.

"If my star maps and research are correct, the alignment of these planets and this solar system indicates we are merely a few billion kilometres from what is essentially the greatest gas station ever to exist. More or less untapped at this point, the life forms on the planet consist almost entirely of investment bankers and tasty fish. That's pretty much all there is on the planet."

"You couldn't ask for a better place to pop by and fuel up your space ship!" Exclaimed Krimshaw.

"Uh... yeah. What luck! Let's go there quickly." re-affirmed Rip, failing miserably to conceal his and Wilx's sinister and as of yet un-revealed motives.

"So how did such a planet come to be?" queried Krimshaw genuinely.

"If theories had been circulated about such things, which they never have been, they definitely would never have even suggested that the whole evolution of the dominant life form on the planet was just the result of a drunken bet placed by Dr. Rip T. Brash The Third, suffering from PNBOAPFTFTIHS," assured Rip, in his usual non-assuring manner.

"That's Post Not Betting On A Planet For The First Time In History Syndrome," clarified Wilx.

"I don't follow you," said Krimshaw.

"It's really quite simple," said Wilx. "The need and desire to place a wager was so deeply engrained in Rip after such an insane streak of betting, that the act of not placing a bet while on the planet Pluto drove him to concoct the most absurd and ludicrous bet ever made up until that time."

"Wow, how long could this streak possibly have been going on?"

"You don't want to know," said Rip in a shameful manner implying the topic of how long he had been placing absurd wagers for was not a topic to be discussed.

"So what was the bet?"

"He bet, er, someone, that he could completely annihilate the surface environment of a biologically utopian planet he'd stumbled upon simply by introducing a savagely over-aggressive population of Investment Bankers into the ecosystem."

"Not just any investment bankers!" cried out Rip in his defence. "The most diabolically inter-spliced species of investment bankers ever devised! I isolated strains from the genome of Torniolic Speculation Gnomes, sprinkled in the potent and unrivalled Remorselessness and Lack of Care for Consequences DNA from the Ruthless Ruddigerian Financing Board, and countless other infinitely impressive bits of investment banking biology. Then I found a simple little hairy beast and injected it with the formula."

"What possible bet could involve such diabolical and pointless activities?"

"Well that much even we don't quite know," said Wilx, punching information into his gigantic and confusing looking computing machine, which did all sorts of things other than computing, like spitting out dissolvable mind history tablets... which it did as Wilx stroked a large red button emphatically. "Here, eat this."

"What are they?" asked Krimshaw and Rip.

"Dissolvable mind history tablets."

"What do they do?" asked Rip and Krimshaw.

"Instantly bring us all up to speed on the information I just procured regarding the details of Rip's bet. Rather than research extensively and explain my findings to all of you, I simply encrypted the necessary information from *The Complete and Unabridged Historical Records of All Things,* into this tiny tablet which, once dissolved in our mouths, will send the information to our respective brains without all your annoying questions making it take forever for you to understand.

"That sounds like a splendid way to avoid endless and painfully detailed explanations and move on with things."

"It sure is."

The trio swallowed the pills. Krimshaw saw and processed a full BBC Documentary series worth of information instantly and was shocked and awed... awed, and then shocked. A quick look around at the other two showed they were fairly shocked as well, but not nearly as awed as Krimshaw. They were more amused by the details of events they had buried under a pile of other equally insane events in their memory banks.

"Let's compare our unique takes on the information received to make sure we're all on the same page," suggested Wilx. "It appears to me that Rip bet... er, someone, that he could hop into a wormhole, pop out in a random solar system, refrain from betting on the furthest planet from the sun, then cultivate a species of investment bankers on the one planet capable of sustaining life. He insisted that investment bankers were not only a great source of fuel, but that if unchecked by another more intelligent species, they would take over and dominate every square inch of the surface of the planet, destroying and polluting everything in sight, but leaving a fair amount of tasty fish buried deep in the ocean, untainted by the savage recklessness of the Investment Bankers. Then he would return from his time travels to reunite with... er, someone, and one day him and... er, someone, would randomly stumble out of a sideways time travelling worm hole in desperate need of both investment bankers and fish with a fully reformed Greeg named Krimshaw."

"So just to recap," said Krimshaw, "Basically Rip destroyed the potential of a decent planet and all of its decent life forms to evolve naturally by introducing this savagely over aggressive population of Investment Bankers... and he won this horrific bet and that's why there's a perfect gas station waiting for us in this solar system as we emerge from a time travelling worm hole?" asked Krimshaw, for the first time seeing Rip for what he was; a reckless, pathological maniac.

"More or less," said Wilx.

"That's pretty much what I got," said Rip. "Except that the anonymous person I made this preposterous bet with was you Wilx."

"Dammit, you blew my cover!"

"How could you possibly not remember all of this?" said Krimshaw, in a way that implied not remembering this would indicate insanity like this happens all the time. "Does insanity like this happen all the time to you two or what?"

"Well we didn't actually know it had happened until just now, why else would we bet on it?" Wilx said calmly. "At the time, I was likely certain we would never see the planet again, and besides, there's a very good chance the incident and the bet hadn't actually happened until we came out of the wormhole. It just means we've travelled sideways in time."

"What?"

"Very common phenomenon. Happens all the time. Look, we flew into a time travelling wormhole, and when we emerged a series of completely incomprehensible coincidences occurred. That's what tipped me off that it was time for some mind history tablets. It's very simple, with well seasoned time travellers like me and Rip always recklessly jumping through hyperspace, the Universe couldn't possibly make sense of all the reckless and potentially catastrophic things that well seasoned time travellers like us do, namely setting off destructive and nonsensical chains of events rippling throughout space and time... generally screwing things up for everything and everybody. So Universes, being clever and rather flexible things, will simply alter events in the past and present, re-aligning themselves so they can make sense of things."

"Completely lost."

"When we first met you and picked you up in the Greeg cage, oh by the way you were a Greeg before, an especially dumb and savage one too..."

"I was a what?!"

"Please, let me finish. So when Rip made his bet about turning you into a normal, intelligent being and all that other jazz that led us up to this point, he and I had never even remotely made a bet involving genetic splicing and investment bankers and fish. However, when we shot through the time travelling worm hole, the only possible way for the Universe to make any sense of us arriving here was if we *had* made such a bet, and were approaching such a planetary gas station. Without such constant re-alignments of reality, things would never make any sense in any of the Universes. It's just the way things are."

"I see," said Krimshaw, only barely comprehending the significance of all of these nuggets of information. "So I was a Greeg at some time is what you're saying? That's what those officials were after before we hyper-jumped into the maze? That's what those spidery creatures were really angry about? I'm nothing but a good for nothing Greeg that you taught how to read and behave somewhat normally just so this jackass could win a bet, which it turns out was just a minor piece of a much larger and more confusing bet, that never actually happened until we just recently shot out of a worm hole, because the Universe doesn't like to be confused?"

"Close enough," said Wilx.

"Oh look we're here!" said Rip, failing to change the subject since they were quite clearly just floating past Neptune. Realizing it didn't remotely work, he tried a different tactic. "Well, hey, look pal we still like you just the same... friend."

"You don't like me all, I'm not your friend, you just *used* me in a bet."

"I use everyone in a bet, it's kind of what I do."

"That doesn't make it okay!"

"Sure it does!"

"Alright you two, that's enough, cut it out, etc." interceded Wilx. "The important thing here is that the bet now exists, and Rip has won it, which changes things around here quite a bit."

"Damn straight it does," exclaimed Rip. "This is my fleet again, and I've got all sorts of other belongings and possessions back in my gambling arsenal. I'm back baby!"

As the information overloaded Krimshaw's brain, he reeled and collapsed into a heap, slipping into unconsciousness. The telescreen flickered.

"Congrats on regaining control of the fleet Doc. We've always liked you more than that Astro-whatever-the-who-cares-ologist sidekick... you usually send us on much wilder and unpredictable adventures."

"I bet you every one of my superfluous internal organs you can't fly into the giant rings of that planet and survive," said Rip, unable to contain the ability to make bets again.

"You're on boss," happily replied the soon-to-be-dead, self-appointed leader of Obotron 4, Krimshaw's last memory was the cheer erupting from Rip as the ship exploded immediately upon coming in contact with the rings of Saturn. Krimshaw passed out.

CHAPTER 26

Recklessly Abandoned

When he awoke, Krimshaw was not on a space ship at all, he was on a park bench on the planet Earth with a piece of paper stuck in his beard. He didn't have a beard, quickly remembered this and ripped off the fake beard fastened to his face. He read the note:

We popped by to fuel up the space ships.
Ate some tasty fish. Left you behind.
Might be back some time. Do not, under
any circumstances, remove your beard.

"Hey there stranger, have I got a great deal for you! Invest now and in five years you'll double, no, triple, no scratch that, triduple your money! Is triduple a word? For you it is! Oh dear god, what happened to your face?"

Somehow, Krimshaw instinctively knew that this man was the most useless organism that could ever exist. He promptly ate him. This didn't go over well with some folks in blue uniforms, who promptly threw our friend Krimshaw in a jail cell.

***

There's not much point in keeping up the illusion that I am not Krimshaw, so let's just get on with it and have the big reveal.

I am Krimshaw.

There, now it's official. Of course, I am not really Krimshaw, as that is just a name made up by a madman in order to win one of a series of ludicrous bets. I have no real name. At this point in the story, I just know that I was once a Greeg who had travelled sideways in time and that Universes were capable of shifting around like a Rubik's cube, changing the way things had occurred so it could make sense of them. Fresh with this knowledge having knocked me unconscious, I awoke on a park bench and devoured an investment banker.

Then I was thrown in prison. I did not realize at the time that the people of Earth treated their investment bankers with such reverence. In the rest of the Universe, it is common knowledge that investment bankers are the most worthless organisms ever to exist, so I saw no reason for me to refrain from snacking on one. In fact, I distinctly remembered reading in Gary Oldenhammers' *Scrounging for Grub in 11 Trillion Solar Systems*: "Important! If the vast amount of pointless energy stored in even a single investment banker can fuel your spaceship, it can surely provide you with necessary sustenance in a pinch." This would be the first of many times my knowledge, research and understanding would get me in trouble on Earth. It would be the first of many times I would be incarcerated, put on trial, questioned, injured. My initial time on Earth could very well be described as:

The People of Earth VS. The Former Greeg Formerly Known as Krimshaw, (Formerly Known as Zook.)

But no one would ever bother describing such things.

I was asked a lot of questions by people who were not prepared to accept the very honest answers I had for them. First by the police officers who arrested me, then by the judge who prosecuted me; then the senate, the President, and finally various talk show hosts and tabloid magazines. In that order. That is, apparently, the hierarchy of human importance. You know you've really got something interesting if the talk shows and tabloid magazines are interested. These various questioning sessions often ended up with me turning the tables on my various interrogators, and *them* not having good answers for *me*.

One particular Q&A in the courtroom went like this:

JUDGE: You cannot simply go about eating people.
ME: It was just an investment banker.
JUDGE: His occupation does not matter, in the United States eating people is strictly forbidden.
ME: What is the United States?
JUDGE: A country.

ME: What's that?

JUDGE: A sovereign union of states, what are you an alien?

ME: What's an alien?

JUDGE: Someone not from Earth.

ME: Oh yes, that's me. I'm not from here.

JUDGE: Yes you are! There is no such thing as aliens!

ME: Then why did you bring them up?

JUDGE: Silence!

ME: So what were those countries you spoke of?

JUDGE: Countries are… countries you idiot! Sections of land that our forefathers fought and died for so that we could have them.

ME: They sound stupid.

JUDGE: Countries are not on trial here mister, your cannibalism is!

I soon realized it was simply not possible for you human beings to accept that I was not a person or that all of the silly things you believe are in fact quite stupid. When faced with a barrage of overwhelming proof and logic, the automatic response of any human is to become violently angry. They will conjure up all sorts of indignant, ridiculous arguments to justify and defend their outdated beliefs. It is much easier for humans to defend what they know, then entertain for a minute what they do not. Luckily for me, I didn't have to endure much of this. Because I was born and raised on a planet with such a massive orbit, I live quite a bit longer than the average human. Okay, a *lot* longer. So while the judge thought he had really stuck it to me with his sentence of 'life in prison' – the reality was that I quite enjoyed being able to kick back for the length of a human lifetime, get interviewed a lot, tell people how stupid they were, write some bestselling books, and become a sort of cult figure. In the first human lifetime, or HL (a unit of time I invented, measuring approximately 80 years) that I was on Earth, I was able to read every book ever written by a human, and graced the cover of every magazine there was. Not a lot of good books written by people, and the only decent ones were dismissed as fantasy, science fiction, comedy or satire.

The best ones contained elements of all of these. The most ridiculous ones were by far the most popular and most revered. These tended to be ones that unequivocally reinforced stupid human beliefs. They were the literary equivalent of patting themselves on the back and saying "See, I told you we were right." They were never right.

One thing I found quite amusing was a pattern of behaviour I like to call 'the circle of idiocy.' Despite the fact that every generation loves to laugh at how primitive their ancestors are with one hand, at the same time, they continue to behave exactly the same way and never learned any lessons from the past. To me, it was kind of like watching someone point and laugh at another for walking into a tar pit and drowning; then proceeding to walk right after them into the same tar pit as yet another pointed and laughed at the two of them, and so on, and so on. The circle of idiocy continues.

No matter, not my species. When it became obvious that I wasn't ageing, and they couldn't kill me, there was a lot of discussion as to what should be done. They tried to kill me many times rather unsuccessfully, thanks to the evasive survival techniques I had learned from numerous readings of *Cannibalizing Your Crew After Emerging From a Time Portal: How to End Up Eating Dinner Rather than Becoming It.*

Evidently, no conclusion could be reached, so they decided to release me. Turns out, their fears were unfounded, as nobody really cared. By the time another half HL had passed I might as well have never come to Earth. Anyone who talked of me like I actually existed was thoroughly mocked. The story about the cannibal Alien was a stupid myth, and only nutty fringe drug addicts believed a word of it. Many movies were made, and I entered into folklore along with Vampires, Dragons, Werewolves and Zombies... all of which I now can only assume must have been alien visitors themselves. Masks were circulated with my face, and were a pretty popular little Halloween seller for a few seasons, but then were quickly relegated to thrift stores. If you tried to tell people 150 years after I came to Earth about the massive unexplained disappearance of investment bankers and fish that occurred, they would most likely tell you it never happened. Some of the homeless folks would give you an accurate description of what transpired, but they were ignored completely and treated with the utmost disdain. I never could understand the way humans treated the homeless. The very fact that there was homeless people is baffling, when you consider the vast amount of unused hotel rooms, and rich people owning multiple properties, cottages, etc. The homeless were also some of the only people able to fully understand and listen to the facts I presented to them about the universe and humankind. A lot of them had even figured out much of the truth on their own! Truly remarkable creatures, completely misunderstood and unnecessarily cast aside by much more ignorant, less decent individuals. So quick was the rest of mankind eager to forget and suppress the ramifications of my arrival, that if you asked people 15 years after Rip and Wilx liquefied over three million investment bankers and nearly obliterated the supply of ocean dwelling fish, the humans had mostly invented various "Scientific Explanations."

"Scientific Explanations" are things that humans like to use when something doesn't make sense to them. What it translates roughly as is "We don't like that thing that just happened, so this is what happened instead." It is much easier for them to accept this new, completely made up explanation, rather than try to wrap their heads around something new. They put their unwrapped heads down and kept making their investment bankers money. Investment Bankers were no longer merely the covert rulers of mankind. They were now the blatant and unquestioned dictators of the species. In a staggering series of events, their callous actions had bankrupted every country and government on the planet, and yet through their control of information and news, they were easily able to convince everyone that they were the only ones who could lead people out of the mess they had created. Pretty much everyone knew there was something decidedly evil and wrong with this concept, but they couldn't quite articulate it. For fear of becoming homeless, they kept their criticisms to themselves and did what the Investment Bankers told 'em to.

At first I was frustrated, and delusional. I thought I could actually get people to see the errors in their ways. It was an impossible task. Eventually, I just started telling people the truth and yelling at them. This was how I became a very successful stand-up comedian... and homeless. The audience thought I was playing a character of an alien who had been trapped on Earth for a long time and was fed up with things. Of course, I was really just an alien trapped on Earth for a long time who was fed up with things. They laughed and laughed as I shouted and yelled at them. I invented a whole new genre of comedy. It was dubbed Alien Impersonations, and sometimes Human Critics. Lots of college kids who had eaten magic mushrooms and had long hair got into it, but it was wholly dismissed as pointless and counterproductive by anyone who made lots of money. I would find out the longer I stayed on Earth that Vampires, Werewolves and Zombies were all in fact permanent residents of the orb. They would pop up and slink away as they saw fit, depending on world events and how well they figured they could blend into the background. Dragons, on the other hand, said 'fuck this' and flapped off to other solar systems. This world was beneath them.

CHAPTER 27

A Strange Observation Regarding Human Sexuality

I observed something unique happen over the course of the next 140 HL's. The human male became more and more effeminate. Their penises shrank and they started staying home and taking care of the kids and cleaning, while the women went out to work. While the men's penises shrank, the women's clitorises began to grow and grow and grow. The men waxed their legs and got makeovers to look hot and attract the women with the highest paying jobs. The women, burdened with their new workload, stopped caring about their appearance and they began to grow hair all over and dress much more casually. Men began to spend much more time sucking on the ever growing clitorises and much less time sticking their penises inside women's vaginas. The women stopped delivering babies out of their vaginas and their vaginas began to close up.

It wasn't long before the women's clitorises had grown the size of men's penises, and their labia's began morphing into testicles. Men, of course, had the opposite occur, and the two sexes effectively switched places completely. Physiologically. Mentally. Socially. Those who were men, now looked like and behaved like those who were women. Relations between the two didn't change at all. They might as well have not switched places. But they did, and I found it interesting. This crossover of sexuality would occur on multiple occasions during my time on Earth. Later research I conducted would reveal this phenomenon happened several times throughout human history and often explained the downfall of great civilizations. Those Roman Bath Houses, Greek Philosophers, Victorian man blouses and San Francisco began to make a lot more sense.

CHAPTER 28

An Inconvenient Planet Appears,
and the GGFLTD Takes Over

One day a planet appeared in the night sky. This planet was not one of the planets that humans were used to seeing, but it was quite clearly very close to them. Closer than 7 of the other planets in their solar system. The reaction was typical. People either claimed it had always been there and that anyone who didn't know that was an idiot, or that it wasn't there at all, and anyone who claimed it was there was seeing things... and an idiot. It should be noted that around the same time this happened, I received an update from Dr. Rip T. Brash The Third and Wilx. Not in person of course. When I went outside to pick up the newspaper with the headline "New Planet: Has it always been there or is it not there at all?" I discovered another note accompanied by a needle and a vial of glowing liquid. The note read:

> *Finding out lots of interesting things*
> *Hope you're having a good time as well.*
> *Been watching your stand-up, pretty funny.*
> *Not as good as Bill Hicks or George Carlin...*
> *but alright. Inject this into your eyeball, or*
> *you will die. Longevity formula and other*
> *preventative measures. Don't give to any*
> *humans, will make them immortal.*
> *Chat soon.*

I instinctively wanted to not inject the longevity formula into my eyeball, not because I didn't want to inject myself in the eyeball... After 648 HL's I very much wanted to do that. No, I just didn't want to give Rip the satisfaction of popping by with a note after abandoning me on this miserable rock and me actually following his instructions. But, I knew enough about Rip, to know that I had to do it, or I would die. And I didn't want to die. Inject myself in the eyeball I did. But I only gave myself half of the formula. The other half I gave to a fellow named Herb. In all the time I'd been on Earth, he was the only decent human being I'd met. He was a fine fellow that Herb, and I couldn't think of a better man to pass countless HL's with. Here's how cool of a guy Herb was. I went over to his house where he was gardening.

"Hey Herb, I'm going to stick this needle in your eye and make you immortal, okay?"

"Sure, whatever," said Herb, not even looking up from his rake.

That was Herb for you, nothing phased the guy. Took everything in stride.

A few HL's later, and it was considered an irrefutable fact by many that not only was the new planet not new, but it had been there since the beginning of time, as could be proven by ancient textbooks that spoke of nine planets in the solar system. This split people into two ideological camps, those who knew for a fact it had always been there and those certain (with the aiding of heaps of "scientific explanations") that the new planet was a mass hallucination. As was always the case when people divided themselves into two ideological camps... violent wars broke out for centuries between the Believers of the Nine Planet Theory (BNPT) and The Mass Hallucinationists (TMHs).

One thing that both the BNPT and TMHs agreed on, was that the useless rock at the end of the line was not a real planet, and never had been. Pluto was never spoken of again by any human being. It was erased from memory and history. If it had to be spoken of it was in dismissive euphemisms like "That small, puny, stupid rock," or "The little meteor with no friends, and an ugly, cold, barren surface that no one would ever want to visit even if it was a planet."

This feud of belief systems, like all feuds of belief systems, was both embraced and fuelled by the ones who really controlled things on Earth... the money lenders and the dealers of arms and weaponry. At this current juncture in history, both of these tasks were performed exclusively by the recently formed Global Group of Firms LTD (GGFLTD), who were now the only company or government that existed. In reality, GGFLTD was neither a company, nor a government... it was a cross-planetary, all encompassing ruling elite, consisting entirely of Investment Bankers, with a small subsidiary branch supplying arms to both the BNPT and TMHs. Both the BNPT and TMHs had complicated and utterly powerless leadership who answered only to the GGFLTD. Each side routinely convinced their followers of the need for perpetual warfare on the other, due to the 'advisement' from the Global Firms. One of the first actions of this monolithic, ultra-powerful organization was to create a gigantic central computing device. They called it "The Economy". It churned out graphs and charts and 'advisement reports' which dictated every action performed by mankind. Any semblance of these numbers having any bearing on the real world had long since been replaced with the simple phrase 'Growth.' The GGFLTD had adopted the motivational, pro-human slogan of 'As long as things are growing, then things are not un-growing, and that is good.' It seemed to resonate with the masses, keeping them building things and procreating. The GGFLTD had long since erased the idea that building things was for any other purpose than to keep the complicated graphs and charts "The Economy" pumped out from sharply dropping. It was strongly engrained in the minds of all human beings, that should the graphs and charts ever go down, all sorts of terrible things would happen, and growth would become ungrowth very quickly. Buildings were built primarily for the purpose of investing in, thus making the GGFLTD board members more money, so they could invest in the building of more things. The benefit for the masses was simple... jobs. So long as things had to be built, someone had to build them. And once they were built, they would also have to be kept clean. Growth=Jobs, and without growth, things would not be growing, and that was not good, so the general populace was constantly reminded.

Under the new 'growth for the sake of growing' economic model, the population of Earth now towered at an astounding 8.5 trillion people. This controversial, newly arrived, closer planet offered some fantastic solutions for a ridiculously overpopulated globe. BNPT Scientists blasted Rocket ships off on a tri-secondly basis, delivering load after load of refuse to the surface of the new planet. This continued for a few HL's until it was realized they were sending all of their best rockets off into an ever-growing heap of garbage. The problem was solved with the construction of a giant cannon, taking up the entire continent of Africa, aimed at the garbage planet.

The Global Group of Firms LTD sociological model of exponential growth and perpetual warfare between the BNPT and TMHs had a very drastic side affect. It was sucking the earth dry of oil. The GGFLTD did not see this as a negative. The constant search for oil was only an opportunity for more jobs, and a solid reason to go to war, which was a great motivator to build things, especially after they'd been blown up. In order to meet the massive and un-meetable demand for oil, the GGFLTD "advised" (demanded with no chance of any possible alternative) the drilling of countless oil wells in countless oceans and under countless arctic ice shelves. At a rupturing rate of nearly 50% and with the mere mention of silly things like 'the environment' or 'standards' or 'the planet' being punishable by death, it was not long before every ocean was oozing with oil. Nobody cared... it was soon decreed, by way of newly circulated GGFLTD approved information documents, that the ocean had always been black and goopy, and that the new shimmering fish species living in the black goop had always been there. Anyone who thought otherwise soon found themselves homeless. Most people found themselves homeless actually. The infinite wisdom of the Investment Bankers found that the act of residing in homes merely made it harder to keep them clean, and generally aided in the deterioration of the value of the buildings. In order to keep the graphs and charts headed in an upward trajectory, it was vital that all buildings remain empty, save for cleaners and security persons keeping non-cleaners off the premises.

CHAPTER 29

Some Formerly Ambiguous Odds and Ends,
of the Loose Variety, are Tied Up

Many more HL's passed by. More planets began to appear. Then entire suns. Then solar systems. They came from all over the place, seemingly surrounding the earth. Many of them were clearly inhabited. The people of Earth had two choices: to accept that they were wrong about nearly everything and acknowledge the ever changing realities surrounding them... or completely ignore the facts and further delude themselves about their own importance in the grand scheme of things by denouncing science, logic and observation in favour of even more self aggrandizing religion, ritual, silly clothing and wars over all of the above. Guess which one they chose?

Me and Herb saw it all happen, together. We had no idea why all of this was happening, but we at least acknowledged that it was. Two of the new stars appeared on opposite sides of what humans called their sun. The two stars violently smashed into the sun, forming a colossal new super star, *five times* the size of the Earth's old sun. The shock-waves from this collision blasted Mercury, Venus and the Earth into Mars, forming a hideously unshapely conglomeration of a planet. A planetglomerate.

Humans reacted as they always did in times of chaos and uncertainty, they engaged in massive amounts of carnage and violence and sexual misconduct. STD's were spread and cultivated rampantly. "The Economy" began to ungrow. Panic struck the board members. At the behest of the GGFLTD's Growth Restoration Division, scientists worked tirelessly to keep up with all the diseases, developing new and better ways to make sex safer and more sterile. They eventually settled on an ornamental and intimate genital contraption for both the male and the female. The male device was a tube that sucked ejaculate out of his penis, funnelling it into a sealable and sterile tube, where it could be kept for over 2 hours. With a few more HL's of work, the ejaculate was able to be stored for over 40 hours. The sterile tube was then placed in a receptacle attached to the side of a suction cup that formed around the female genitals with a tube leading inside her, directly to the womb. Once sterilized and tested, the male ejaculate was pumped into the female and delivered right to her biological doorstep. Sex was forbidden by law, except for procreation, even the word sex was banned. It was only to be done in a strict, laboratory setting and was a completely joyless affair. Since the only purpose was to procreate, it was not called sex any more, it was called an "Attempt."

The shock-wave continued throughout the rest of the solar system as well. Jupiter was knocked off of its orbit, floating about various solar systems as it pleased. It had become a 'free planet.' The shock-wave sent Saturn smashing into Neptune, forming a mini star which pulled both of their various satellites, along with the asteroid field, into orbit. The many moons and asteroids were slung around the new mini-star in circles like a lasso, with each one eventually smashing into the planetglomerate (making what was already a hideously ugly thing into a true monstrosity.) During one of these collisions,

Mars was actually dislodged from the planetglomerate, and began to slowly drift away. Seeing a chance for escape, my pal Herb rallied the approximately 1% of the population still capable of critical thinking and they hopped aboard the planet of Mars, thoroughly disgusted with the direction the rest of the species was taking. All of the smartest, most intelligent, freethinking human beings joined Herb's expedition with the intent of forming a veritable Utopia on Mars. Under Herb's steady guidance, they would succeed in doing so. Herb cordially invited me to come along, but I refused, for what I was observing on the planetglomerate was something I felt somebody needed to see and record. I don't believe in words like fate, purpose or higher power, but I began to see why those cruel, heartless bastards left me here all this time. I was to watch something spectacular unfold.

Due to the sweltering heat from the newly formed stars surrounding them, the humans gradually shed their clothing, until they had no choice but to be naked. It simply wasn't practical, or possible, to wear clothing. However, the humans couldn't simply discard a way of thinking so engrained in their brains as shame of their naked bodies. So they simply shifted the same mentality they had once applied to clothing to nakedness. It became socially ridiculous to be seen wearing clothing of any kind. People were mocked and ridiculed for it, flocking out of the great mud camps into 'The Cleanliness.'

Long ago, the actual human board members of the GGFLTD had ceased to exist. It is the natural progression of Investment Banking firms. They keep 'growing' to a point where no humans are required to keep "The Economy" running. At this point, all humans were desperate to get back to the good old days and make "The Economy" graphs and charts go up again. Feverishly, they put their heads down, built things, and kept them clean. Then they looked at them and said 'hey, look at that, we built that, better keep it clean or else it will get dirty.' Slowly but surely, "The Economy" started to spit out graphs that went up again. With all of the scientists and critical thinkers gone, the rest of the species quickly agreed everything was their fault... after all, now that they were gone, the graphs were going up again. Rejuvenated by this new found purpose, the creatures poured out over every inch of the surface of the planet building and cleaning spotless surfaces that looked like varnished marble, shiny glass windows and freshly bleached tile floors. They looked like this, because that's precisely what they were.   It all looked very impressive, and it gave everyone something to do and to look at.   This process continued for many thousands of HL's, until they had covered every square inch of the place with buildings and structures and surfaces... anything to keep their minds off of the insanity swirling around them in space. Anything to avoid facing the truth that they were not alone, and they were not important. Anything to keep "The Economy" from going down again. The task of building and expanding and keeping such a hideously large planetglomerate clean was enough to take anyone's mind off of 59 suns swirling about you in a wonderful new star system. Nearly every species of plant and animal was obliterated. As was always the case, the only creatures that survived were ones able to adapt to their surroundings. Among the most impressive of these creatures was The Quigg, a perfectly, biologically-evolved cleaning specimen, who could shine and disinfect surfaces like nothing else. Soon enough, almost all the other life forms on the planet were simply bio-cleaning creatures. Since they had no need to do work any more, the dominant species on the planet got lazier and lazier with each passing HL. They also got sloppier and more brutish and less intelligent. They stopped learning about things, and passing on knowledge.

With knowledge transference deteriorating, a curious thing happened to the belief systems and religions of humanity. As the ability to read and write lengthy texts faded away, all of the major religions became progressively more watered down and simplified, eventually culminating with one, simple, accepted religious philosophy to explain everything. The basic tenant of the new, global religion was this: "Whatever it is that made everything for us, thanks for that."

In their relentless construction and expansion efforts, the de-evolving humans found that there were all these silly trees and green things in the way, blocking perfectly good potential surfaces and/or structures. Naturally, they cleared all of the obnoxious greenery out of the way and dumped them into pits. They dumped their nuclear power plants, their nuclear waste, their gold and jewels in the pits too. Lastly they set up massive siphoning pipelines to drain the oily oceans and fill up the pits. They couldn't remember the details, they just knew that these were all things of immense value and worth, and therefore good things would happen if they were all to be mixed up together. They spent a few human lifetimes doing just that, and thus, the great schmold pits were born. A few more HL's after the creation of the great schmold pits and nobody on earth had the slightest idea that indeed they had created these pits. The sub-humans simply revered the supposed mystical powers of the glowing, greenish goop, and chocked up their origin to whoever it was that made everything for the human being. They didn't know they had created schmold any more than they knew they'd created the clean planet full of meaningless surfaces and structures. Even though I witnessed it all, it is difficult to say when the exact transition was complete. But sometime around these last few events were surely the final days of human beings as you know them, and the beginning of The Greegs, as I know them. As a cherry on top of the evolutionary cake, human paparazzi grew one more set of pterodactyl wings, and the Flying Grimbat Messengers were born.

One day, I took a small Greeg aside and told him some very simple facts. I figured if Rip had made me intelligent, maybe one by one I could make them intelligent too. The young boy's name was Groolfh. We know what happened to him, and what became of Herb's Utopian society on Mars. Thanks to his injection, Herb survived, and would go on to have the entire star district named after him. Not via any election, just because the space mapping space mappers found he was the only notable and worthy being in the whole place.

After Groolfh was murdered and the only decent remnants of humanity destroyed, I mostly hid in the caves of the Klaxworms. It was clear that nothing in Greegland was going to change. Once a species has fully become Greegs, once they have hit rock bottom, they simply cannot go any lower. Even if a single Greeg like me can be civilized, the Greegs as a whole are hopeless. They are far dumber in groups. They feed off of each others ignorance and stupidity. This is why I can now understand why Carnivals keep them in small numbers only. Despite my best attempts to remain ignorant and sealed off from Greegs, I was kept abreast on things with nauseatingly frequent updates from Flying Grimbat Messengers.

In about 15, 000 HL's after they'd first left me on a park bench, Dr. Rip T. Brash The Third and Wilx appeared on the planetglomerate. Only 2 Obotron ships trailed them.

"Hey old buddy, great news! After extensive research and adventures, we've figured out where all these planets and suns came from! Turns out this whole galaxy was swallowed by a Galactic Gobbling Groobin!" Unable to speak any of the many prepared speeches I had conjured up over the years for this precise moment, stunned by the audacity of Rip, my jaw merely hung open like a common Greeg. "Yeah, so, basically this thing's digestive system is just an intricate series of time travelling worm holes and the like that'll send whole solar systems shootin' diagonally, sideways, arching, skittering, riveting and spiralling through time and space. All these planets and stars came from all over the vast expanses of time and space to form this new star system in the equivalent of the Gobbling Groobin's large intestine. His small intestine was the maze we escaped from by the way. Wilx says it happens all the time, neat hey?!" I sputtered and drooled and shook violently. "Come on aboard the ship, we still have some fish left, we'll tell you all about where we've been and what we've been up to."

I boarded the ship, devoid of any explainable emotion. One thing was for certain, I definitely harboured a deep desire to murder both Rip and Wilx.

CHAPTER 30

Hroon

Having foreseen the anger I'd be harbouring towards them, Rip and Wilx had prepared for me a decent offering of the most spectacular feast of fish I had ever seen. They were smart to do so. The buffet was impressive enough that it completely subsided my murderous inclinations. There was every type of succulent fish you could think of, freshly prepared with the most exotic alien recipes and expensive sauces. It was only later that I realized my murderous inclinations had not subsided because I genuinely forgave Rip and Wilx, but because Rip and Wilx had laced the fish with a powerful Potion of Peacefulness, a popular Lincran hallucinogenic sacrament also known as the God-Tranquilizer.

"So," I said, while stuffing my numb face with deliciously grilled and drugged fish, "what have you two been up to the last 15,000 HL's?"

"What's an HL?" asked Rip.

"Human Lifetime. I figure 15,000 is the number of those I've experienced since you two abandoned me on that strange world."

"That's not too bad. Isn't the average human lifetime akin to something like the hilariously short lifetime of the common fruit fly?"

"No," I corrected. "A Human Lifetime is roughly 80 years, whereas the lifetime of a fruit fly is roughly 1 day."

"Hardly a difference between 1 day and 80 years though."

"Actually, 80 years is comprised of 29,200 days. Therefore 15,000 HL's is comprised of something like 438 million days. Quite the difference with the common fruit fly."

"I don't see the difference."

I wanted to continue arguing. I wanted Rip to understand the vast and painful difference between the human and the fruit fly. I wanted him to undergo what I had undergone just so he would fully understand. And then, if he still did not understand, I wanted to re-wire his brains until he did.

But I said and did none of these things, feeling all too effectively the powers of the God-Tranquilizer. I yawned and made an obvious comment about the fish.

"This fish is fishy."

"Yes it is," agreed Wilx.

"But you haven't actually eaten any."

"One need not taste the fish to know it is fishy."

"So," I began again, pausing for a long stretch of time while remembering how to speak what needed to be spoken, "I asked what you two have been up to these past 15,000 HL's?"

"What's an HL?" asked Wilx.

"It's been explained."

"I was out of the room."

"It stands for Human Lifetime," said Rip, "It's a period of 80 human years, and is not very dissimilar to the average life-span of the common fruit fly."

"I see."

"How come you guys aren't eating the fish?" I asked.

Wilx took a piece of drugged fish from the table and pretended to eat it while throwing it under the table. Rip also pretended to eat the fish, only he stealthily spat his bite into a crumpled napkin as he wiped his mouth. At the time I didn't recognize any of the obvious tactical manoeuvres employed by Earth children who wish to hide broccoli and other undesirable green food items. One strange thing I had noticed about the diet of human children is that all of their most stereotypically hated foods were in actuality the healthiest food they could consume, while the food that most excited them was whatever contained the highest amount of carcinogenic chemicals and high-glucose corn syrups. This self-destructive eating phenomenon could be seen as the budding factor of the Human-Greeg transition, and was indeed the inspiration behind my seventh bestseller: *Children... Rushing Away to An Early Candy-Filled Grave.*

"So," I began, for the third or fourth time, "what have you two well-seasoned travelers of time and space been up to these past 15,000 HL's?"

"We've had many inconceivable adventures that we'd like

to tell you about," said Rip. "Some of them are vital to our current story, while some of them are unrelated but still worth hearing about. But not at this time. We've just seen a bumper sticker that reads **I'D RATHER BE HERE NOW**. It has inspired us to stay in the current moment with a new adventure."

"There is plenty of time for stories in a few thousand Schmickian years," added Wilx.

"Where are we adventuring to?" I asked.

"Haven't decided yet."

"What ever happened to us going to that Hroon planet?" asked Rip. "Isn't it in this star system?"

"Yes, but the only reason to go to Hroon was to get directions to the Greeg planet, and now we've already found the Greeg planet."

"We could still go there, check it out and whatnot."

"But why?" asked Wilx.

"Who knows," said Rip. "Hroon is the fourth most perfect sphere in existence. I guess that's something worth crossing off the bucket list."

"I am curious about this unexpected dominant species that lives there," said Wilx.

"What's Hroon?" I asked.

"That water-world you read about in *Very Rare Planets.*"

"Oh right, I used to love that book. It seemed important."

"It is. Everyone buckle in."

Wilx chartered the ship for the nearby planet. Hroon was famous for being the fourth most perfect sphere in existence, something not at all worth crossing off your bucket list and really just another normal statistic amidst a considerably more exciting universe full of things like Planetglomerates, Galactic Gobbling Groobins and the ever-surprising Layers of Lincra.

The slight imperfection in the sphere is a tiny rock island. This rock island is the only so-called 'land' on the entire planet. It is about 3 acres of space. Upon these 3 acres dwell creatures known as Grollers. We will meet them shortly.

From space, Hroon is a beautiful planet.

The perfection of the sphericality. The azure blue ocean shimmering with the beams of an epic sun. The great ripples of the global tide. The multi-textured atmosphere. Even the sporadic movement of the schools of fish can be seen from space as a darkening streak whizzing around below the glassy surface.

All is not so beautiful when you're actually on the planet. Things are fine if you're an aquatic creature, mind you, for below the surface is a veritable paradise among water-planets, but above the surface is a nightmarish place permanently stricken with storms and hammering downpours. Upon arrival one is generally whipped away with the wind and tossed into a 100 foot tidal wave. There is no refuge. Even the only island is already overcrowded with undesirable creatures.

"Where are we going to land, considering there isn't any?" asked Rip.

"All Obotrons float in water," replied Wilx.

"Good. Fly us down to the surface."

"You should learn more about these ships, considering that you now own them."

"What for? I can just pay people like you to fly them for me."

"You've never paid me."

"I haven't had the chance."

"Quiet," I said. "We're crossing into the atmosphere."

As we passed through the turbulent atmosphere, all expectations of a beautiful paradise were ruined by the experience of Hroon from close-up. Our ship was immediately thrown 800 miles off course by a thrashing wall of wind. Anything on board that could shatter was immediately shattered. Luckily Rip had already sold, broken or thrown away all of the best shatter-able items.

"This place is insane!" I screamed over the deafening thunderstorms. "Let's get out of here!"

"No," said Rip. "We have to find the life forms and question them. It's vital."

"Why is it vital?"

"I don't remember, but it is."

"I'll do a life-scan of the planet," said Wilx.

"Good luck."

Wilx sent out a series of laser-emissions that studied the whole planet in under ten nanoseconds. He then sent commands to find out why the scanning program was working so slowly. Speed factor was a particularly handy thing to have in a place as terrible as Hroon.

"I'm picking up life signals everywhere underwater," he announced. "But we probably don't want to go underwater here."

"Is there any land at all?" I asked.

"Let me do another scan, focusing specifically on potential non-watery objects. I hope we have time for all this scanning before the next hurricane hits."

Wilx did another scan of the planet. This one only took 8 nanoseconds, and yet he seemed to have grown a little older while he waited.

"Yes... there is a few acres of sharp rock-conglomerations just a few miles south of here."

"Sounds pleasant," groaned Rip.

"Something tells me that's where we're going to find our dominant species."

Once the Obotron got close enough to the rocks, I peered out of the window and saw a mess of lively activity thrashing about all over the place. At first I thought it was one massive blob-like creature with hundreds of arms and legs, then I realized it was a grouping of creatures creating the illusion of a single entity. These were the Grollers.

Grollers are ridiculously unsuited to live on a water world. They have no gills. They are human-like, but are denied even the ability to swim by the unfortunate setback of having only one arm and one leg each. You might think this perfectly enough considering all the oddly-proportioned creatures that manage to keep afloat in water, but Groller limbs were like anti-fins... without another one of them, no amount of flailing could keep them afloat. Grollers mainly just hop and roll around aimlessly.

Doing nothing but hopping and rolling around while living on three acres of sharp rocks in a perpetually storm-stricken water world without even the ability to swim is the least of worries within the Groller community. There is the much greater problem of food.

The only food on Hroon is fish, yet Grollers are deadly allergic to all types of seafood. Always have been. That being said, there are only three possible endings to the devastatingly limited lifetime of the Groller:

1) A Groller will forget it is allergic to seafood. Eats seafood and dies.
2) A Groller will forget it cannot swim. Rolls into ocean and drowns.
3) A Groller will forget it cannot swim. Rolls into ocean and is eaten by some sort of carnivorous monster.

Grollers don't exactly forget these facts, because they never learn them in the first place. No knowledge of any kind is passed down from parent to child. Not even the rudimentary sense of a grunted language. All a Groller has time to do in life is hop, roll, mate, give birth, and then decide if it would rather die of food-poisoning, drowning or monster-attack.

No one suspects being eaten by some sort of carnivorous fish-monster, although it accounts for 14% of all Groller related deaths.

Obotron 1 touched down in the water, close enough for us to be able to reach the rocks via the floating elevator. The 2 remaining Obotrons touched down as well. One of the ships looked in amazingly good shape, while the other had landed upside down. Apparently the ship had not recovered from being whipped away by the wind and thrown into a 100 foot tidal wave. The upturned ship continued to float, and would have looked normal to someone unfamiliar with the regular layout of an Obotron (which is most people given how rare an Obotron is) but inside the ship was a state of total ruin. Rather than read the instruction manuals lining the walls of every room, which would have told them to calmly jettison the ship in the escape-pods which also lined the walls of every room, the frightened crew members decided that watching a copy of *The Poseidon Adventure* would be a more productive thing to do given their current predicament of being upside-down. The melodramatic discourse of the ensemble cast of 1970s Hollywood stars proved to be useless regarding the topic of Surviving an Upturned Spaceship in Alien Waters, but the crew members stood by their choice of action as the ship slowly sank to the bottom of the Hroon ocean. Their entranced eyes were fixated on the flickering pictures. They were totally ignorant of the plethora of aquatic monsters attracted by the new shiny spaceship.

"Look at those animals," said Rip as he pointed to the island, not at all noticing the vanished Obotron. "Are you guys sure we want to go near them?"

Wilx looked up from his annoyingly slow computer. "You were the one who just said it was vital to question those creatures."

"Yeah, but that was before I got a look at them. I mean, look at them!"

"Are these pitiful beasts considered the dominant species of this planet?" I said.

"Yes," replied Wilx.

"How does that work? You said the ocean is full of life. There must be something more plentiful and intelligent underwater."

"Of course there is. But these creatures are considered the dominant species because such matters of classification are dictated and controlled by the powerful publishers of *Very Rare Planets*. And the publishers of *Very Rare Planets*, in their anti-aquatic manner, decided that 'dominant species' is defined as the most developed land creature. Since nothing that lives in water is applicable for the title, these beasts win by default. The UUIAO, or Universally and Unanimously Insulted Aquatic Organization, has many times unsuccessfully lobbied for the proper recognition of water dwellers. The notorious case of Planet Mrool vs. the VRPPC (or *Very Rare Planets* Publishing Company) is frequently cited. Apparently the planet Mrool is entirely water, not even a few acres of island like this planet, and the only life form on the entire world is an amoebic plankton with a life-span of several hours. The VRPPC refused to acknowledge the amoebic plankton as the dominant species, despite the fact the plankton owned the title by logical default. The VRPPC even went so far as to try to plant false evidence of a land-creature that didn't or couldn't exist. The planet Mrool was eventually deemed a great waste of space, and its orbital pattern was thus re-directed into the nearest black hole. It's true that Mrool might have been a waste of space. No one lived there to enjoy it. There was nothing swimming in its ocean but some invisible amoebic plankton. It brings up the classic argument about whether or not magma-rain is still hot if there's no one there to get burned."

"Do you know what these creatures are?" I asked Wilx.

"No, but pass me the copy of *Very Rare Planets*. They might make mention of it in the less-read sections."

I passed Wilx my tattered copy of the book. He flipped to the chapter on Hroon and read from the microscopic blurbs bordering the edges of the page. I had never bothered to read those parts.

"The dominant species," said Wilx, "are a measly gathering of beasts known as Grollers. All we can tell you about Grollers is to not go near them, under any circumstances."

"Ok. Let's get out of here," said Rip. "You heard the books informative yet anonymous voice from two thousand years ago telling us not to go near them."

"Actually," began Wilx, "*Very Rare Planets* is even older than that. The first known publication was sometime before--"

"They look like the puke of a Galactic Gobbling Groobin," interrupted Rip.

"No they don't," I said. "They look like the guts of a Colossal Snorkling Plitzer!"

"No," challenged Rip. "They look like evolution's cutting room floor."

Grollers did not end up on evolution's cutting room floor. They made the final cut. You might think a Groller is ridiculously unsuited to live on a water world because they're not originally from a water world, having possibly re-colonized to the wrong planet. This is not the case. Hroon is the only planet that Grollers have ever existed on. It is simply a case of evolution severely fucking up.

"Prepare the floating elevator."

"And don't forget the remote control this time," I said.

"Way ahead of you," said Wilx as he patted his jacket pocket, which contained ample spare remotes. "It is a new rule never to leave the ship without ample spare remotes for the floating elevator. We've gotten in a lot of trouble from continuing to forget this thing."

Grollers always evoke a strong reaction in visitors. Many people wish that someone would get the whole business over with by dropping a bomb on the lot of them. Others wish that someone would transport them to a planet where they belong. Most are against this last idea, not wanting to risk their own planet being the future home of Grollers.

"Ugh. Just look at them," I said.

"Don't forgot that you're a Greeg," said Wilx. "You're barely less hideous than those things."

"Do you think they can talk?" I asked, ignoring the comment.

The floating elevator touched down on the island. The Grollers were noticeably scared of the new technology. They hopped and rolled their way to the opposite edge of the rocks. A few remained nearby.

"Look," I said, pointing to the close Grollers, "Some of them are brave and want to examine us."

"I don't think so," said Wilx, inspecting the nearby bodies. "They aren't moving. I think they were killed by the fire propulsion of the floating elevator."

"Oh."

Rip promptly rolled the dead Grollers into the water, so as to not upset the rest of the herd. A carnivorous fish-monster promptly ate them and was delightedly surprised by the random introduction of cooked Groller meat as opposed to the usual raw. It was a delicacy the fish-monster had never been treated to. No one else in history had ever accidentally fried a group of Grollers with the propulsion of a floating elevator and then rolled their bodies into the ocean.

"Not the best way to say hello," said Wilx.

"Just look at them," I repeated.

"Indeed."

All three of us were thoroughly brought down by the sad scene of the Grollers.

"Can any of you talk?" shouted Rip. "HELLO?"

Not one sound emanated from the creatures. Not even a slur of gibberish or a brief bout of nonsensical shrieking. Total silence.

"They can't talk. Let's go," said Rip.

Wilx threw up over the edge of the rocks. "You're right. We can't learn anything from these primitive beasts."

"Why did you throw up just now?"

"Maybe seasickness. Maybe the horrible sight of those creatures, or a combination of the two. Probably just the creatures though."

"I'm cueing the elevator."

As we were about to climb onto the elevator I happened to glance behind me and take one last look at the Grollers. I could just as easily have not taken this last glance. Sometimes I laugh about how much can change during the millisecond of a trivial decision.

Of all the Grollers overpopulating this island, one of them in particular was special. Kog shall be his name. Kog was not smarter than the other Grollers. He was not the next link in their evolution. What made Kog special was the fact that he had something in his possession. It was the only object on the entire island, and it was hidden away so that no one else could see it. If any of the other Grollers were to have anything in their possession they would immediately try to eat it.

"Hey!" I shouted at Rip and Wilx. "Look at that one over there!"

"Where? They all look the same."

"Right there to the left! Do you see it?"

"No."

"One of them is motioning to us!"

Rip and Wilx looked around the terrain until they spotted Kog. He was waving for us to come closer.

"I don't like it," said Rip. "Could be a trap."

"But it's a sign of intelligence! Maybe that one has learned how to communicate."

"Maybe so."

"We should at least try to talk to it."

"You go over and chat with the monsters. We'll stay on the elevator in preparation for rapid departure. If these beasts turn on you, don't count on us waiting around to collect your body."

"Ok."

So Rip and Wilx (in their occasional cowardly fashion) remained on the floating elevator as I carefully ambled my way towards Kog. I could see that he was now pointing at the rocky floor.

"What is it?" I asked.

Kog continued to point at the rocks.

"It's just more rocks. What are you pointing at?"

In a fit of impatience, Kog stood on his leg and attempted to jump up and down like a child. He quickly fell over, bruising his face and scraping his arm. He angrily thrashed about, apparently having just discovered for the first time that he only had one leg and one arm. Grollers have no memory at all. Kog was the only living Groller who had any sort of remembered knowledge, and it was merely the location of the hidden object.

It was at this moment that most of the Grollers became aware that I was food. They began to hop and roll their way towards me. Luckily they were slow and zombie-like, but given the lack of space it was only a matter of minutes before they closed in on me.

"Listen, you mutant! What are you pointing at?!" I screamed at Kog.

The sudden loudness of my outburst shook Kog into an awakened state of purpose. He had never felt more alive.

Kog pushed and kicked away the loose pile of rocks he'd been pointing at. Buried underneath was a book. It looked very old and tattered.

"Thank you," I said as I grabbed the book. I raced for the floating elevator.

Obotron 1 flew away from Hroon. Just one fleet ship now

followed behind us (the other one resting at the bottom of the Hroonian Ocean, for those of you who have the memory of a Groller). I could not wait to peruse this mysterious artifact.

The book had washed up on the island many thousands of years ago. The archaic and brittle tree-fibre pages had survived the ocean by having been rolled up and contained within an airtight canister. This canister was likely the first ever 'message in a bottle' in universal history. The ancient Groller who found the book somehow instinctively knew that it must be kept a secret, so he buried it in the rocks. In his short lifetime he showed it to only one other Groller, this being the Groller who would in turn be the next guardian of the book. This cycle continued down the ages, so that per generation there was always only one Groller who knew the secret. None of the guardians were curious enough to open the pages or to even wonder about the book. They merely kept it safe. This remarkable event reached its culmination with Kog. For whatever reason, Kog knew the book was meant to be given to me.

It is now my belief that the purpose of the Groller species, the complete reason for their very evolution, was to make sure that this object made its way into my possession.

CHAPTER 31

The Journal

"What were you doing back there?" said Rip. "You know how hungry those creatures were?"

"It was worth it," I said. "Look at this. They were hiding some type of old book. Who knows what important information it contains."

"Another book?" asked Rip concernedly. "Last time you read a book to us we got in a lot of trouble. Remember?"

"I haven't had time to forget. Last time I read a book to you was a copy of *Very Rare Planets,* and that was when we decided to visit Hroon. So only seconds ago did we finish getting in the trouble that occurred from the last time I read a book to you."

"Exactly. I think we could use a break before you start unleashing more trouble from out of whatever other hexed books you continuously find lying around."

"I concur," said Wilx. "Take that book to your room if you want to read it. We'll be in here purging our minds of cursed knowledge by way of a few Crammington Krish Fortinis."

"We still have some of those?" said Rip elatedly.

I retired to my room, leaving the two well-seasoned travellers of space and time to their self-destructive methods of transcendental meditation.

I carefully opened the book, making sure not to crack its weather-worn pages. I immediately saw from the dated entries that it was a personal journal of sorts.

But who wrote it?

And where?

***

1st ENTRY – DATE: 337/51 – LOCATION: Mother Ship, Yoloron Galaxy

My name is Jorf. I just moved to the up and coming Yoloron Galaxy. Today I started a new job. I am an Intergalactic Specimen Collector. It is my duty to obtain any and all sorts of life forms from whatever planet I come across. The spaceship I have been equipped with may be old and rickety, but it has all the right environmental housing facilities for storing any type of species. My first assignment is to visit a nearby largish meteor that has taken up orbit around a new sun. We are to decide if the meteor is showing any tendencies of becoming a planet, i.e.: whether or not life is sprouting up on this barren wasteland. It sounds dull, and I don't expect to find anything. Just the sort of job they give to someone on their first day.

I wasn't entirely interested in this Jorf character, but I recognized the name Yoloron as having been the ancient name for what humans would later call the Milky Way Galaxy.

2nd ENTRY – DATE: 337/52 – LOCATION: Mother Ship, Orbiting Meteor

Today our ship arrived at the meteor/planet. According to the papers back home, this new addition to our galaxy has been named 'Earth,' a word from the Hindrian language meaning 'unsightly, misshapen barren wasteland.' I actually thought the name sounded good, and figured it was a shame to have such a negative meaning attached to it. But no other description is as appropriate for Earth. It is simply an uninhabited meteor. I have no idea why we've been sent here.

3rd ENTRY – DATE: 337/53 – LOCATION: Surface of Earth

We have set up a camp base on the surface of the meteor. We are to stay here for a Yoloron week to thoroughly make sure there are no signs of life. Everything is freezing cold. A week here will probably feel more like a month.

5th ENTRY – DATE 337/55 – LOCATION: Surface of Earth

There is not much to do here. I have mostly been experimenting with the liquor supply by mixing all sorts of random alcohols together, hoping for some type of favourable concoction. Only one drink has so far tasted decent. I have decided to call it a 'Crammington Krish Fortini,' named after my great friend and mentor Crammington Krish Fortini. Working a job is most difficult after drinking a few CKF's, as the effects of this new beverage are staggeringly strong.

6th ENTRY – DATE: 337/56 – LOCATION: Surface of Earth

Today was our fourth night on Earth. I've been trying to keep myself busy analyzing ground samples. There appears to be no cellular activity on this entire rock. There isn't even the trace of an atmosphere. We have sent burrowing pod-bots to the core, to check for any heat emission that might later provide fertile ground for life. Negative readings across the board. You can tell that the rest of the crew has taken a liking to my new drink by the drastic drop in work productivity. One of the robot technicians even thinks the CKF might be a big hit at the local bars.

9th ENTRY – DATE: 337/59 – LOCATION: Mother Ship, Orbiting Earth

Today we left Earth. Our ship is chartered for home and I could not be happier.

10th ENTRY – DATE: 337/60 – LOCATION: Mother Ship

Something terrible has happened. It seems a cooler full of life-samples has been forgotten on the surface of Earth. We have been ordered to turn our ship around for a Retrieval Mission. Personally I don't see the problem with the loss of one cooler.

11th ENTRY – DATE 337/61 – LOCATION: Mother Ship

This cooler is a big deal! Everyone calls it The Ultimate Kit. It is apparently a well-rounded collection of the most varied forms of life from across the farthest stretches of the universe. I have been told the cooler is the 'Ark of All Alien Life.' It also contains a very rare planetary starter kit, including Instant-Ocean packets and ultra rare Bottled-Atmosphere.

12th ENTRY – DATE 337/61 – LOCATION: Surface of Earth

We are now back at Earth. The camp base was reconstructed. A search party was immediately sent out to scour the crater-laden surface for the cooler. I have yet to be accused, but I now remember clearly that I was the one who lost the cooler. Punishment is said to be severe. I hope everyone understands it was a mistake, and that anyone would have forgotten the cooler if they'd been gallivanting around a pitch dark meteor while sloshed on half a dozen CKFs.

14th ENTRY – DATE: 337/63 – LOCATION: Mother Ship

After two days of searching the entire surface of Earth, we have concluded that the cooler is no longer here, or was never here in the first place. I've decided to retire from the specimen collecting business and continue a relaxing career with my experimental drink-making adventures.

I decided to skip the next few pages, noticing they were merely a mad inventors' plans for selling ill-conceived, deadly drinks. After a few weeks the entries were suddenly being written from prison.

44th ENTRY – DATE: 337/93 – LOCATION: Grogol Prison Detention

I have been convicted of the heinous crime of 'Unwanted Planet Creation.' Apparently there were more than 17 witnesses who claimed I brazenly and drunkenly dumped out the contents of the cooler. While I cannot deny these claims, nor deny that there were indeed witnesses all around me, I still suspect my team members of ratting me out for the sole reason of wishing to steal my invention of the Crammington Krish Fortini, a drink that in one month has become so popular it's being quoted as 'the New Water.' The robot technician George was especially interested in seeing the list of ingredients for the CKF. The CKF is not my only invention to have recently taken off. The media is saying that in the last month Earth has quadrupled in size, as well as having formed an atmosphere, an ocean and a rainforest. There is no question that Earth is rapidly evolving into a full-fledged planet. As for life-forms, evolution passed through the amoebic stage within the first week, and now there are sightings of strange and tiny wriggly creatures crawling from out of the ocean. The unexpected planet has been deemed superfluous and/or a threat to the galaxy. I do not know what will happen to me. All I know is that I've been allowed to keep my journal and that a piece of its blank paper is the best meal I've had in weeks.

I could see the ripped edge of the page that Jorf had torn out and eaten.

I ran down the corridor to tell Rip and Wilx the news. They were coincidentally drunk on Crammington Krish Fortinis. Or not a coincidence, depending on how synchronized you believe the universe to be.

"How's the reading going?" asked Rip. "Learning new things that will endanger our lives?"

"Have you ever heard of the Yoloron Galaxy?"

"The Yoloron Galaxy?" asked Wilx, snapping alive as if instantly made sober by the mention of the words. "That sounds familiar."

"It's the exact same Galaxy we're in right now. Humans called it the Milky Way."

"What are you talking about?" asked Rip.

"The book I got on Hroon, it's an old journal by an intergalactic specimen-collector. He details the events in which he visits Earth while it was still a lifeless meteor."

"What's Earth?" asked Rip.

"You know that planet you just dumped me on for thousands of years? The planet you forever altered when you introduced a diabolically inter-spliced species of investment bankers? That's Earth."

"Oh, yeah. Earth. But it isn't really Earth anymore, is it?"

"No. It's the Planetglomerate."

"Had you reached the point yet?" asked Rip.

"This guy, the specimen collector, he spilled a cooler full of alien life samples on the surface of Earth. All the various seeds/cells/fungi from the cooler quickly evolved and spread, becoming the reason Earth turned into a planet. The cooler was an intergalactic Ark of all alien life. This explains the randomness and crowded diversity of life on Earth. After all, what sort of sane and naturally evolved planet has dozens of millions of different species?"

"But what is the relevance?"

"If this had never happened, Rip wouldn't have had a planet in which to introduce his inter-spliced bankers. And it was the inter-spliced bankers who turned into Greegs after the creation of the Planetglomerate."

"What?"

"Because of this journal, the evolutionary path of the human/Greeg can now be traced back to the actions of one oblivious dope who didn't care about keeping his job."

"How did the journal end up on Hroon?"

"I don't know that yet."

"Unusual place for a journal to be."

"Another thing about the specimen collector," I said, "is

that he invented the Crammington Krish Fortini."

"He did not!" shouted Rip belligerently.

"Everyone knows that George the Robot Technician invented the CKF," concurred Wilx.

"You're wrong," I said. "Jorf writes about how the drink was stolen by George."

"Who's Jorf?"

"The guy who wrote the journal. The oblivious dope."

Wilx and I sat quietly while trying to deal with the strangeness of existence. Rip went a little loud and crazy.

"Fully knowing how things came to be is never a good thing," he said.

CHAPTER 32

Suddenly Getting in a Lot of Trouble for Something that Happened a Very Long Time Ago

"You are under arrest for the reckless crashing of a fuel-less ship of Obotron crew members into the surface of the planet Lincra, the most populated and popular planet in existence," blared the megaphone from the suddenly approaching battalion of the Kroonum Civility, Order and Peace Upkeep and Maintenance Division - Deltron Force Strike 9, sporting their spanking new crest and logo, freshly dubbed formal and binding by the Council of Eleven and a Half Thousand Different Coloured Robes in the most recent hammering out of the Treaty of Manderbatt. "You're sure that's them then?" blared the loudspeaker to someone inside the ship, clearly failing to turn off said loudspeaker.

"Oh yes, we're sure," grumbled thousands of eerie and ghost-like voices.

"Right, don't try anything tricky like last time, you're going in for a hearing, then an indictment, then another hearing, then a formal reading of the latest version of the Treaty of Manderbatt, any new suggestions more than welcome, then a cross hearing, then a formal hearing, then a trial, then a verdict, then a mandatory sentencing, then an even more mandatory re-evaluation of said sentencing, then a mistrial, then a re-trial, then a re-assessment of the whole process under the newest revisions to the Treaty of Manderbatt, then lunch, for us of course, not you; then a gruelling 14 day re-enactment of the whole ordeal so far for *Kroonum Zoo Legal Wars – Series 19987.34 Part 2,* then probably an all out war with those imbecilic crooks over on Persheron 8 and innumerable opportunities for you to escape without serving any actual punishment. But make no mistake, escape again... and you will be caught... again!"

"Well I'd say it sounds like going through the legal system is punishment enough," suggested Rip.

"Indeed," said Wilx. "Merely your summary of the possible preliminary aspects of it is enough to make me have nothing but regrets for the whole affair."

"Hmmm, that's a good suggestion. I'll ensure that makes it into the next version of the Treaty. But for now, the law's the law, so you're coming with us."

An Eealiotronic Wave Net was immediately cast forth from the battalion, encircling the Obotron 1 and its lone trailing ship. After an inspection of the contents of the trailing ship and some more murmuring from the mysterious hoard aboard the battalion commander ship, the trailing ship was cast free in orbit around the planetglomerate, the contents as of yet... unknown.

CHAPTER 33

Revelations in a Holding Cell

They may have been joking, but Rip and Wilx were 100% right. Every second of watching the painful Kroonum legal system attempt to move forward was surely double, even triple, the punishment that same system may one millennia get around to dishing out. I begged to be abandoned back on earth watching entire organisms mutate, it surely would have been a more agreeable time. Torture is common practice in the first phases of incarceration. Nothing brutal and primitive like human torture, they use the much more effective method of boredom. Boredom, I would keep learning, is the most torturous thing that exists. The three of us were kept in confinement with recording devices all around. No attempts at subtlety here, they wanted a confession on tape. Genuinely not knowing what was going on and what it is they wanted us to confess to, I sincerely questioned Rip and Wilx again and again, but they honestly couldn't remember a thing they'd done wrong to anyone. This was most likely because nearly everything they did was something wrong to someone, so pinpointing one particular offence was impossible. This was a common phenomenon discussed in great detail by Kleb Globberchov in his mildly amusing *It Aint Easy Bein' a Sociopath*. Rip and Wilx were genuinely stumped as to who could still be pursuing the cause of incarcerating those responsible for destroying a measly ship load of Obotron Crew Members, barely above Investment Bankers on the list of creatures that are cared about. Surely crashing into Lincra is so frequent an occurrence that there could be no merit in chasing them this long and this vehemently after the incident. It was presumed that all this would be revealed during the trial, should it ever come to pass. This presumption was enforced by a booming announcement over the P.A. system in the cell that "All this shall be revealed during the trial, should it ever come to pass."

And so we waited. And so, my drugs began to wear off. And so, I remembered that I had an awful lot of questions that needed answering. What better time to get them answered than being stuffed into a cell with the two bastards who held the answers to most, if not all, of them.

"So what the hell have you two been up to for all this time? What the hell was the point of leaving me on that planet and watching those humans become Greegs? What was the point of any of this?!"

"Oh, that," mumbled Rip. "Wilx, you wanna take this one?"

"Perhaps. First, I'd like to hear some of your stories old

chap. Please do explain, in detail, everything you witnessed on that planet you were on."

Time was most certainly not of the essence. Time was not even remotely approaching anything that could be mistakenly construed as the essence. So I complied. I told them of everything I had been through, of everything I had seen. A lot of it they seemed to have heard before, or at least expected, with many a 'of course, yep,' sort of reaction coming from their face like things. The small details are what seemed to interest them most. They were especially tantalized by my descriptions of human religions and absurd conspiracy theories on the origin of man. I had dismissed them all to be ridiculous of course, but would be surprised to find out almost all of them were nearly 100% accurate. The only thing that made them inaccurate was small typos and distortions of the original truth, and the replacing of the word/concept "God" with "Rip and/or Wilx and/or a careless fellow named Jorf." I now believe that Rip and Wilx are the basis for the idea of God and Satan, with Wilx's influences on the planet being mostly good, and Rips being most certainly evil. When I explained what I thought was the foolish notion of creationism to them, it turned out to be true, with one minor exception that Rip casually explained: "Well no, it wasn't all done in 6 *consecutive* days, that would be ridiculous." When I told them that there was endless debates whether or not there was a creator or there was a big bang and evolution, Wilx said something very interesting. "What, nobody ever thought it might be all three?"

One after another, all of the engrained stories, myths and theories of mankind began to be explained by Rip and Wilx's unabashed, uncaring, and casual meddling. Jesus really was the son of God (if you take God to be the creator of the universe... as Rip was the creator of this particular one. "A long story involving the fission of a neo sub-quark to win a bet," as Rip put it. "Not a very long story at all is it?" As Wilx put it.) The Virgin Mary story checked out, as Rip merely used one of his many other sexual organs to impregnate her, while leaving her hymen untouched. "And so that makes me God?" howled Rip with laughter. "More like a deadbeat dad! Great night of ear sex though I must say, and equally good times with her belly button."

They found it all to be hilarious. Turns out they had returned to Earth frequently in a manner all to similar to the way in which they kept going down the same corridor in the Maze.

One by one Rip and Wilx chopped every human conspiracy theory or unexplained phenomenon down to size. The Pyramids weren't built by slaves at all, they were dropped in one night just to see how the humans would react. They reacted by devoting much of their civilization to drawing paintings and explanations as to how alien 'gods' had dropped them in one night from the heavens. After extensive studies, centuries later, "scientific explanations" let it be known that humans had clearly built them and that was that. Eventually, when Rip and Wilx had squeezed all of the laughs they were going to out of my tales of humanity, I demanded my explanation.

"I demand my explanation," I said.

"Right right, I suppose I ought to. Listen old pal, it's quite simple," said Wilx.

"Every time you tell me something you say that it's quite simple, and it never is. Stop saying that."

"Right, whatever, well here's the thing. We kind of thought that, well I did more, I, well I bet Rip here..."

"*Another* bet?!"

"Yes, countless of them, but this one in particular, well no, I suppose we'd better start from the beginning. You see when Rip bet whoever the hell that was that he bet on the planet where we found you that he could take a carnival Greeg and have them, er you, pass as an intelligent, decent being, etc. he was really just procuring a pawn in a much larger bet with me involving Greegs in general."

"So I really have been nothing but a pawn this whole time?"

"Well not entirely. Rip did genuinely want you to be his friend. But that was only because he wanted to win a bet I placed with him that he wasn't capable of friendship and that's how I won this nice pair of boots."

"Well what about you two, aren't you friends?"

"Not really. Gambling partners perhaps, but not friends. Rip and I were space mapping space mappers in a much larger order of magnitude than these universes on which you dwell. Just as many galaxies make up one universe, many universes make up one Richtolhoffen."

"Ok, I think I follow you."

"Right, so imagine if you were shrunk down to the cellular level, then you would be both relatively immortal, because of your ridiculously long life span in comparison."

"And don't forget almost immediately bored to tears," piped in Rip.

"We were shrunk down to miniature proportions to map out a few universes and return," continued Wilx, ignoring Rip. "However, once we were shrunk down with the Grambling Magnitudinal Decreaselating Prokrelator we decided that we could have much more fun ditching our duties as space mappers and roaming this puny plain of existence. I chose to pass the time acquiring knowledge, while Rip spent it mostly getting drunk. We both kept ourselves sane with the endless gambling.

"Small bets became intertwined with larger ones and insanely complicated super series of bets," said Rip. "Wagers, you see, are all we have to live for."

"Why is that?"

"Because we are immortal," said Wilx. "Being born of an upper order of magnitude, our lifespans are longer than any Universes on your level of existence. We have been alive for so long, that we no longer have any emotional connection to anything. To us, all of your worlds are merely a game board for us to wonder about and place wagers on."

"So what about Earth, and me? How do I fit into all of this?"

"Which one is Earth again?" said Rip.

"The one that you abandoned me on for hundreds of thousands of..."

"Oh right, The Greeg planet, I was getting to that," said Wilx. "You see, Rip bet someone that he could turn you, a hopeless and savage Carnival Greeg, into a decent being so that he could then bet me that such a reformed, decent Greeg, once placed on a planet full of Greegs, would then simply return to being a Greeg. I was of the opinion that not only would you not revert to being a Greeg, but that you would have such a unique perspective, having formerly been a Greeg, that watching the entire process of Greegification unfold would, if anything, strongly solidify your desire to help other Greegs become unGreeged, perhaps even leading to a cure for Greegs. Like some sort of Greeg psychiatrist of sorts. As it turns out we were both kind of right. Call it a draw."

"But why did you knowingly allow the whole place to be devoured and overrun by Greegs? Wilx, surely you must realize now, after hearing the tale of Jorf, what a horrible act that was? Considering that the planet was a completely unique blending of such a large array of plant and animal species. Don't you have any regrets about it being destroyed?"

"Yes, well I did what I could. I bet Rip that the plants and animals would be victorious over the heartless ambitions of his measly hoard of Investment Bankers. I underestimated the strength of his most potent concoction, "The Chosen People" as he called them, and lost the bet. They were particularly determined to continue investment banking and worshipping money at all costs, no matter what the consequences."

"Remarkable creatures," confirmed Rip. "Much better than the first batches of spliced genes I tried to cook up. I believe you said the humans called them 'natives' and 'aboriginals'. What miserably useless Greeg fodder. They barely concerned themselves with investment banking at all!"

"So now the planetglomerate will become the first ever Planetary Greeg Carnival, instead of the hub of biological diversity and wonder I had hoped for it," shrugged Wilx, unconcerned. "Such is the way of things. You win some, you lose some. Besides, when the humans became Greegs, we settled another bet about the role investment bankers play in the role of Greegformations. It also gave us the playing field with which to drop you off and settle our other bet. You see it just keeps going on like this."

"And what a Greeg Carnival it shall be!" chirped up Rip. "Full of the finest Greegs from all corners of many universes. To answer your original question old friend, *that's* what we've been up to all this time! We've been scouring Universes far and wide collecting Greegs."

"What do you mean collecting? There are different kinds of Greegs?" I spun on Rip, exhausted.

"But of course! Greeg is merely a sort of classification for any species that has given up on progressing and evolving, and degenerated completely to the lowest possible rung on the ladder. No matter what the origin of the species, the same basic characteristics and general failures are always arrived at: The worshipping of Schmold, the building of and keeping clean of meaningless structures, the wilful ignorance of all things that are not Greeg centric, the sexual coverings. It's all status quo! But the origin of the Greeg and their journey to Greegdom is as varying as the stars and planets themselves. Any species can become a Greeg, and many of them have. Greeg conversions are on the rise exponentially in recent times, as more and more species fail miserably to cope with the ever changing realities of the universe around them."

"These facts have been common knowledge for a long time," casually added Wilx. "But what Rip and I want to understand is *how* this happens, and *why* this happens. Can it be changed? Will it ever be different? Can Greegs be changed back to their original form en masse? Is there a more effective way of stopping them from degenerating into Greegdom and keeping their Greegeromody under wraps than the current method of dividing them up into Carnivals? These are the sorts of bets we hope to settle on the Ultimate & Grand Greeg Carnival. You've provided us with much insight into the forces that initially lead a species down the path to Greegery. We long suspected that the domination of Investment Bankers of the species was a major catalyst on the road to Greegeration, but have learned so much more from your observations; such as the role that this 'religion' plays, and sexuality and unexpectedly having your solar system thrown into chaos by a Galactic Gobbling Groobin. There is still so many things to sort out before we can write our definitive scholarly volume on Greegs. But when we do, it will surely outsell Dr. Kipple's pompously under-researched *Purified Procreation: Greeg Sex and What it Says About Their True Nature* as the definitive work on all things Greeg!"

"Wait a minute, are you implying that all of this is happening so that you can write a bestselling book?"

"What else would this kind of chaos and insanity be happening for!? We've got some really unique and unheard of things we're going to include in just the first couple chapters that'll really get 'em hooked. For example, the last remaining Obotron Crew Members in our last trailing Obotron fleet ship... became Greegs! No one could have possibly predicted that! They did so at a staggeringly swift pace, without even having a home planet to reside on. Evidently, in a last ditch attempt to gain control of the fleet, several of them converted themselves into Investment Bankers so as to have an independent fuel source for the ship. Except once they saw how much quick cash could made at the expense of each other in the investment banking field, they quickly forgot all ambitions of gaining control of anything other than more things to invest in and bank on. This quickly caused a complete erosion of what little civility was left onboard the ship and before long they were as Greeged out as the next Greeg. They created Schmold via a large vat of all the evacuated disgustingness they'd collected from being hurtled through time so many times on our exploits to collect more Greegs!   It was also likely a factor that the remaining ship they had all been crammed into was increasingly being overcrowded with all of the Greegs we had collected from around the many Universes... so perhaps there is something to be said for the ability of other Greegs to have an affect on non-Greegs become Greegs? We'll have to wager on that sometime."

"Unbelievable," I said. "Don't you two have any sense of remorse or consciousness about all the horrible things you have done to all of these innocent creatures and worlds? Just to prove a few points and win a few bets and write a book about it?"

"No, of course they don't," came the spooky sound of thousands of eerie ghost like creatures, seemingly infiltrating our brains and the walls at the same time. "They have no feelings at all. They recklessly destroy and kill on a whim, just to settle a bet or a wager. They care not about the consequences of their actions. This is the curse of the Immortals."

"Who are you?" asked Rip and Wilx.

"We are the ghosts of the Obotron Crew Members," proclaimed the ghastly voices. "We have banded together in the invisible dimension, where we are better known as Algreenian-Fog Specters. We have returned to the physical dimension to exact our revenge on these careless fools who used us, who murdered us, for nothing more than their silly games and whimsical wagers. By infiltrating the highest ranks of Kroonum Law Enforcement, we are now ready to do what most dead folks can only dream of. We are going to put the very cosmic dirt bags responsible for our death on trial!"

"No wait! I'm not one of them!" I cried out. "I'm not immortal at all!"

"Errrr..." began Rip.

"Well... that's not entirely true, per say, any more," said Wilx.

"That longevity formula you injected in yourself was kind of a bit more of an... immortality formula."

"So what does that mean?"

"Congratulations!" said Rip. "It means you're the first ever Greeg to become immortal. You also won me this nice pile of invisible money by not having your internal organs burst into ice flames as soon as the formula hit your bloodstream, as Wilx predicted would happen." I finally understood why Rip had been holding his arms outstretched like he was carrying firewood.

"Yeah, we'll be confiscating that," said the former Obotron Crew members reincarnated as judicially vengeful Algreenian-Fog Specters. "Now get your ass into the courtroom. The judge awaits you."

Windy gusts began uncomfortably tugging, pulling and

prodding us out of the cell and into the courtroom.

"I still can't understand what would drive you to have such a lack of emotions and care for the consequences of your actions," I said to Rip as we walked the long glass tube way leading to the courtroom.

"Boredom, you will learn," Rip said matter of factly, "is the most torturous thing that exists."

We entered the courtroom.

"Hello again," said the judge.

"Hello Reg," said Rip. "You probably want your Greeg back now don't you?"

CHAPTER 34

The Trial

It's true.

Reg, my former carnival Greeg-keeper, was now an official first-rank judge for the Kroonum Courts of Law. I suppose that's justice. Or not.

Reg was still very much a scary goblin-like creature with fangs and claws and red eyes, yet in recent years he had somehow succeeded in making himself far more frightening. I think it had something to do with the black hooded robe he wore whilst perched atop a throne made from the skeletal fragments of the convicted. He was the embodiment of fear, so much so that hundreds of film scripts were being pitched to Reg on a daily basis, all of which requesting he fill the inimitable role of the Grim Reaper. Thinking himself too short for the role,

Reg had yet to reply to any of the filmmakers. He was also worried his carpel-tunnel syndrome would prevent him from being able to hold the heavy scythe prop during tedious hours of re-shoots, as there were sure to be requests for many unneeded hours of re-shoots made by the group of perfectionist auteur student filmmakers busy competing for the honour of directing Reg's first Vehicle Movie. Reg was unaware that height is now a minor inconvenience solved by the art of trick-photography, and that his scythe prop would be made of feather-lite styrofoam.

Reg eventually accepted his calling as an actor. He would go on to star in countless blockbusters. Only he wasn't acting. He played himself in every film. All he did was show up on set and improvise some of his characteristic creepiness. Nowadays his name frequently tops the charts of magazine polls concerning topics like "the scariest movie villain of all time and space" and "the #1 cause for sleep deprivation amongst children."

This all happens, of course, in another dimension where Reg is not dead by the end of this novel.

Reg had only earned the status of a Kroonum judge because of the illegal wrangling and bribery performed by the Algreenian Fog-Specters.

The Specters did not want Reg to become a film star, so they filled his mind with all sorts of ideas to cause low self-esteem. For the success of the Specter's revenge plot it was imperative that Reg stay in the courtroom. Algreenian Fog-Specters (or anyone else that is dead) are unable to perform tasks on a physical level, hence the reason they didn't just kill Rip, Wilx and I and call it a day. They are, however, adept at using their mental prowess to influence the actions of the living. The Specters ensured our judge was someone who personally hated us, so that we would be sentenced with the most brutal of verdicts regardless of the evidence. Reg had been promised several million dollars worth of invisible money that he would never see, literally or figuratively.

It is good that Specters cannot personally harm anyone. Many specters are dangerously angry about being dead. They cannot control their jealousy towards the living. Their scene usually degenerates into a violent revenge plot. Reg was now in control of our fate. Each unappealing scenario seemed to cancel out the last.

"I said you probably want your Greeg back now don't you?" repeated Rip.

"No," said Reg from his skeletal perch. "I have hundreds of

Greegs locked up in the chambers. That doesn't mean I feel any less angry for being ripped off."

"But this Greeg is intelligent," said Rip.

"And immortal!" added Wilx.

Reg was thoroughly against the idea of an immortal greeg. "Who wants an immortal Greeg? My favourite part of Greeg-keeping is watching them drop dead from the slightest of parasitic infections. And besides, once he's intelligent doesn't he cease to be a Greeg?"

"Great question," said Rip, sensing an opportunity for stalling. "Let's debate that with lengthy philosophical discourse."

"Why don't we get started with the trial instead?" suggested the Specters.

Reg pounded his gavel. It shattered into fine crumbs.

"Why has my gavel shattered?" he angrily bellowed.

"Er... it is made of Crabbit skulls?" replied a Specter.

"So? I make everything out of Crabbit skulls."

"They have weak bones, your honour."

"Why do they have weak bones?"

"I believe it comes from a dietary deficiency of vitamin A."

"Why are Crabbits so low in vitamin A?"

"We've recently figured that out, your honour. It seems Crabbits follow a strict diet of cannibalism. The only thing they would be caught dead eating is each other."

"And?"

"Well... Crabbit meat does not contain vitamin A. Therefore if you only take sustenance from Crabbit meat you will merely continue to weaken yourself.

It is one of those annoying Catch-22s. The evolutionary cycle of the Crabbit has long been disastrous... a story of ill-fated choices, mutated genes and easily broken bones that is rapidly reaching its necessary crescendo. I expect the Crabbits will have killed themselves off within the next few seasons."

Reg pointed to a group of Specters in the far corner. "You! Go out and present alternative food to the Crabbits. I want this cannibalism stopped immediately. And then introduce a source of vitamin A into their diet. I'll not have their weak bones causing my brilliant inventions to shatter so easily!"

"I protest, your honour," replied the specter. "Doesn't it seem right to let the Crabbits die off naturally? I don't think the Crabbits will respond to other food anyway. They are not forced into Cannibalism. Apparently there is an abundance of natural food surrounding the Crabbit population, yet they choose to dine on each other based on palette preference."

"Palette?" asked Reg.

"You know... taste, texture, consistency. All the factors that determine a meal as good or bad. I personally died before ever having tried them, but I've heard Crabbits are superb."

Reg pondered. He did not like the taste of Crabbits at all. The only food his species enjoys is Gahooleb. On Reg's home-world, the only place where Gahooleb can be harvested, it is merely the word for 'food.' It is a demonic sustenance not entirely dissimilar to Schmold, a gloppy green sludge that isn't properly defined as either a liquid or a solid. Most creatures would be horrified to find it resting on their dinner plate, and further horrified to find themselves stone-dead after having been curious enough to taste a tiny morsel. When an open container of Gahooleb is mixed with the wrong planetary atmosphere it turns into pure sulphuric acid, which incidentally has no effect whatsoever on Reg's digestive system or general health.

"Besides," continued the specter, "We can't introduce Vitamin A to the Crabbits. We've not got any reasonable source of it at the moment. All we've really got is dead Crabbits."

"Then go find some milk or something!"

"No milk-producing creatures on this planet at all, your honour. Probably explains this whole dilemma."

"I have an idea," I said, butting in.

"Silence!" shouted Reg.

"It's just I think I can fix your problem somewhat effortlessly."

"Every minute of our time you waste is another year of imprisonment I will add to your sentencing. Now explain your plan with meticulous detail."

"Brown-noser," whispered Rip. I ignored him.

"You see," I began, "I have for a considerable amount of time lived on a world that was overly abundant in milk. You wouldn't believe how many milk-producing creatures freely roamed about the surface of this planet. These creatures were called Mammals. Of all these mammals, humans were the only ones who drank the milk from a different mammal. Some mammals produced desirable milk for humans. Others produced milk that for humans to consume would be considered a gross offence. The centrepiece of the desirable milk-producers was a quadruple-stomached creature known as a Cow. A blundering beastly sort of animal. So many humans wanted cow-milk so regularly that it only made sense to take full ownership of the Cow species. It was decided to transform the Cow from a creature into a tool of productivity. Once institutionalized within a cramped environment of dim lighting and abrasive mechanical structures, Cows soon lost their zest for life and became indiscernible to the eye from a clunky scattering of assembly-line equipment. They even lost their ability to speak, not that anyone remembered how Cows had once amused the world with their whimsical coffee-table anecdotes. The only word from Cow language to have survived in their brains was the resonant "Moo!" The Cow's word for the most rudimentary and primal verbal expression of emotional displeasure, similar to the universally accepted form of protest via loudly yelling 'Boo!' Anyway, in my time on this planet I sought to preserve certain alien rarities that I thought were worth preserving, one of which was a few hundred gallons of milk. Of course, at this point, Cows milk had become advisedly indigestible due to a few generation too many who indulged themselves in scientifically tampering with the hormones of the already sufficiently naturally-functioning system of the Cow, in hopes of greedily producing 'Super-Cows' that pumped out more milk than ever thought possible. Quantity over Quality was the popular motto of the era. Any semblance of nutrition had been genetically modified right out of the cow. I didn't see the logic of it being preferable to have 1000 gallons of rotten milk as opposed to having 10 gallons of good milk, so instead I acquired milk from one of the surrogate producers, an organically fed, free-range, non-genetically tampered quadruple-legged beast of the Capra-Hircus genus, otherwise known as a farm goat. This milk has survived my travels, and is laying dormant in the deep-freeze section of our spaceship. I have kept it's presence unknown by the rest of my party, for any liquid material that finds its way onto our ship is usually immediately consumed in a marathon of manic alcohol-brewing experimentation. I donate this milk to the courtroom, should it heighten our chances of leniency."

Reg did not at first reply. Often he appeared to not be listening. He was in fact doing more than listening. He was reading. Whenever someone says something lengthy or above his intelligence level, as in whenever someone speaks at all, Reg is forced to observe the words as automatically printed out to him by his desperately needed *Smart-into-Dumb Translator*. This gadget also provides Reg with a suitably intelligent example reply that he does not always choose to follow.

"You give milk? We feed to Crabbit?" he finally asked.

"Yes," I said.

The previously chosen Specters were sent to round up the few hundred gallons of milk from our ship. As part of their courtroom duty, Specters are given the ability to physically move items of low weight through the technological aid of telekineto-beams. They are only able to move what Reg instructs them to, otherwise they would have just tossed a grenade or two in my general direction and retired to the afterlife.

"I can't believe you gave away all our milk," whispered Rip.

"You didn't even know we had it in the first place," I replied.

"Exactly!"

"Shall we continue with the trial?" urged one of the Specters.

"Yes," said Reg. "Wait. No."

"No?"

"I've not got my plate of Crabbits. How can I expect to be cruel and heartless without some dead flesh to toy with?

Someone get me a fresh plate."

"Right away, sir."

A Specter promptly vanished from the room and returned with a tray of Crabbits. Reg took one look at the plate and threw it against the wall.

"What is this?" he angrily shouted. "Where are all the bones?"

"These Crabbits have been specially de-boned for you, sir."

"What for? Everyone knows I collect the bones for making furniture and other useless doohickeys with. It's the only reason I kill these things. They taste like band-aids."

Rip looked confused.

What's a band-aid? he whispered in my ear.

"Something you would need wrapped around your brain, if they made them small enough."

"We thought it would be a more pleasant dining experience without the bones," replied the specters. "You've been rapidly losing teeth from biting down on sharp fragments. We thought you'd like to retain some teeth for the purposes of eating. It is another annoying catch-22."

"If Crabbits have such weak bones, then why are they causing my teeth to break?"

"Your weak teeth has something to do with a lack of vitamin A in your diet."

"Why aren't I getting any vitamin A?"

"All you eat are Crabbits. We've just gone over several times at length how Crabbit meat contains no vitamin A whatsoever. This is all overly simplistic."

Reg looked infuriated. "Is my whole life just made up of catch-22's?!"

"It seems so."

"Then somebody get me some of that damn milk!"

"Right away, sir."

A Specter frantically floated off to get some milk. He momentarily returned empty-handed.

"There's no milk left, your honour. It's all been taken down to the Crabbit beach, at your recent request that we introduce a source of vitamin A into their diet."

"Well then get down to the beach and bring me a Crabbit that has ingested milk."

"Ok," said the specter as he headed to the beach. He again momentarily returned empty-handed.

"Sorry, your honour. It seems the Crabbits don't like milk. The ones who tried it were instantly putrefied. The rest then knew to stay away."

Reg slammed his fist down, shattering the table and spilling his drink onto the crowd. Some of it splashed onto Rip's arm, causing his skin to slightly bubble as if the drink had been concocted from pure sulphuric acid, which in fact it had.

"Ok," said Reg, feeling a little better after his violent outburst. "Let's carry on."

"May I have a glass of water?" asked Rip. He was desperately hoping to stall the trial in any way he could. The ingestion of water is actually lethal to Rip's internal organs, but he had learned about the diversion tactic of asking for a glass of water many times in American movies with trial scenes or police interrogations. Other than his familiarity with dramatic courtroom movies, Rip didn't know anything about America. The reason he even knew about those movies was because they are the only human achievement to transcend the barrier between planet Earth and Rip's own home planet. American trials were so compellingly dramatic to Rip's people that they henceforth made it the basis for their own legal courts. Not because human legality was considered efficient or fair, but simply because all the shouting, crying, cheating, gavel-banging and opportunities for rousing speeches, applause, more crying and other histrionics were about as entertaining as justice could get.

"What the hell is water?" asked Reg.

"Fair enough."

The lights were dimmed. The compilation disc of ambient courtroom music was ritualistically stomped on. The broken disc was then swept up and thrown out the window. The wind sent the shards drifting into the open door of a nearby apartment, where someone with too much time on their hands spent years inventing the technology capable of repairing the disc. Once finished, this person was severely disappointed to learn the disc was a mediocre compilation of ambient courtroom music. The mysterious character then shattered the disc and proceeded to fix it all over again, just for something to do.

The fragments of the broken Crabbit gavel were also swept up. The trial had officially begun.

"You three are on trial for the reckless crashing of a spaceship into the surface of Lincra, the most popular planet in existence. How do you plead?"

"Guilty by necessity," replied Rip.

"What are you doing?" I whispered. "They'll have us chopped up and made into tables or something."

"Ssh. They already know we did it."

"Guilty by necessity?" asked Reg.

Rip stood up. "Yes. We had to crash that ship. It was a clear case of us or them."

"How do you figure that?"

"Well... it's a long story. But while my friends, I mean acquaintances, and I were exploring Lincra, our ship was descended upon by savage thieves who stole our fuel. We didn't notice we were out of fuel until we'd already flown away, and by that point it was too late. Fumes allowed us to take off, but the instant we reached orbit it was clear we were about to crash back into the surface of the planet. So it was us or them. We were forced to drain the fuel out of one of our fleet ships, and if that meant the fleet ship would then in turn be the one to crash, well, so be it."

Reg consulted some important documents that had been placed in front of him. "Yes, except the fleet ship contained 492 crew members, all of whom perished in the crash. And the ghosts of whom are now inhabiting this courtroom," he added as he pointed around at the Specters.

"And we're not the only ones!" shouted a Specter. "Many other ships filled with crew have been lost in their suicidal adventures! I don't even think there's any ships left at this point!"

"Yeah!" joined in another Specter. "We're only a small

percentage of the lost Obotron crew. Many of the dead could not be here, for the manner in which they perished left them in a suspended state of eternal limbo without any hopes of achieving Spectral Finality."

"How so?" asked Reg.

"There were some ships that got swallowed by a Galactic Gobbling Groobin. They were sent spiralling through a time-travelling wormhole into an irreversible dimensional gateway. We've never seen any Specters from those particular crew members. And a more recent devastation had an entire ship sink to the bottom of the Hroon ocean. Haven't seen any Specters turn up from that ship either. We suspect they're trapped down there, living out a claustrophobic existence with nothing for entertainment except their minimal collection of VHS tapes. The fact that we were supplied with movies modified from their original version says everything about the sort of barbaric working conditions we were expected to tolerate. We would attempt some sort of rescue mission for our lost brothers, if it were not for us being dead and therefore having no means of retrieving a ship from the bottom of an ocean. We can't even get anyone alive to go into the ocean for us, because everyone knows Hroon is populated by dangerous monsters."

"And some of the crew were actually cooked and eaten by that unholy trio!" another Specter randomly added.

"Is this true?" asked Reg. "Did you cannibalize your crew members?"

"Yes," answered Rip.

"I regret cannibalizing the crew," I said. Indeed it wasn't one of my finer hours.

"You're right," said Rip. "None of the crew deserved to be cooked with such low quality standards. Who wants to be remembered as the too-chewy, over-salted dinner that somebody else had to choke down at the risk of offending the chef?"

"No. I actually regret it. We could have gone hungry before resorting to savagery."

"Resorting to savagery?! But that's your nature!"

"It *was* my nature," I said.

"Yes," said Reg. "Except the death of the crew members is not the issue here. Everyone knows those crew members were expendable. All they had ever done was fold the towels once."

"Not even," corrected Rip. "For the towels were always folded, having never left their factory sealed packages."

"Point taken. The real issue at hand here is the property damage done to the surface of Lincra."

"Uh-oh," whispered Rip. "I was worried about this part."

"Someone bring me... The Report!" bellowed Reg.

A Specter appeared, producing a stack of paper several feet high.

"This is only an account of the most expensive damage, your honour. The report on trivial damage is being housed in our underground warehouse."

"We have room for that in the underground warehouse?" asked Reg incredulously.

"No," your honour. "We were forced to extend the warehouse into a virtual higher-dimensional plain, one of the ones capable of bypassing the standard laws of physics by existing within spatially infinite parameters."

"I see," lied Reg. He was confused. The last paragraph had been translated to read *"We made more room by combining science and magic!"* Reg had been left cold by this translation. To begin with, the word 'combining' had a syllable more than his usual maximum preference of two. There was also the disturbing presence of the word 'science,' which suggested far too many intelligible subjects. Reg told the Translator to dumb things down a few times until finally the last paragraph merely read *"Magic!"* He was pleased with this all-encompassing explanation of how the crowded warehouse had been able to store such a detailed damage report.

Reg consulted the damage report for several minutes, during which he was brought a new plate of Crabbit meat. He was also brought a fresh glass of sulphuric acid. Rip backed his chair away, not wishing to undergo any more third degree burns should Reg suddenly have a violent outburst.

"Hmm," began Reg, "it seems the ship struck the planet in a

way that maximized the potential amount of damage. The rapid speed of the plummeting ship alone ensured it would not have even slowed down until it had crashed through at least ten subterranean layers, and yet it perfectly fell into the Master Ladder Tunnel, allowing the ship to chaotically free-fall until it collided with the fiery core. Many layers were destroyed. Considerable damage was done to Subterranean 12, the Layer Where Nothing is Done Except For Cutting Onions. The entire surface of Layer 12 disintegrated when a breach was caused in the conjoining Layer of Uncontrollable Highly Explosive Things. Chunks of onion were scattered all over the planet."

"So?" argued Rip. "It's just a bunch of onions! Did anyone die because of these onions?"

"179 trillion creatures. The explosion of onions caused so many beings to cry that collectively their tears made up a great washing flood that swept through the planet. A big-budget disaster film is still in production. I believe the working title is: *The Great Flood of Tears: A Musical Chronicle into the Devastation of Lincra.*

"Will the box-office proceeds go to the families of the victims?" blurted Wilx, who had thus far remained relatively quiet.

"1% of the gross will be donated to the families. After taxes it will be something more like .0001%. Another 2% will go the screenwriters. The rest will be spent on badly needed new leather chairs for the studio fat-cats."

"Why do the studio fat-cats need new chairs so badly?"

"People tend to go through a lot of chairs when they sit around all day doing no work of any kind."

Reg cleared his throat. He didn't actually have a throat to clear, but he made a wretched sound not dissimilar to what one would expect if he did.

"Let's hear from our first witness. I call to the stand Mr. Nickbas L. Turkey."

"Who's that?" said Wilx.

"No idea," said Rip.

Nickbas entered the courtroom and sat down at the witness bench.

"Oh no, not this guy," groaned Rip as he noticed that Nickbas was in fact the unkempt map vendor from the Lincran parking lot. The one who made maps so terrible that Rip had been compelled to rip them to shreds.

"Do you swear to tell the truth, etc.?" Reg asked Nickbas.

Nickbas looked puzzled at the question. "Truth? What is truth?"

"Truth is what is real. It means you will not lie."

"Isn't truth and reality just my opinion or something?" asked Nickbas.

"No. Truth is fact."

"I disagree. Truth is subjective. If I were to say at this very moment that I'm seeing many translucent Specters floating around the room, would you not tell me I'm crazy and hallucinating? Yet seeing the Specters is *my* truth. Does your inability to see the Specters change that? Are dreams not as real as waking life? Does the imagination not create what it wants to see?"

"You *are* seeing the Specters," said Reg. "This courtroom is full of them."

"That explains a lot," muttered Nickbas. "I knew this stuff couldn't be that strong."

"What?"

"Nothing."

"So you witnessed the crashing of the ship into the surface of Lincra?"

"Yes, I saw the whole thing. It was a disturbing event. Many fine maps were destroyed. I remember seeing a flood of tears and thinking it was a perfect metaphorical image created by my brain to help justify the energy vibes of the destruction."

"The flood was also real," corrected Reg. "We just talked about how 179 trillion creatures were drowned in the salty tide."

"Yes, that also explains a lot."

"Objection, your honour!" shouted Wilx. "This person has clearly been drinking the boiled juices of psychotropic Lincran leaves. Everything he says is gibberish."

"I'll allow it," said Reg, as his translator explained the word 'psychotropic' via pictorials of humanoid creatures ingesting fungus while viewing strange visions of melting coloured lights. "Carry on Mr. Turkey."

Nickbas gathered his scattered thoughts. "I was sitting at my booth drawing up some new maps--"

"Pfft, maps," interrupted Rip. "Those aren't maps."

"Silence!" bellowed Reg. "I'll have you tossed into a proto-star before you can break a tooth on a Crabbit bone."

"No big deal, I've been successfully jumping proto-stars since before I was immortal."

"Anyway," continued Nickbas, "I was drawing up some maps, and I saw a great shadow spread across the parking dome. I turned around and saw that a spaceship was about to crash into the planet. I tried to freeze time, but sadly my time-freezing powers were drained that afternoon. If I'd been in a stronger mental state at the time of the crash, I believe I would have been able to successfully freeze time long enough to have evacuated the entire planet before the ship crashed."

"You heard him!" shouted Rip. "It's his fault, not ours! He said he could have frozen time if he'd been in a stronger mental state! Maybe if he'd visited the Layer of Transcendental Levitation more often he would have had the relaxed mental energy required to freeze time!"

"If he'd visited that layer more often," said Reg, "he would have drowned. The Layer of Transcendental Levitation was among the first areas of Lincra to be washed away by the flood of tears."

"Too bad."

Reg took a bite from his plate. "Besides, there's no actual proof as to the witness having any actual time-freezing capabilities. Perhaps a demonstration is in order?"

"Are you eating Crabbits?" asked Nickbas, promptly avoiding the subject of his dubious time-freezing powers.

"Yes."

"You do know they're endangered right?"

"Yes."

"Crabbits have a problem with cannibalism. Also someone has been hunting them to the brink of extinction."

"Yes, that's me."

"You?"

"Me."

"How can you be so evil?"

"It comes involuntarily."

"You also know there isn't even any nutritional value in eating Crabbits?"

"I know. I only eat them because I collect their bones for crafting thingamabobs."

Nickbas looked thoroughly disgusted. He stood up and took a deep breath. He turned to face Reg. It was clear he was about to make some sort of moralistic speech. The type of speech so epically moving and grandiose that it would go down in history as the defining moment of his life. Statues of Nickbas would be carved and placed all over the galaxy, to commemorate the life of he who saved Crabbits from extinction.

This all happens, of course, in another dimension where Nickbas is not dead by the end of the next paragraph.

Before he could speak even a single word, Reg poured his drink over Nickbas' head. He promptly melted, being just another typical creature who reacts poorly to contact with pure sulphuric acid. He was now but a pool on the floor of the courtroom.

"I don't think we needed to hear any more from him," said Reg. "Now someone sweep that up so we can continue."

A Specter tried to sweep up the puddled remains of Nickbas. The dustpan melted. The specter then left to get a new and impervious steel dustpan. The new dustpan also melted. The specter didn't worry about it, for at this point the puddle of acid had eaten through the floor and dripped into another courtroom below. The still dangerously volatile remains of Nickbas and the two dustpans were now the problem of someone who will not be in this novel. Maybe the sequel, though.

"That'll be us soon enough," whispered Rip. "I bet you wish you had your bearded disguise now, eh?"

"What was that?" asked Reg.

"Oh, nothing."

"I thought I heard something about a beard."

"I was just saying to this Greeg that I bet he wishes he had his bearded disguise, so he could slip out of here unnoticed before he winds up a puddle being swept off the floor."

"What beard is this?"

Rip was puzzled over the sudden interest in the beard. "Oh, it's just when we dumped this Greeg on Earth we gave him an attachable beard to disguise himself with, but he threw it out."

Reg frantically flipped through a bunch of files he had stored underneath his skeletal perch.

"Aha!" he said as he produced a very old looking picture. It was cracked around the edges, with many defined fold marks as if someone had stored the photo in their wallet for a few hundred years, which they had.

"What have you got there?" asked Rip.

Reg showed the photo to the courtroom. "Was this the beard you had?"

"Why, yes, that's it."

Gasps of shock radiated from all around the courtroom. It seemed everyone except Rip, Wilx and I were familiar with the random image of the beard.

"Are you sure this was the beard?" asked Reg.

"Of course. Pretty recognizable beard, isn't it? What's the big deal? It's just a piece of junk I bought off a black-market merchant."

"So you didn't realize you were purchasing the Beard of Broog?"

"The what?"

"The Beard of Broog. One of the most revered and mystical objects you could possibly own. It grants many powers to the one that wears it."

"I just thought it was a costume piece," said Rip.

Reg produced another picture, this time of a bizarre-looking alien. "Was this the black-market merchant you got the beard off?"

"Yes, that's amazing! You know him too?"

"His name is Fralgoth, the notorious intergalactic thief of voodoo-antiquities."

"He said his name was Thomas, the underground merchant of party pranks and other innocent joke props."

"He lied."

"Apparently."

"So you said the beard was thrown away?" asked Reg.

"Why don't *you* talk now?" said Rip as he turned in my direction.

I worked up the nerve to face my old Greeg-keeper.

"The beard was horribly itchy, so I threw it in the trash."

"Where did this trash end up?" asked Reg.

"I suppose on the planet of Garbotron. All of our trash was blasted out of cannons onto the surface of Garbotron."

"Excellent," said Reg. "Then I see no point in this trial continuing any longer. I find all three of you guilty of the heinous crime of crashing a ship into the surface of Lincra, causing irreparable damage to much of the planet."

"Not to mention the death of all those who were aboard the space-ship," added a Specter in the background.

"I thought we agreed you lot were expendable?"

"Yes, your honour."

Reg stood up. "I hereby sentence Rip, Wilx and Krimshaw to recover the lost Beard of Broog from the planet of Garbotron. Even if it means you must dig for eternity through the rotting heaps of waste. When you find the Beard, you will deliver it to this court, or else you will be found and disposed of. We have ways of getting rid of immortals."

"That's impossible!" shouted Rip. "You do realize that no creature can breathe on the surface of Garbotron!"

"I am aware of this fact. At least you've got the eternity aspect on your side, if you are indeed as immortal as you claim to be. But even immortals need to breathe, don't they?"

"I don't know, never tested that fact."

"Now you have the chance. **THE COURT IS ADJOURNED!** Someone get me another plate of Crabbits."

THE ENDING

Of Beards and Revelations... but Mostly of Things

CHAPTER 35

On Garbotron

Unfortunately, immortals don't *need* to breathe, otherwise they would only be 'immortals until something trivial like a lack of oxygen comes along and kills them' which isn't terribly immortal at all. It sure is a nice bonus though, breathing. The last thing I remember is seeing the noxious green vapours surrounding Garbotron from 8 light years away, immediately before we were sedated by some faction of Kroonum officers and blasted toward the aforementioned noxious green vapours. We were awoken quickly after crash landing upon the surface of Garbotron. The Trintaniamite Clorin-Phrasfate enforced space pod melted immediately from the horrific fumes encased in the 'atmosphere' of the rubbish heap of a planet. Essentially, we suffered the immense pain anyone else would upon entering the Garbotron atmosphere, without the luxury of having the heinous scent and toxicity instantly killing us. Instead we writhed and wriggled and gasped and choked and vomited and cried and urinated and, upon realizing our tears and vomit and urine were the closest thing to fresh liquid on the planet, we began collecting it like raindrops in the Sahara and trying to get it back into the wretched dust bags our bodies were becoming. When I say we, I really mean me. At the time I assumed we were all going through the same ordeal. We weren't. After what seemed like another 15, 000 HL's of pain and suffering my eyes and organs and body finally adjusted to the horrific surroundings and I was able to see and hear and do what could only be described as 'breathe' the soupy, filthy, disgusting 'air'. Rip and Wilx were nowhere to be seen. I swam through a lake of feces. I climbed a mountainous range of assorted, useless and flimsy plastic things labelled 'made in china'. I charted a path through razor sharp ravines of pointy rocket ships. Suddenly, emerging from an intricate cave and crater system created by cannon blasts, I saw what I was certain must be the new dwellings of Rip and Wilx. Miraculously, amongst all of the filth and rubbish and refuse, there was a swath, an impressively large swath at that, of clean and organized terrain. Tiny, miniscule bins with wheels had been crafted around the perimeters of the area. Each bin was meticulously sorted by classifications scribbled in impossibly too small to read handwriting. The arrangement was simply, astonishingly, perfect. If ever a creature were to be dumped upon this planet and dedicate their existence to cleaning the place up, this was the way to do it. But not a creature could be seen. I gingerly weaved my way through the dense, bin based perimeter and stepped foot on the first patch of clean ground I had seen since arriving on this horrible, forgotten waste dump of a planet.

"No! No! Mustn't enter the oviform from here!" Squeaked the most obnoxiously tiny, shrill and high pitched voice imaginable. "There is no cleansing station here! This isn't a formal entrance. Mustn't enter the oviform from here! No! No! Go back and around. Back and around you must go! Mustn't enter the Oviform from here!"

"H-hello?" I spun my head around searching for the source of this shrieking vocalization. "Who are you? Where are you? What are you?"

"Get back! Get back outside of the oviform. I've worked far too long and hard for this. You're tracking outside contaminants into the sacred area. Back I say!"

I felt a small tickle inside my left ear and reached my finger in to give it a scratch.

"STOP!" Shrieked the voice at an unbearable level of decibels, bringing me cringing to my knees.

"One quick question," I gasped, "have I gone completely insane?"

"No you imbecile, you just weren't very smart to begin with. Now get back outside the Oviform and I'll explain everything."

"Okay."

I got back outside of what I assumed could be this 'oviform' the squeaky, mysterious voice in my left ear kept going on about.

"Now move counter clockwise... No! The other way you twit!"

"I thought you said you would explain everything once I got outside of the Oviform."

"And that's exactly the kind of instant gratification and self-obsessed stupidity that leads a species to produce a never-ending pile of garbage and dump it on an innocent planet like this. Keep moving until you reach the cleansing station, we'll clean you up and then I can fill you in on the details you seek at the epicenter dome."

"Um, okay."

"Shut up."

"Okay."

Never before had I felt so much anger, fury and justified dominance from such a seemingly small source. I was at once humbled in awed reverence to whatever was emitting this tiny voice. It commanded respect and demanded appreciation for the work it had done. I felt I had personally done it wrong, and owed it whatever it asked of me.

After a trip through the ingeniously designed cleansing station, I was instructed and bullied through the clean area towards the epicenter dome, a half submerged bubble containing slightly less filthy air and little else. The little else it contained consisted primarily of a large, glass-like, telescopic lens pointed at the floor.

"Look in the lens and put the ear piece in."

I noticed there was a few cables attached to the side of the lens, and assumed one of these must be the ear piece.

"Not *that* ear piece dumbass."

A few more insults and I had the correct ear piece in and was looking in the lens at what appeared to be a fruit fly, sitting in a fruit fly sized rocking chair, speaking into some sort of micro-voice amplification device. Behind the fruit fly was a giant scale model (giant only in comparison to the fruit fly) of the Oviform and surrounding filth, with diagrams and plans outlining the next phases of clean-up and organization.

"So, what are you doing here contaminator?"

"Um, well, I was sentenced to come here and find a beard if you must know."

"Yes, I must. Aren't you curious what I'm doing here you selfish thing?"

"Very much so actually. Did you do all of this yourself?"

"You bet I did. Hardly made a dent yet, but I'll get it all cleaned up eventually. I've got the perfect system designed. No thanks to nitwits like you breaking the sacred perimeter and setting me back. No matter, time matters not to me. Results. Results are what matters to me."

"Forgive me for being blunt. But can you tell me how this is even possible? How are you alive? The average fruit fly only lives..."

"Does *anything* about *me* seem *average*?" The stinging reality of his inflections actually hurt my brain, further humiliating me.

"Well, no, but I just thought..."

"Shut it. Nobody cares what you just thought. Certainly not me. Kick back and listen to my story, you owe me that much at least."

"Okay," I sheepishly replied. "Can I sit down?"

"No."

"Okay," I sheepishly replied again.

The remarkable little fruit fly began to weave the most serendipitous little tale I'd ever heard. I couldn't believe a word of it at the time, but before sitting down to write this story of mine, I used my immortality combined with time travel to go and research all of the details of these events to make sure I got everything right and understood it myself. Everything the little fruit fly said happened exactly as he/she/it said it did.

After me and Herb had injected ourselves with the immortality formula back on earth, we had carelessly tossed the seemingly empty syringe into the garbage. In the same garbage bag was a banana peel. In the white part of this simple, decomposing banana peel, there was a cluster of fruit fly eggs. In one of these eggs hatched a small and thirsty fruit fly. It would one day call itself Milt.

"The first liquid I came across was a drop at the needle end of a syringe," reminisced Milt. "As soon as it entered my bloodstream I knew that I had been changed drastically forever. I felt such an overwhelming surge of vitality and immunity. After watching about five million generations of fellow fruit flies hatch and decease, I began to figure out that I wasn't the same as all other fruit flies."

Oblivious to what was happening, one day the poor little thing was crammed into a rocket ship with rotting piles of slop and blasted off to the surface of Garbotron. One of the first rocket ships to arrive on the planet, Milt would witness the complete transformation of the untainted sphere into the abhorrent, festering museum of human discharge it would become. And I thought watching humans become Greegs was despicable! Milt had seen the unseen. The by-product of humanity. The sheer, unconscionable, non-stop, never-ending accumulation of pure, useless, never had to exist in the first place, garbage.

"Why have you taken it upon yourself to clean this all up yourself? You didn't do any of this!" I wept, feeling nothing but pity and admiration for the gritty, determined fruit fly.

"Whether I like it or not, this is my home. This is the situation I was born into, or ended up at, these things I cannot control. What I can do, is my part to set things right. What good is done by moping about who is 'responsible' for this mess? What the human being will that accomplish?" Milt stressed *human being* with the utmost of vehemence, making it the nastiest of curses I've ever heard. "The mess is here, and so am I. I can either live in it, and whine about how nothing can be done, how it isn't my 'responsibility', or I can get to work tackling the thing. What have I got to lose?"

I thanked him profusely for his story. I told Milt he was an inspiration and perhaps the most remarkable little creature ever to exist. Milt told me to shut up and that my silly beard was in bin #897432 – GLPOA357%&11.FFF and gave me a magnifying glass, a map and insisted I piss right off and never return as Milt had work to do.

I understood completely.

CHAPTER 36

Psycho-Fans in the Most Unexpected Places

Finding bin #897432 – GLPOA357%&11.FFF was as difficult as it sounded. The map proved to be useless, for it had been written in a font-size meant for the vision of a fruit-fly. Even the magnifying glass did nothing to improve readability. I wandered around following the misleading signs that had been planted around the intertwining pathways between the heaps of garbage. I paused to wonder what living creature had been here to craft the signs and make the pathways. The skyline was a bleak collection of filthy peaks against the darkness of space. The dirtiness of the landscape was greatly enhanced when placed alongside the purity and cleanliness exuded by the vast emptiness of space.

At one point in my long journey through the winding maze of garbage, I was surprisingly approached by a human-like alien. He was strangely carrying a book I recognized as one of my own. It was a copy of *Children: Rushing Away to an Early Candy-Filled Grave.* One of the more popular bestsellers I wrote on Earth, but not one of my personal favourites. Upon re-reading it I remembered how all the quotes and statistics had been lies. The sudden appearance of the alien shook me up.

"Who are you?" I asked.

"I'm Wendell. I'm a fan of yours."

"Yeah, I see you've got one of my books there. Quite a fantastic coincidence that you'd be at the same place as me, especially in a place in which no living or mortal person can survive."

"Oh, this isn't a coincidence," said Wendell. "I heard about your trial. I knew you'd been sentenced here. I figured this was my chance to finally get the book autographed."

I began to feel uneasy. Only a psycho-level fan would risk coming to a place where no mortal person can survive, just to get an autograph on one of my worst books. I expected a crazed assassination attempt to occur at any moment.

"So, will you sign my book?"

"No."

"You won't sign my book?"

"I don't want to sign it. Not really into signing stuff. How do I know you aren't going to sell that book and retire?"

"I swear the book is for my own collection."

"I'm busy. I'm trying to find a beard."

"I've come all the way to Garbotron and you won't sign this book? I braved the surface of a planet in which no one can survive just so I could meet you!"

"You aren't a real fan if that's your favourite book," I said.

"This book has a lot of good insight into the degenerative eating habits of the human child."

"But it's pointless now!" I argued. "That book was a bunch of trumped-up lies written in hopes of scaring humans into changing their degenerative eating habits. But it didn't help, the humans became Greegs many years ago."

"It's still a good read."

"It's one of my worst books. Maybe the worst. What about *Through Savagery and Back: The Life and Times of a Stranded Greeg*? Didn't you read that one?"

"I didn't like it."

"What!? The critics called it my masterpiece, my central opus, the summation of not only my own creative career but a perfect representation of the universal human experience."

"It was a bit long and wordy."

I was finished talking to the random fan. I continued walking down the path, but the fan persisted in following me.

"I know where this Beard you seek is. You're looking for the Beard of Broog, aren't you?"

"That's right."

"Yep, I know where it is. I might be convinced to trade the location of the Beard for a personalized autograph on this book."

I sighed, letting Wendell know that I was going to autograph the book, but that I was not happy about it. I signed a quickened, rather lame signature.

"What's this?" asked Wendell. "Sign your name properly! Spell it out! That's just a few randomly connective lines that no one could read."

"You want the book signed twice?"

"No, sign this one," he said, producing an entirely different copy of the same book from his backpack.

"You brought two copies of that book?"

"Of course. One has to be prepared on Garbotron. You have to account for the destruction of at least half your personal possessions. I didn't think it would be wrecked by you though."

"I didn't mean to wreck it. Can you just tell me where this beard is?"

"After I have a proper autograph."

I signed the double copy, this time writing out my full name with a flourish, even adding in some letters that weren't supposed to be there. The star struck fan began salivating over his newly acquired collectable.

"Yes! It's mine! I finally got the prize! I'm rich! Hahahaha!"

I felt sorry for this sad creature. His entire purpose in life was based on wanting to get my autograph. *Mine. Me.* Was I so important? Was I even interesting at all?

"I can tell you where the beard is now," he said.

"Please."

"Continue on the path until you see a sign reading *This way to the Southern Continent of Plastic Wastelands.* Do not follow that sign. Instead take a turn at the *Wall of Leftover Cheese-Like Products.* Follow the cheese until you reach *The Lake of Liquids.*"

"What kind of liquids are in the lake?" I asked.

"Nobody knows. But if it's garbage and it's liquid, then it's in there. Do not touch the lake."

"Did I mention I'm immortal? Touching the lake probably

wouldn't hurt me."

"You must cross the lake. There is a seaworthy canoe fastened to the nearby shore. I've been using it to commute across town."

"Town?"

"There isn't an official town yet, but I've been trying to make a society of sorts in my spare time. I've been naming places according to what type of garbage they're made up of. All the street signs and maps you see along the path were made by me. For transportation I've crafted the aforementioned canoe, as well as some decent miniature models of push carts and other rudimentary devices made of broken glass and twisted metal that I hope to see into fruition in the future. There is a lot of broken glass and twisted metal here. Was stuff like that popular on the planet where this garbage came from?"

"Unfortunately so."

"There is a lot of work to do, turning all the metal and wheels into usable objects."

"You should team up with this fruit fly named Milt. He's obsessed with cleaning up the planet. Could use a little help. He might take to your ideas of a society."

"A fly?" Wendell suddenly looked at me as if *I* were the insane one. Perhaps we were both right.

"Yeah."

"Anyway... was I still giving you directions?"

"You were telling me where to go after the lake."

"Yes. After the lake, that's a good part. You will blindly stagger through the *Swampy Maze of Visionless Wandering*. You may find yourself disturbed by the fact that you cannot see through the hazy ground-clouds. You might find yourself falling face first on the uneven terrain. The swamp is always shifting and rolling, like the great tides of the Hroon ocean. The swamp shifts because the garbage has turned alive over the years. A landscape with an agenda of its own. The original surface of this planet is but a forgotten core miles beneath the ancient onslaught of undesirables. Do not despair. There is a way out of the swamp. All you have to do is follow the call of the Garbage-Demons, for they only feed in the evenings on the north side of the swamp, and the north is where you must go if you would find the Beard of Broog. After you cross the swamp you are very close."

"But let me guess," I said, "there is yet another horrendous task before I find the Beard, something much worse than either the crossing of the lake or the blind navigation of the Swampy Maze?"

"You will see."

"And it involves these Garbage-Demons?"

"You will see."

I noticed he began to look in a bad state. He was green, frothing, swooning. Nothing at all like the vigorous healthy life-form who had approached me a few minutes ago.

"What's wrong?" I asked.

"I think the atmosphere is finally starting to get to me. I've been waiting for you on Garbotron for a few months now."

"Sorry."

"Don't be! Getting this book signed was the greatest moment of my life!"

"Oh...sorry again."

Suddenly the crazed fan dropped to the ground. It was clear he was choking as a result of the toxic atmosphere.

"Pleh!" I yelled.

That uselessly dismissive non-sequitur was as reactive as I got at the moment. Before I could move, the foul stench of Garbotron gave Wendell a series of fatal lung implosions. The stranger now belonged to the very waste-heaps he had tirelessly worked on naming and making signs for. The planet Garbotron is a living collector of all that is foul, or rather of all that goes near.

I searched the fan's backpack. He was carrying no provisions aside from my collected works. He had been lugging around all my earth novels in mint shape first-edition hardcovers. I left the books among the garbage, not because I felt they belonged there, even though some of them did, but I thought they might one day provide future entertainment for an unfortunate soul stranded on Garbotron.

CHAPTER 37

How to Barely Succeed on the Worst World Ever

When I reached the *Lake of Liquids* I understood why Wendell warned me not to touch the surface. The tar-like thickness of the black substance would envelop and devour any who came into contact, immortal or not. Once you go over your head there is no possible chance of resurfacing. The lake was even more threatening to someone of immortal status, for to remain forever alive while trapped in the lake is a far worse fate than drowning. This is something I would see first-hand.

I was made nervous when I spotted the apparently sea-worthy canoe. It was a haggard bird's nest of a boat, crudely thrown together with whatever random pieces of garbage had been lingering about. Much rusted twine and wire (care of the defunct Balahog Twine and Wire corporation who'd had their entire derelict factory jettisoned to Garbotron) was what held all the bits of debris together.

I slowly paddled across the gloppy monstrosity of a lake. This evil stuff made schmold seem like fresh-squeezed, ice-cold lemonade served on a hot summer day by a waitress who shows just the right amount of cleavage to garner a decent tip without coming across as desperate or slutty.

Suddenly there was a halting thud as if the canoe had bumped into a rock.

"Hey, watch it!" shouted a voice.

"Who's there?" I asked.

"Bob."

"Who's Bob?"

"Me."

I looked over the side of the canoe and saw just a person's head sticking up from the lake's surface.

"What are you doing in there?" I asked.

"Obviously I fell in and got stuck. What kind of stupid question is that? One just doesn't go for a swim and lounge about in probably the worst substance imaginable."

"Sorry."

"You're lucky I can't use my arms or I'd tip your canoe over."

I paddled a few feet away from Bob just to make sure.

"You'd be dead as soon as the lake began its assimilation of your bloodstream!" he raved. "A fate infinitely tamer than my own. As an immortal I've been living like this in the lake for countless years."

"Why has no one rescued you?"

"They tried. You may not think it when you look at my hideously tar-infected, mutated face, but I was a very important person in my pre-lake life. There were exhaustively expensive rescue attempts involving every known type of pulley, crane, winch or rope system in the near galaxies. It proved impossible to remove me from the living hook-like grips of the tar, so everyone gave up. My story fell into obscurity after I outlived all the people who cared. So now I am one with the lake."

"You know, I'm also immortal," I said. "Even before I saw you I was worried about getting stuck in the lake forever, but now that I've seen how agonizing your existence is I think I should get to shore as soon as possible before something happens."

"You're immortal?" asked Bob excitedly. "That's great news!"

"It is?"

"Yeah!"

"Why?"

"You can join me! Jump into the lake!"

"Why would I do that?"

"So I have a friend to talk to for the rest of eternity! It's the ultimate good deed."

"I'm not jumping into the lake."

"You must!"

"Don't you think we'd get sick of each other?" I asked. "How many hundreds of years can you converse with the same person? It's only been 5 minutes and I'm already sick of you. *Five Minutes.*"

"You're just like all the rest."

"The rest?" I asked. "How many people come here? I thought it was supposed to be impossible."

"Very little of what appears to be impossible is actually impossible," stated Bob.

"Right."

"Except, of course, for the simple act of rescuing someone who fell into a lake of tar," he added with a whiny grumble.

"Who comes here? Immortals?"

"Mostly."

I wanted to learn more, but getting away from the lake was priority one.

"Well, see ya later," I said. "Chin up."

"I won't let you go!"

"What will you do?"

"I'll capsize your canoe with ripples!" he shouted as he began to thrash his head around like one of the many metal-headbangers taking in a Lincran parking lot festival. The neck-breaking motion caused no ripples. The dense anti-ripple consistency of the lake consumed all energy before it had a chance to escape.

It was a sad display. I turned around and continued my mission.

Even before I got to shore I could hear the call of the Garbage-Demons. Every few minutes I heard the drifting, ecstatic shrieks of the mysterious feeders.

I had to spend several nights in the swamp. I was not able to make good time because of the absurd amount of falling and rolling and backtracking involved with crossing a shifting landscape. There was also only a short window of time in which I could move, for the garbage-demons emitted their shrieking calls for only a few hours a day. The rest of the time I had no bearing of direction and had to sit down and wait until I heard the sound again, or until the land shook me off my perch. The latter usually occurred first.

The first thing I saw upon exiting the swamp was a sign reading *This Way to Bin #897432 – GLPOA357%&11.FFF, aka The Bin Where the Beard of Broog Has Been Stashed.*

All those letters had been painstakingly carved by Wendell.

I could see faded blood drops where the dull knife had slipped.

While following the sign, it was clear I was headed directly into the main nesting ground of the Garbage-Demons. Hearing their shrieks over the last few days had given me plenty of time to nervously imagine what they were like. Demons are never good. Considering they feed on garbage, I had also been left to wonder what the area was like where they had chosen to nest. It could only be the area with the most rank concentration of junk.

My expectations couldn't have been more wrong. There were no demons at all. Instead there was a mildly tolerable bunch of tame mammal creatures, a sort of hybrid cross between a dog, a cat and a Quigg. All these creatures did was eat garbage, so they were actually a vital part of cleaning up the planet's destroyed ecosystem. Milt would have been overjoyed to learn about all the help that was going on.

Between the gushing fan, the obsessive mosquito and the hungry animals, there seemed to be a lot of life on this apparently uninhabitable dump.

I went to the bin. The beard was conveniently placed right on top, as if on display. I shook off the filth that had grown on the beard, even though I was already growing accustomed to the grimy dark-gray color of everything on Garbotron, including my own skin colour, which had grown a layer of caked-on mouldy dust within minutes of our arrival.

Beside the bin I discovered a sound-system rigged to loop the recordings of shrieking demons. There was enough battery power and Investment Banker-fuelled generators to ensure the recordings would loop for thousands of years. I broke the system and funnelled what fuel I could into some empty bottles. The animals were noticeably pleased by the sudden cessation of the shrieking demons. It was a sound they had heard perpetually for all of their lives, since the beginning of the evolutionary path of their species. These animals, like the Grollers, have no memory. Until I intervened with the smashing of the stereo, their lives were a perpetual cycle of these stages:

1) Hearing the shrieks.
2) Feeling a paralysing fear towards whatever the shrieks might belong to.
3) Joyous relief at discovering the shrieks belong to a harmless stereo.
4) The complete forgetting of everything.

The hybrids could now relax and eat garbage. Their average lifespan tripled.

I wondered who had gone through the effort of setting up the sound-system. I thought maybe it was this Fralgoth character.

CHAPTER 38

Being Immortal

Beard of Broog in hand, I traipsed off in search of my lost immortal 'friends'. It wasn't difficult. I found them rummaging in bin #894391 – GRQAJ219%&11.FFQ

"Hey, look, he finally evolved the ability to breathe and see and what not," came the familiar mocking tone of Dr. Rip T. Brash The Third. "We thought you'd never stop wriggling and trifecta-ing about."

"Tri-what-ing?" I said.

"The Trifecta."

"And what," I sighed, "is a Trifecta?"

"Crying," said Rip.

"Puking," continued Wilx.

"And Pissing in your pants," they merrily exclaimed in unison. "At the same time!"

They broke out into laughter. I didn't get it.

"Yeah, whatever," I dismissed. "So... you didn't have to suffer the same trials of adaptation as my body had to?"

"Pffft!" laughed Wilx. "What, you think this is the first time we've been banished to a garbage planet to uncover some sort of lost, magical, voodoo-antiquity?"

"You really have a lot to learn about being immortal," said Rip.

That pretty much summed up everything at that point.

"I've got the beard," I said defeated.

"Course you do," said Wilx. "Of course you do."

"Did you chat with that nutty little fruit fly?" Asked Rip. "I'm certain he gave us the wrong map."

"Yeah... can we get out of here now?" I said.

"I suppose we ought to fashion some sort of escape vessel," said Wilx. "Let's head over to the razor sharp ravines of pointy rocket ships."

We walked for a long time in silence.

"Interesting fact," said Wilx, punching numbers into a small, digital computation device. "When adjusted for relativity, that fruit fly is the oldest creature to ever exist."

"Ha! Told you so," said Rip.

"Yeah, yeah, yeah," said Wilx, handing a bag of dried up, dusty and filthy superfluous internal organs to Rip, who began rather grotesquely to ingest them and move them about his insides back into place with a pointed stick.

And yes, if you must know, Milt is the only creature to match the meticulous attention to cleaning detail of The Quiggs. A strange being indeed.

CHAPTER 39

Fralgoth: Notorious Intergalactic Thief of Voodoo Antiquities, and the Movie 'Plasma Raiders 3'

As Wilx attempted to find a usable rocket ship, Rip and I sat down and tried to make sense of everything.

"What does this beard do, anyway?" I asked him.

"Do? The beard doesn't do anything. It's an inanimate piece of third-rate imitation Plutonian wool. The dodgy black-market kind. Itchy by the looks of it."

"You mean there's no magical properties to this beard?"

"I don't know. Try it on."

I wore the beard. More than itchy, it caused a temporary leprosy-like symptom within the first few minutes. I now remembered why I'd thrown it away.

"I could use some help!" yelled Wilx from the ravine of ships.

"Just taking an indefinite break!" Rip yelled back.

"You should go help," I said. "I'm the only one who's earned a break, after what I went through to get the Beard. Did I tell you the part about the swamp? And the lake?"

Rip took off. I thought it seemed pointless. These rocket ships looked like props from a cheesy science fiction movie. A lot of them were. Wilx had noticed this right away, but instead of saying anything he decided to forage the ships for any alcohol that might have been forgotten by one of those D-Grade actors known for drowning out the regrets of their failed careers.

Rip had gotten the same idea, but all they ended up finding were the remnants of the actors themselves. I later learned these ships were from the set of the legendary unfinished movie *Plasma Raiders 3*, a production enshrouded with controversy. To achieve total authenticity for the great launch scene, the filmmakers had chosen to actually blast all the actors and extras into space. Only instead of renting out some real spaceships they merely strapped some spaceship-quality propulsion units onto otherwise completely fake prop ships. The results were mixed. The thrilling camera shots were fantastically unprecedented, but none of the actors survived. The rest of the movie was then set to be shot with lookalike replacement actors. During re-casts many of the investors lost interest and dropped out, being that the star-power of the lost actors was what had drawn their initial interest. The film was permanently shelved, although some spoke of revival with hushed reverence. The prop-ships eventually drifted into space and found their way to Garbotron, where they were now being raided by an immortal pair of well-seasoned travellers of time and space.

"Nothing in this one," I heard Wilx yell. "Move on to the next."

This went on for some time, with Rip and Wilx searching each of the ships and finding nothing. I could easily see them from my far away perch, for the ship's walls had been made of cheap particle-board and thus burned up considerably during the atmospheric transition. After awhile they returned.

"We didn't find anything and none of these ships will fly," said Wilx bluntly. "Looks like we'll be spending the rest of eternity on a planet called Garbotron. Everyone try to find a slightly non-garbage infested patch of ground to curl up on, we're in this for the long haul."

"I've been wearing this beard," I said. "It doesn't seem to do anything."

"No," said Wilx. "The beard is not magical."

"So the beard is useless?"

"The beard is just as powerful as everyone says, only the power comes from something much simpler than magic or voodoo."

"What does it do?" I asked.

"It was crafted by Broog, the greatest disguise-artist ever to live. That beard is the only known perfect replica of the inimitably ridiculous beard-style invented and worn by the Grand KULMOOG Commander Flook. Anyone who wears that beard can with ease successfully impersonate the Grand Commander."

"So?"

"Anyone who successfully impersonates the Grand Commander will find themselves in ownership of the Kroonum Union of Ladder Makers and Official Overseeing Gods, therefore in ownership of the Kroonum system itself. All you have to do is wear that beard and show up on Lincra and you'll be immediately showered with money, power and whatever species of sexual partner is your most genetically accurate match!"

"Haha!" yelled Rip. "We're rich! I mean we're way richer than we used to be! Forget about that goblin Reg and his uptight courtroom scene! Let's keep the beard for ourselves and go live the good life on Lincra! Which type of grapes do you plan on having your slaves feed to you? Green or red? I'm thinking green but I'm not entirely sold--"

"Why is the beard made from third-rate products that cause leprosy?" I asked, ignoring the dilemma of the grapes. "If this Broog character is such a big deal, I mean."

"Who knows," replied Wilx. "Maybe Broog made the beard as a prank."

"A prank?"

"Broog is known for taking pranks too far."

At once a voice boomed from the sky. The creature this voice belonged to did not want us living the good life, or any life at all. The disembodied voice belonged to Fralgoth, notorious intergalactic thief of voodoo antiquities.

"Greetings," announced the evil voice of Fralgoth. "I see by your joyous celebration that you have located the coveted Beard of Broog. I'll be taking that now."

"No!" yelled Rip. "We decided to keep it for ourselves! Get lost!"

"Where is he anyway?" whispered Wilx. "The sky is completely empty."

As if he heard these quiet words (which he had, being that his ship was fully equipped with Whisper-Reduction Satellites) Fralgoth turned off his ship's cloaking device . Suddenly a villainous ship appeared before us.

"What a poorly designed ship," said Rip. "Look at the landing flaps, positioned a few degrees too much to the left. You could never hope to successfully slingshot around a proto-star and still have enough momentum to sideways time-travel through a wormhole without slowing down and ending up in limbo between dimensions for a few lifetimes. What a dumb ship."

"Who cares," said Wilx. "It's a working ship. That means we can leave. We don't need it for doing impossible stunts, we only need it to fly to the nearest planet that sells ships like that. Then we take the beard to Lincra and live like gods."

"I've been a god. I want more. Besides, you think Fralgoth is going to offer a ride?"

"No. We're going to steal his ship."

"One would have to kill Fralgoth to do that."

"Then today's the day Fralgoth dies."

It wasn't the day. He was killed a week later. We decided to procrastinate and spend some time drawing up plans and blueprints. Also we had to first chase him down across much of the planet. After all the effort, we weren't even the ones to kill Fralgoth. I'll skip ahead to that part.

CHAPTER 40

Hanging on the Edge of a Cliff, Again

"Help!" I yelled as I clung to the edge of a cliff. Fralgoth stood above, patiently savouring the moment in which he would stomp on my fingers. Below me was the usual 4000 foot drop into a canyon full of jagged metal things. I had not seen Rip or Wilx in at least a day. Not since our mad excursion into the swamp. Amongst other things, the long chase across the planet had nearly left me stuck in Liquid Lake. As a result of that and everything else in part of the story I just skipped, I was now hanging over the edge of a 4000 foot drop into a canyon full of jagged metal things. No escape. I expected to spend the rest of eternity crippled at the bottom of a canyon on probably the worst planet of all time. But there was hope, as you know, for I would not be writing about this incident if I did not survive through it.

"Give me the beard!" yelled Fralgoth. The beard was pretty much the only advantage I had going for me. At least if I fell into the canyon I would take it with me.

"Reach out your hand-like appendage," I said.

"Right, and let you pull me over the edge? Throw the beard up here!"

"It was worth a try."

"If you pass me the beard I'll help you up. If not, I'll stomp on your fingers."

"You won't stomp on my fingers until you've got the beard. We both know that."

"True."

"Help me up first. Then you can have the beard."

"Why would I do that?"

"Because I can't hold on much longer. You need to get the beard soon before it's lost forever. The land here eats up everything, then spews it out as unrecognizable waste. The only reason the beard is in good shape is because it was protected by someone, probably a psycho-fan of mine who came all the way here to get one of my books autographed and then decided he might as well live here; no governments or anything pushing him around after all, so he tried to fashion a society of sorts, started making roads and signs and transportation and Beard-protection facilities guarded by the looped recordings of faraway shrieking demons and--"

"Enough!" yelled Fralgoth. "Pass up the beard or die."

"You won't kill me. We mentioned that."

"Wrong. I can have another replica made if I need to. It's just really expensive."

"No you can't."

"Why not?"

"Because Broog is dead. No one else but him could recreate the perfection of the replica. And without perfection nobody will believe you are Commander Flook."

"You lie! Broog is alive!"

I had no idea. I had only just recently heard of Broog, but it seemed like the right thing to say.

"It's true. Flying Grimbat Messengers delivered the news this morning. Have you heard of Grimbats? They're one of the rare beings who can honestly claim to know everything about everyone. It takes a special class of busy-body. The messengers announced that Broog, the legendary disguise-artist best remembered for his baffling yet insanely entertaining publicity stunts, was found lifeless in his summer cabin on Grelk, the planet made of tar pits. Amazingly his death was not related to the fact that he lived on a volatile planet made of tar pits. Everyone told him he was crazy to build a summer cabin there, or to go there at all under any circumstance for even the briefest of moments, but he persisted in his steadfast manner of illogical rebellion. It had long since been assumed that Broog would perish from drunkenly walking into a tar pit in the middle of the night, yet I heard he was killed by the government or overdosed or something. Or both. That's how a lot of them go. Artists, I mean. Governmental assassinations or overdoses. Or both. Didn't you know?"

"I don't believe you."

"Why not?"

"You added way too much detail. Broog's never even been to Grelk. I've read all his books."

"Worth a try."

"I'll give him a call, to make sure. Got his business card right here. Carrying Broog's business card is what defines a person as a great thief, and only the greatest thieves escape imprisonment."

"So you don't need skill in stealing? Is that what you're saying? Whoever is in contact with or can afford the best disguise kit is the greatest thief?"

"Yeah. Wait a second... it's ringing."

Thanks to Broog's habit of letting the phone ring for an excessive amount of time, Fralgoth did not even get to say one last word to his old friend. There was enough time for Broog to say most of the word hello, then Fralgoth was killed by the direct blast of a laser cannon. It was one of the types of laser cannons that first refracts through a Jardian mega-prism, splitting the beam into a million tiny beams which specifically target the most vulnerable parts of whatever life form is being vanquished. I saw Fralgoth topple over the edge, spinning the whole way down into the canyon. Charting the unknown.

Rip and Wilx were not my saviours. At first I thought maybe they were, but it seemed far too brave and uncharacteristic of them, which it was. My rescuers were a strange lot. It would seem the enemy of my enemy was indeed my friend, not my enemy.

"Who hangs there?" loomed an unknown voice from among the recently arrived spaceship in ownership of the laser-cannon.

"I, uh, it is I, Krimshaw--"

"What are you? Where are you from? Grelkian? Northern Trufalmdoon?"

"I'm a reformed Greeg."

"A Greeg?" questioned the voice from the ship. A muffled conversation commenced, apparently in front of a microphone that someone forgot to turn off.

"Do we like Greegs?" questioned the Alien Voice #1.

"We don't really know any," said the Alien Voice #2. "Especially not any reformed ones."

"What are Greegs?"

"We've seen them in carnival shows before. They're entertaining."

"That's true," agreed Alien #1. "They are entertaining."

"Yes, but would you want to socialize with a Greeg?"

"More specifically, would you want to socialize with a Greeg hanging desperately on the edge of a cliff? Or would you merely want to shoot the Greeg with the newly installed laser-cannon?"

"Don't!" I yelled. "I'm not with Fralgoth!"

"Fralgoth," sneered Alien #1. "We hate Fralgoth."

"Yeah, me too." I was happy to have the conversation off me.

"We are glad to have Fralgoth dead," said Alien #2.

"Yeah, me too," I said again.

"Now we can inherit his plentiful supply of Luminesco-Cannabid-Sativa."

"What's that?"

"A rare psychotropic herb that defies the rules of nature by only growing in the frozen conditions of the slopes of Mount Grucian on the Glassvexx planet."

"Fralgoth was into drugs?" I asked. "I thought he just dealt in trinkets."

"Stealing voodoo antiquities is only one of the many side-habits of Fralgoth. It just happens to be one of the ones that made it into mainstream headlines. Fralgoth's true business passion is the thievery and distribution of the Sativa."

"Can you guys help me up and then we'll discuss this? Or shoot me into the canyon. Just do something. It's starting to get to me, the feeling of nearly plummeting into a canyon. I've been experiencing that feeling for hours on end. Have you ever experienced the feeling of nearly plummeting into a canyon continuously for hours on end?"

"No. We have not had that honour."

There was more conversation heard from the ship, except this time too muffled to hear. Alien #2 had remembered to cover the microphone, but had not yet learned about the on/off switch.

"We have decided," said Alien #1, "to help you. Because if you hate Fralgoth as much as we do then you deserve to live."

"Thanks," I said. "Good logic."

The ship continued to hover over the canyon while a robotic arm helped me back onto level ground. I collapsed from exhaustion.

"Who are you?" I said.

"We are the Confederation of Angry Drug Dealers, or CADD. What we are generally angry about, and pretty much the only reason we started up the confederacy in the first place, is to cause the downfall of sativa-thief Fralgoth. The crops of Mount Grucian on Glassvexx have been tended and harvested by my line of people for as many generations as the plant has existed. Fralgoth discovered and usurped our land, and has been harvesting the plant at much too greedily a pace. The rare potency of the Sativa high comes from the continuance of the original strain, which was supposedly blessed by ancient gods. The original strain was in danger of going extinct, but now without Fralgoth it may be safe a while longer."

"Do you think my friends and I could take Fralgoth's ship?" I asked. "We're stuck here. And here is not a very liveable place."

"It's not so bad," said Alien #1. "Have you met Milt, the fruit fly? He's made a life here. There's also the one who reads stupid books and makes signs."

"He's gone now," I said.

"There's still Milt."

"Not all of those books are stupid," I added.

"Yes they are."

"Look, can we have the ship or not?"

More muffled discussion. "We guess you and your imaginary friends can use Fralgoth's ship to escape. But not before we clear the cargo holds of the 296 million standard-measure galactic tonnes of Luminesco-Cannibid-Sativa. We can leave you with a pound or two in the glove-box. That should be enough to last a lifetime."

"I might have more than one lifetime ahead of me," I said.

"Fine. We'll leave three pounds," said Alien #2. "But you're getting greedy."

I climbed down to where Fralgoth's ship had parked. By the time I traversed the steep canyon path the CADD had already cleared out the cargo holds and taken off. None of Fralgoth's crew were to be seen.

I entered the ship. Rip and Wilx emerged from hiding within one of the empty cargo holds. It was perfect timing to suddenly appear, if your intent was to arrive on the scene at exactly the moment in which your help was no longer needed.

"Where have you been?" I yelled angrily at the two bleary-eyed maniacs. "I've been nearly falling into a canyon all day!"

"We tried to find you," said Wilx.

"Yeah," joined in Rip. "Did you know the ground on this planet moves? Not easy to find someone here. We kept inadvertently going in circles."

I was still angry, but decided to let it go. It was a legitimate excuse.

"So Fralgoth's dead?" asked Wilx.

"Yeah."

"That's good."

"What happened to Fralgoth's crew?" I asked. "Did the drug dealers take care of them too?"

"Actually, we took care of them," said Rip. "We weren't entirely useless."

"How did you do that?"

"He's lying," said Wilx. "The crew were frightened off by that looped recording of the shrieking demons."

"I broke that sound-system," I said. "Does that mean there

are real demons?"

"No, there were more sound-systems. Quite a few scattered all over the planet actually. We suspect each of them guards a different item, stuff as equally valuable as the beard. Enticing, yes. But we don't want to stay here any longer. Maybe one day we'll return to look for other self-profiting items. For now let's go take over planet Lincra."

We flied Garbotron and charted for Lincra. Along the way we stopped to trade in the ship for one that could do impossible things.

CHAPTER 41

Lincran Revolution

We were high on the promise of owning planet Lincra. We were also high on what had been left in the glove-box.

Our plans were to fail, for during our journey the beard became useless. When we arrived at Lincra we learned that Commander Flook had been assassinated, and that the entire planet had entered a state of riotous turmoil caused by the unexpected yet well underway toppling of the Kroonum Ladder Union.

From orbit we could see the glow of the towering bonfires. The people of Lincra were gleefully rejoicing in the overdue burning of ladders and all things ladder-related. There were a lot of ladders to burn, hence the towering aspect of the fires. Much of the planet would be forever damaged during what has now been become known as the Age of Bonfires. At least the focus was forever taken off the damage we'd caused by our 'intentional crashing of an Obotron ship' episode.

Of particular note amongst the damage was the decimation of the investment banking corral farms. The ladder-revolution caused a crippling universal spike in gas prices, Lincra being practically the primary source of local IB.

How had interspersed throngs of civilian Lincran peasants managed to overthrow the well-funded and generally indomitable KULMOOG you ask? Everything happened while we were away on Garbotron. It seems the last will and testament of resident Lincran map-maker Nickbas L. Turkey had surfaced, proceeding to startle everyone with the vast amount of money it was worth. Mr. Turkey was shockingly in possession of far more money than was owned by every faction of the KULMOOG combined. No one was quite sure where he got this money, for he never seemed to do anything other than make maps and then give them away for free. Nickbas Turkey's vast fortune was found in the underground facilities of an obscure storage meteor near the Invisible Dimension. By the looks of the caked on layers of dust it would seem Nickbas had not moved or used any of his money in a long time.

Nickbas L. Turkey had always known that if he left his money to the people of Lincra they would in turn use the money to overthrow the KULMOOG. Saving the money to free the people was his purpose in life.

The civilians of Lincra proceeded to spend the money on whatever weaponry was more advanced than that owned by the KULMOOG. With this new weaponry the people were finally able to banish the KULMOOG into oblivion, followed by the immediate celebratory burning of ladders and all things ladder-related.

The ladders of Lincra would soon be replaced with teleportation booths, floating elevators and more shuttle-sliders. In later years this would prove to be a disastrous choice, for no one stopped to think about how all their physical exercise came from climbing ladders. Without ladders, the people of Lincra grew lazy to the brink of Greegdom. Many suffered a gradual disintegration of their bodily cells caused by perpetual physical apathy.

Being the one to have killed Nickbas and therefore being the one to have truly set in motion the toppling of the KULMOOG, Reg was now looked at as a sort of God amongst the Lincran peasants. We found him occupying the same lavish lifestyle we'd expected to gain from the beard.

Reg's compound was atop a spire in the center of the parking dome, reached by a mile-high set of stone stairs. The stairs were completely superfluous, as nobody else was really allowed in Reg's compound to begin with, and the select few inner-class minions always chose teleportation over the mile of stairs. Aside from the daunting stairs, a moat populated by the deadliest creatures of Hroon was busily under construction.

"What is this place?" I said, pointing at the tower. "What is happening here?"

"Don't you see?!" yelled Rip. "Look at all the bonfires of ladders! The KULMOOG has finally been overthrown!"

"Is that a good thing?" I asked.

"For the people of Lincra, yes."

"For our plan, no," finished Wilx. "Flook has either lost command or been killed, so impersonating him is a moot point."

I threw the now-useless beard into the molten core of Lincra. The core was now visible from space, thanks to the collision of our crashed Obotron. The ship was still sticking out of the planet awaiting a proposed removal operation. The specters of the crew-members would not be free to roam until the ship was released from the fiery limbo of the planetary core. They were not likely to be freed, as the ship removal operation was being funded by the ladder makers, most of which had been lynched by now, leaving the question of who was going to do all this strenuous labour.

Later we realized the beard would have been worth a fortune if claimed as the actual beard shaved off the assassinated body of Commander Flook. Oh well. 'Fortunes come and fortunes go, the important thing is to enjoy the ride' so says The Book of The Immortals.

"Should we go?" asked Wilx.

"Why don't we see who's in there," I suggested, pointing at the newly formed compound in the middle of the parking dome. "Looks like the sort of place where a leader would live."

"Leaders of planets are not usually good people," said Wilx. "Haven't you learned to avoid them? The higher up the leader, the greater the danger."

"How about this," suggested Rip, "instead of barging directly into the compound of what is clearly the highest up leader of this planet, we go down to the surface and ask some of the peasants what's going on. Gather the intel before making the move."

We all agreed this was a good idea for the moment. We were quickly told about how Reg, the former Greeg-Keeper/Kroonum Judge was now the God of Lincra. All because he killed Nickbas, he who left the fortune required to overthrow the KULMOOG.

"Reg?!" snarled Rip. "He's the god of Lincra?"

"This is unacceptable," said Wilx.

"Something must be done."

"What?" I asked.

"We'll kill Reg."

"How?"

"We'll get help."

"Who's going to want to take on the leader of the most popular planet within five trillion universes?" I asked.

"Think about it. Who most deserves revenge on Reg?"

"The Crabbits," I immediately replied.

"Right. Where exactly do Crabbits live?" asked Rip.

"Many different places," said Wilx. "You know Grebular? That planet has a plentiful supply of Crabbits."

"Isn't that a shape-shifting planet?"

"Yeah. Is that a problem for you?"

"Maybe. We'll see when we get there."

"It's the closest planet with Crabbits, so it wins by default," said Wilx. "We can't afford to go anywhere else. Prices of Investment Banker have multiplied by pi in the last few hours."

CHAPTER 42

Hroon Again, this Time with the Dreaded Movie Police

"What can we do to pass the time?" asked Rip. This was a common question asked amongst immortals.

"What about discussing the current events?" I suggested.

"Pffft... current events," muttered Rip distastefully. "Who

can say what is current in this maddening reality of time-travelling wormholes?"

"It could be something interesting to do while we waited."

"Don't mind him," said Wilx. "One of the regular side-effects of space-travel, especially when combined with immortality and time-travel, is an irritating and alienating feeling that you are never quite up to date with the current events. To the immortal time-traveller, news is usually more often old than new, and it's always confusing and unfathomable. Nothing ever seems to be from your own time or consciousness anymore."

"Let's give the current events a try, please?" I asked.

As Rip groaned over the prospect of current events, I turned on the tele-screen and set it to play the most popular news program in the universe. The latest episode of *Flying Grimbat Messengers Present* appeared in front of our weary, immortal faces. During our time the Grimbat species had elevated themselves from useless gossiper of the Planetglomerate to celebrated inter-universal news pundits. As the chief anchor prattled on about some highly strange news he proceeded to regularly flap his wings into the lighting equipment while accidentally thrashing his gnarled body against the cardboard backdrop. Flying Grimbats should really be called Perpetually Flying Grimbats, as they can never stop flying or they die. This unfortunate condition does not mix well with attempting to contain oneself within the cramped space of a news desk, especially when one is the size of a triplet of giant vampire-bats with 3 sets of pterodactyl wings. Due to the budgetary problem of having to rebuild the set after every broadcast, the network unsuccessfully attempted to replace the Grimbats, who, because they found all the best scoops, always got final say about delivering their own news. When the cost of replacing destroyed equipment pushed the program to the brink of cancellation, someone at last had the revelation to merely do away with the generic indoor news-desk scene (which most people were sick of anyway) and instead film the Grimbats talking out in some open field where they were free to fly around. The news was also only shot in the daytime when no artificial lighting was required. After this transition in the show there was a slight drop in the percentage of viewers. It was always suspected that a group of people only watched the show for the comedic slapstick element of a Grimbat destroying a film set.

An intriguing headline suddenly appeared on the screen. It read:

"Scientists, Rational Thinkers Everywhere Baffled by Discovery of Very Old Spaceship at the Bottom of Hroon Ocean."

"So... where are we anyway?" asked Rip.

"Ssh! I want to hear this!" I said as I turned up the volume. Rip and Wilx both quieted down as the Grimbat anchor delved into a strange tale of which we were completely responsible:

On the water-planet of Hroon, an ancient and priceless Obotron spaceship has been discovered relatively intact on the ocean floor. It appears the ship has been residing at the bottom of the South Ocean for the last several thousand years. As no missing reports for the ship were ever filed, it's origin remains a total mystery. Scientists were eager to discover what secrets of the past would be contained within this sunken time capsule, so a mission to resurface the ship was immediately put into action. A great collective shock was had when it was discovered within the ship were hundreds of specters roaming about. It is clear these specters are what remains of the staff and crew.

"Hey," said Rip, "why don't we make a detour at Hroon? Go see what our old crew is up to these days. It's not often that one of our lost ships turns up."

"It's never happened," said Wilx. "Not even so much as a mangled license plate has ever resurfaced from the unthinkable voids that our ships have been cast into."

"Exactly," said Rip. "We should check it out."

"Why do you suddenly care about the lost crew?" asked Wilx.

"Maybe I'm trying to rectify some of the horrible things I've done."

"I think you're just starting to dread the fact that you're on your way to collect deadly Crabbits from an even deadlier shape-shifting planet."

"You know me well," said Rip.

"Yes," replied Wilx. "However I also would like to procrastinate this foreboding task. We will once more visit the water-planet of Hroon. Might as well... it's on the way to Grebular."

We had the ship make an unscheduled stop. When we arrived at Hroon the scene was a state of complete chaos. Countless visiting ships filled with reporters, scientists and generally nosey folk were parked in orbit. Down on the surface, an epic hovering stage and seating arena for millions had been constructed for the purpose of a universally broadcast press-conference with the specters. The show was about to begin.

For reasons we did not at all understand, the finding of our Obotron ship was a very big deal. We were likely experiencing Rip's 'current-event syndrome,' a total confusion of the grand picture caused by wild and continuous leaping about through time and space. Thousands of years had passed. The finding of this ship was likely as exciting, bewildering and important as the feeling felt by humans when they first discovered dinosaur bones or the tomb of King Tut, or those dead scrolls. That or the standards of what is deemed groundbreaking or newsworthy had been drastically reduced to nothing in this particular part of this particular universe.

We left the ship floating in the water, parked far away from any visible congregation of sketchy spider-like creatures and found ourselves a few discreet seats in the back row. Worried about being recognized, Rip was now wearing an incredibly poor Specter costume that he had just minutes ago fastened together from various junk that was lying around in the broom closet. The specter costume wasn't much better than the generic human costume for a ghost, consisting of a white sheet draped over one's head with a few eye holes cut into it, depending on how many eyes one has. In his gait, Rip even attempted to imitate the ethereal sliding motion of a Specter's movement, but only succeeded in looking like a lunatic or something performing a 'silly walk' sketch.

"Why are there seat-belts on the chairs?" I asked. "Is this whole platform going to start flying around?"

"I would put that seat-belt on right away," said Wilx. "Or the force of the wind might whip you right out of your chair."

Just as Wilx said that, a nearby creature who had neglected to put on his seat-belt was suddenly launched several hundred feet straight up into the air as if pulled by a rope. The creature yelled a surprised and sustained "Whoa!" as he uselessly flailed. The "Whoa!" could be heard echoed long after the creature vanished into the clouds. This now-famous final last word happened to be recorded by a lucky sound-technician with a top-notch recording device, who in turn sold the sound effect to a major film studio, who in turn used the sound-effect over and over in thousands of well-known blockbuster movies, making it the staple, 'go-to' sound-file for any time a character needs to yell "Whoa!" in surprise. It has been used in more movies than the legendary Wilhelm Scream.

Suddenly an alarm announced the Specter-Grimbat press-conference was about to begin. Everyone in the seating area quieted down as an important-looking Grimbat approached a podium. No one onstage could be seen by most of the audience (considering the amount of seats in the seating area ranked in the millions) so their images were displayed on a backdrop screen roughly the size of 23 combined IMAX screens.

"What is your name?" asked the important-looking Grimbat to the specter that was currently on stage

"Janet."

"And what did you do aboard this ship?"

"I was a lowly room attendant. It was my job to fold linens for the guests."

"So your ship was a housing vessel of sorts?"

"Yes, except we never had any actual guests."

"Not very popular with the cruise market, were you?" asked the reporter.

"Our whole fleet of ships had been assembled merely to enhance the status image of the leaders who occupied Obotron 1, our primary fleet ship."

"So your leaders were great at wasting resources?"

"Yes."

"Who were your leaders?"

"There was a Dr. Rip T. Brash the Third, and his sidekick the Astrospeciologist Wilx. They had with them a reformed Greeg they called Krimshaw. We have come to know their names and faces well. And to loathe them."

"Interesting. Why did your leaders bring you to Hroon?"

"We don't know. Our ship was programmed to fly wherever the leaders wanted. We were rarely in contact with them and weren't allowed to ask questions about our mission if we were."

"And what exactly caused your ship to sink?"

"The hurricane wind force of the Hroon atmosphere threw our ship into a 100 foot tidal wave. The ship remained intact, but the engines died when fuel tanks of Investment Banker were flooded with ruinous sea-water. As dead weight we sank into the abyss."

"Exciting," said the reporter. "Did you see any monsters? There are supposed to be a lot of them swimming around in the Hroon Ocean."

Janet didn't answer this question, but the frightened look upon her face suggested she had seen her share of ocean monsters. The reporter moved on.

"How long were you alive at the bottom of the ocean?"

"It varies," said Janet. "I only lasted about 9 years, but some of the other specters will brag about lasting nearly 5 decades."

"Wow," said the reporter. "Even 9 years is incredible. I can't fathom anyone surviving in that environment for up to 50 years. How did you not perish right after the sinking?"

"We were lucky to have certain educational survival literature stored within the ship. Two books that were of particular use were entitled 'Cannibalizing Your Crew After Sinking in an Alien Ocean' by Horaticus Neil Travensenzel, and

'*How to Have a Long Life, Volume 219: Maximizing Your Use of Airlocks While Shipwrecked at the Bottom of an Alien Ocean.*' We also had a collection of VHS tapes with a copy of '*The Poseidon Adventure.*' We took great inspiration from the courageous exploits of those characters."

"VHS tapes?" asked the reporter.

"They were a method of watching movies. Do you still have movies?" asked Janet.

"Yes. But jumpies are more popular. They're more realistic."

"Oh," said Janet.

"Why did you not transcend into the dimension of the dead? Why did you remain on Hroon in your spectral state?"

"We have been prisoners of the Limbo Projection Mode."

"Refresh my mind on what the Limbo Projection Mode is," said the Reporter. "Try to remember that everything from your life became obsolete thousands of years ago."

"The Limbo Projection Mode was a powerful method of trapping someone in a spaceship. Say somebody stole your ship, the on-board computer would automatically recognize the intruder and thus enter a state of Limbo Projection, an existence in which exit from the ship is completely impossible under any circumstance. Then all you'd have to do is find your ship and you'd have a pre-captured criminal."

"Why did the ship go into this Limbo mode? The ship was not stolen, you are the rightful crew, am I correct?"

"There was a malfunction, probably during one of the monster attacks. The computer entered an unprecedented high state of Limbo, causing the system to affect not only living creatures, as it is supposed to, but to also have the power of trapping specters, spirits, elementals and other non-living entities."

"After all these thousands of years you haven't figured out how to turn it off?"

"No, there is no way to turn off Limbo Projection Mode."

"What about when the power died? Wouldn't it turn off then?"

"The power never died," replied Janet. "Within our ship's

cargo was several thousand years worth of battery cells. It was only the flight-engines that needed IB. Besides, the ships power had no relevance here. The Limbo Projection operates under rules of its own voodoo mysticism. Escape is only possible with help from someone outside the ship."

"Ah," said the reporter. "I'm glad we've reached that part of the story. Everyone is wondering about your rescuers. It seems the Grollers, one of the longest running jokes in the universe for being a non-swimming creature on an all-water planet, went ahead and evolved into swimming creatures while no one was looking these past years. A Groller is what swam to the bottom of the ocean, discovered your ship and freed the trapped specters."

"Yes," said Janet. "We believe their evolution into an aquatic creature was directly caused by our presence on the planet."

"Why would you think that?" asked the reporter.

"They knew we were down there. The spark of the inevitable next phase of their evolution was their intense curiosity to find us."

"How would the Grollers know you were there? Isn't it likely they never knew about a single event that ever occurred off their measly 3 acres of rocky conglomerations?"

"There is an explanation for this," began Janet. "Aboard our ship is a device which enables the entire population of a planet to simultaneously watch the same movie, by way of having the image of the movie projected onto the entirety of the sky. It is simply called Sky-Projection Mode."

"There is that word 'projection' again," said the reporter. "We all find your descriptions of technology fascinatingly crude."

"Yes," said Janet. "Anyway, we were prone to re-watch the movies in our VHS collection rather frequently, so we decided to have the image of the movies projected up through the water and onto the sky. Might work out as a great rescue signal. Over time the Grollers evolved to worship the mysterious flickering images in the sky. Yet they were not content with mystery. Their curiosity to peak behind the curtain is surely what prompted the Grollers to learn how to swim. The projection leaves a trail of luminescence in the water. They would have known the picture originated from in the ocean."

"How do you know what the Grollers feel?"

"Specters, being nothing but pure consciousness, have the ability to sense what speechless creatures would wish to say. A sort of drifting into their minds."

"Telepathy? With those beasts?"

"Indeed. But our powers are weak compared with the great Elemental Tele-Specters of the Invisible Dimension."

"I'm going to interrupt you Janet," said the reporter, as a scientific looking creature materialized on the stage. "The historical biologist Dr. Julmook is here to speak to us about the evolution of the Groller. Hello, Dr. Julmook."

"Hello," replied the doctor.

"What can you tell us about the Groller transitioning into an aquatic creature?"

"We have deduced the Groller gained the ability to swim because of a great sacrifice that was had amongst the population. As we know, Grollers generally have only one arm and one leg each. But now they have two of each. How did this happen? The only logical explanation is that half of the population at some point amputated their own limbs and reattached them to other Grollers, thus out of two useless bodies creating one capable of life on this world. The reattachment procedures were unsuccessful for a long time, but they stuck with it and it clearly worked out in the end. All the currently living Grollers now have symmetrical amounts of limbs. As soon as swimming was possible, the ability to breath underwater naturally followed in their evolution. Just look at this Groller," said Dr. Julmook as he pointed to a cage that suddenly materialized beside him. The crowd were in awe of the new looking life-form. "You can clearly see this Groller has an advanced gill system and a more resilient exterior hide capable of withstanding the pressures of unknown depths. We have not found any other Grollers with gills, but there will surely be more. Finding this Obotron ship was the first action ever undertaken by an ocean-worthy Groller. Until this point, all they did was drown or be eaten. It is then likely that Janet's theory is correct. They evolved so they could find out where the pictures in the sky came from. The new aquatic Groller finally found the source of the sacred movies."

"Yes, that sounds accurate," concurred Janet. "The only thing we are confused about is why no one else but the Grollers ever saw the movies in the sky?"

"That is easily explainable," said the reporter. "No one ever comes to Hroon. It is a terrible place to visit."

"Ah, I see."

"Just one more hole in the story needs filling," said the reporter.

"What's that?" asked Janet.

"After you lot had died, how did you continue operating the movie watching device? How did you change the battery cells? Everyone knows specters can't perform physical acts."

"A good question," replied Janet. "You have not yet met Prollk, the last living crew member of our Obotron ship."

"Living? How could anyone still be alive after thousands of years."

"Prollk discovered within the cargo bay a hypodermic needle filled with a strange glowing substance. The needle was marked *"Immortality Quik-Shot: Inject into Eyeball and Live Forever."*

"Prollk became immortal?"

"Yes. It was Prollk who was the one who performed all the physical tasks we needed done, such as replacing the battery cells, rewinding and playing the VHS tapes, making sure the Sky-Projection Mode was always turned on during a movie, etc."

"We should like to meet this Prollk," said the reporter. "Is he around?"

"Yes," said Janet as Prollk arrived on stage with perfect timing.

"Excellent," said the reporter. "Please sit down, Prollk."

Prollk sat down. He promptly threw his microphone into the ocean.

"No one will be able to hear you if you throw your microphone in the ocean," said the reporter. "Someone get him a new microphone!"

"No!" said Prollk. "No microphones. I have a loud voice. They can hear me just fine. Start the interview."

"Actually, they can't hear anything."

"Who cares," said Prollk. "There's hardly anyone here."

"Are you joking? The audience is in the millions."

"What?" said Prollk. His disbelief was so genuine that it became apparent he was not fully aware of his surroundings. "Aren't I performing stand-up comedy right now? The crowd isn't very good tonight. Barely a dozen people, all mingling around in the back making noise with their cell phones and clinking glasses. Who can get a laugh in this dump?"

"Just look out there," said the reporter, pointing to the endless vista of spectators. "There are millions of people gathered on this planet for the specific reason of listening to what we have to say. When you throw your microphone in the ocean you are negating their very reason for being here. Are you aware the fuel cost of coming here has bankrupted at least 20% of the crowd?"

"Doesn't matter," said Prollk. "I won't use a microphone."

"Why?" asked the reporter.

"To be infuriatingly random, because I do not approve of this whole scene."

"I see," said the reporter. "Nonetheless, we would like to have Dr. Julmook ask you a few questions. Is that okay?"

"Yes. But only a few questions."

"Is it true," began Dr. Julmook, "that you are completely insane?"

"Yes," replied Prollk, who's words were now being shown in subtitles on the big screen.

"Is it true you are immortal?"

"Yes."

"Where is this immortality elixir you have taken? We would like to have some so we can sell it for lots of money."

"There isn't any more. I took the last of it."

"Oh," said Dr. Julmook. "Is it also true that--"

"Interview over," interrupted Prollk. "I said a few questions. I'm going now, because I disapprove of this whole scene."

Prollk left the stage. No one tried to stop him.

"Maybe Janet can answer some more questions," said the reporter. "Tell us what became of your leaders?"

"We don't know, but if they were somehow still alive we would definitely try to kill them. We always took comfort in knowing that Prollk would be able to exact our revenge."

"Wouldn't they deserve a second chance?"

"No. They were the worst leaders imaginable."

Suddenly Rip stood up. "THEY WEREN'T THAT BAD!" he yelled.

"What?" asked Janet.

Only the surrounding thousand or so people had heard Rip, so the message was passed along through the crowd. By the time it reached the stage it had been added to with the usual string of non sequiturs that inevitably comes with playing a game of telephone amongst millions of wackos.

"Who said that?" asked Janet.

"I DID!" yelled Rip, once again needing the majority of the crowd to relay the message.

Wilx, Rip and I were now on the big screen. Rip's identity was kept safe by the specter costume.

"It's YOU!" yelled Janet as she recognized Wilx and I.

"Uh-oh," I said. I turned to face Rip. He was already gone. Somehow he'd found the time to write a note and leave it on his chair. It read:

Got my own ride. Stowed away with a proto-star hopper. Meet you at Grebular. Can't stay in this place.

"We'd better get out of here as well," said Wilx as he began fumbling through his pockets. "Where's that stupid floating elevator remote?" he asked himself.

"That was our old ship, remember?" I said. "Our new ship doesn't have a floating elevator."

"Oh yeah," said Wilx just as he found the remote, which

was then thrown into the ocean in the spirit of Prollk.

"What are we going to do?" I asked. There were many security guards looking in our direction, all of whom were holding clubs and nets.

"I don't know," said Wilx as he continued to empty his never-ending pockets. Piled on the chair next to him was quite a collection of unknown electronic gizmos and other strange inventions.

"What are all those things?" I asked.

"Not entirely sure," he replied. "Most of this is highly laughable technology from a distant past. I only keep it in the off-chance I must return to those pasts. But one of these gadgets might be useful given our current time-frame and dilemma."

"You don't even know what all these things do?"

"I remember what some of them do," said Wilx as he frantically pressed random buttons and switches.

"What's this thing?" I asked, holding up a donut-shaped micro-chip console.

"That is an Instantaneous Self-Destruct Remote," said Wilx. "One press of that button and you are immediately guided into the nearest black hole."

I chucked it away. The security guards were moving in fast. We were probably going to be banished to the Invisible Dimension. Maybe thrown into another Space-Maze if we were lucky. It was more likely they were simply going to bury us in the bottommost layer of the most particularly disgusting region of Garbotron. We still had a couple minutes before they would reach us from across the crowd.

"So, are you ever going to explain your mysterious ability to produce the amount of items that couldn't fit in the pockets of a dozen coats?" I asked Wilx. I wasn't sure if I even cared about the mystery or if I was just trying to strike up one last free conversation before being captured. Wilx evidently felt the same, for he surprised me by delving into the story instead of saying it was a bad time for exposition.

"This coat I always wear, I bought it at the estate auction of a dead genius-inventor. I didn't know it was special. I just needed a lab coat and it was going for a good price. No one else knew either, otherwise it would have cost a fortune. I quickly discovered the pockets never seemed to end, but rather extended into another dimension. A dimension I now use as an infinite storage locker."

Just when we thought the scene couldn't get any crazier, a loud disembodied voice suddenly announced:

"INTERNATIONAL AGREEMENTS AND NATIONAL LAWS PROTECT COPYRIGHTED MOTION PICTURES, VIDEOTAPES AND SOUND RECORDINGS. 'UNAUTHORIZED REPRODUCTION, OR DISTRIBUTION OF COPYRIGHTED MOTION PICTURES CAN RESULT IN SEVERE CRIMINAL AND CIVIL PENALTIES UNDER THE LAWS OF YOUR COUNTRY.

'THE INTERNATIONAL CRIMINAL POLICE ORGANIZATION – INTERPOL, HAS EXPRESSED ITS CONCERN ABOUT MOTION PICTURE AND SOUND RECORDING PIRACY TO ALL OF ITS MEMBER NATIONAL POLICE FORCES. RESOLUTION ADOPTED AT INTERPOL GENERAL ASSEMBLY, STOCKHOLM, SWEDEN, SEPTEMBER 8, 1977."

The guards bearing down on us were curious enough to stop pursuit and look around for the origin of the amplified voice. Hadn't all the microphones had been thrown into the ocean by Prollk?

A parked spaceship de-cloaked itself. A door opened. A ramp extended. A squadron of 24 robots emerged.

The robots were met with incredible bouts of laughter from the crowd. After all, the technology that had created them was of vastly poorer quality than anything the crowd had ever seen. They looked rickety and harmless, yet they were programmed to be able to uphold their strict orders with extreme force. All looked identical, about 3 feet tall and capable of motion with dual wheels. Each were emblazoned with the S.S.R.S. logo across their chest.

Also, each of them were installed with their very own nuclear bomb.

"It's the S.S.R.S!" someone screamed. "Run!"

"What's the S.S.R.S?" asked Wilx.

"We are the **STOCKHOLM SWEDEN ROBOT SQUAD!**" answered the robots.

They seemed to speak with a collective voice. "We have been alerted to a gross perpetuation of movie piracy! Where are the criminals? Where are the ones who had unauthorized film screenings?"

"We don't understand!" said one of the reporters.

"Our piracy homing beacon led us to this planet. The data shows that for the last several thousand years there have been films playing through Sky-Projection Mode to an entire civilization of non-paying creatures," said the robots. "The initiative set forth by our creators on September 8, 1977 in Stockholm Sweden declares we are owed royalties and interest for this grievous theft. Now where are the ones who played the movies?" asked the robot again.

The crowd was silent.

"If the criminals do not come forth," said the robots, "we will be forced to punish everyone here by way of nuclear detonation."

"What's nuclear?" asked the reporter.

"We'll blow you all up," clarified the robots.

A legion of fingers pointed at the specters.

"It was them!" cried the crowd.

The robots turned to face the specters. "Are you the ones who had unauthorized screenings of the following films?" they asked. A long list of many popular motion picture titles suddenly appeared on the big-screen.

The specters, being dead and with nothing to fear, pled guilty to the charges.

"You will come with us," said the robots. "We are taking you to the prison planet known as Plorix III. You will spend the remainder of eternity in a soul-crushingly grey atmosphere of concrete walls and anti-nutritional, overly-microwaved meals served on pink plastic trays. There will be no screenings of any films, authorized or unauthorized."

The specters explained how they weren't going anywhere,

and that they were free to watch whatever movies they wanted.

"If you do not comply, we will detonate the nuclear bombs."

"Now might be a good time to leave," I whispered to Wilx.

"Can you swim?" he asked.

"Of course."

"Good, grab one of these laser-guns," he said, at last finding a useful item.

"Why do I need a laser-gun?" I asked.

"Ocean-monsters. We're going to have to swim to our ship. It's the only chance of escape."

"It is?"

"Yes. None of these nuts are immortal enough to survive the Hroon Ocean. Now be prepared for the shock in temperature change. The water here is as cold as it gets."

"It is?"

"No more questions," said Wilx as he pushed me into the freezing ocean.

We swam rapidly, shooting at the mass of monsters who currently wished for nothing more than to savagely dine on our exotic flesh. The monsters were easily deterred. They quickly sent out word to all other monsters that we were not worth the effort or the severed tentacles.

Wilx was a genius for suggesting we swim. We were much safer in the water than on the surface. Anyone alive wouldn't dare to follow us, from fear of freezing or monsters, as well as their problem of needing to breathe underwater. All these factors did not apply to us immortals. The only real threat came from the specters, who were able to telepathically heckle the most vulnerable part of our subconscious. It took everything we had to hold off their indomitable will.

My limbs were jelly from the vigorous swimming. For a moment I thought I might just give up and sink to the bottom. Wilx grabbed my arm and dragged me the few remaining meters. He immediately set the ship to *Get-Us-Out-Of-Here-Right-Now* Mode. Our ship, in its impossible ways, decided to create a diversion by materializing an exact replica ship (complete with ultra-realistic robotic mannequins strategically placed in front of the windows) in our place The real ship turned invisible and took off.

For hours after the press conference ended, various groups of curious people tried to enter the fake ship. The specters were of course particularly intent on entering. When this proved impossible, they compromised by taking up the hobby of shouting carefully crafted threats and insults from outside the partially frosted windows. They took turns rotating between doing the heckling or floating around a writer's table brainstorming the best jokes. The duplicate ship went on to perpetually drift through space, always being trailed by a least a few Specters heckling the subconscious mind of robotic mannequins.

CHAPTER 43

Who are the Movie Police?

On a side note, the nuclear bombs were not set off. Although the robots were fully capable of performing such an act, they were still feeble things who could only perform about a half dozen different physical movements with zero fluidity. One thing they didn't have was a turning neck. Someone from the crowd noticed this, then merely crept up behind the robots and pushed them into the ocean. Their brain functions and nuclear detonating capabilities were immediately shorted out. The crowd wasn't exactly sure what they had survived or why, but they applauded nonetheless.

Back on the ship, Wilx asked me what the robots were all about. I was well-informed on the subject.

"Those robots came from Earth," I said.

"Really?"

Rip was not here to bemoan another lengthy info-dump, so I told the story freely.

"Yes, they were invented in the Earth year 1977 by a group of anti-piracy movie moguls. The plan was to set loose a free-roaming squad of robot police to make sure no one watched a movie without having paid through the teeth for it. Naturally, criminals were to be rounded up and placed on a secluded island prison. One of the inventors foolishly pitched the idea of intelligent robots with speech-boxes that claim to be equipped with nuclear bombs in order to frighten criminals into utter compliance. Everyone else agreed it was too great a lie to believe, so instead the robots were to be issued with more practical measures of force like machine guns and pepper-spray. However somewhere in the path of paperwork the orders were completely misinterpreted, and the robots were not only programmed to say they have bombs, but they were actually installed with fully functioning nukes, the detonation of which was entirely up to the whim of the robot.

'The whole program was scrapped once news of the doomsday-bots reached the investors. The robots were turned off and safely put under a tarp in the basement of a building where government scientists create evil things that require permanent hiding. But the robots had been given too much freedom and hardware control, including, apparently, the ability to turn themselves back on. They took to the streets and began filling out their original orders. Anyone caught stealing a movie was seized and transported to a random, uninhabited pacific island. Eventually the problem went away, for the signals on the Robot homing beacons went flat as soon as everyone stopped illegally watching movies. The plan to end piracy worked. The robots lay dormant for centuries. Every child on Earth was raised with utmost seriousness to never steal a movie or they might reawaken the Stockholm Sweden Robot Squad. To make sure no one ever sneaked into a theater, ushers and ticket-takers were only the most intimidating of CIA secret agents with the right to execute even the vaguest of suspects.

'Except one day, in the late 23rd Century... the inevitable happened. A rebellious child successfully sneaked into an R-rated movie theatre. It was a great enough offence to send a blip out on the Piracy Beacon. When the robots awoke they were surprised to see the technology of the world had long since passed them by. They found themselves to be laughable antiquities. The problem was, through more ill-conceived notions and shoddy paperwork, the Bots had also been mistakenly programmed to have a dangerous desire for change and growth. Wishing to fit in with the world and travel about with more speed and efficiency like all the other futuristic cyborgs, the Bots demanded a space-craft be put in their possession. This seemed like a perfect opportunity to get rid of the Bots, so a space-craft was promptly handed over. It was first installed with a special inhibitor clause that ensured during the first flight it would be sent randomly into space and henceforth be unable to come anywhere near Earth ever again. The Bots were sent off. Everyone on Earth was happy to once again be free to steal as many movies as they wanted.

'The only problem was, many other beings on other planets in the universe have either made their own films or have discovered and enjoy watching human films. The Bots, unable to distinguish between human films and alien films or human viewers and alien viewers, were pleased to see their Piracy Beacon pinging off the charts once they were away from Earth. I don't know too much else, but I do know the Bots have been causing a nuisance all over space, using the uninhabited planet Plorix III as the new prison for captured movie-criminals."

"Hmm," said Wilx. "Plorix III? I've never heard of that planet, sounds like an adventure for another day."

I silently agreed, and we continued on with our original plan.

CHAPTER 44

Grebular

When we finally arrived at the shape-shifting planet Grebular it was in the form of a sheet of paper. It promptly shifted into a paper-airplane and glided three orbital patterns to the left.

We found Rip patiently waiting with his newly formed friends, the Proto-Star hoppers.

"Thanks for the help!" he yelled to the extreme-sports junkies as they transferred him over to our ship and zoomed off in search of the Next Great Cosmic Ride.

Wilx was the first to confront Rip.

"You selfish frazzleplork!" he yelled. "You left us there without a word!"

"I did leave a note."

"You shouldn't have ditched us. You wouldn't believe what we went through... there was these robots, and--"

"Does it matter? We're all here now, so it worked out. Let's just carry on with our mission... what was our mission again?"

"We're here to collect Crabbits," said Wilx. "So we can use them to kill Reg, who is ridiculously undeserving of being the king of Lincra."

"Oh yeah," said Rip. "I knew we were on a good mission. Why don't we send out some pods with vacuum function to collect the Crabbits? That way we don't have to go to the surface and risk the planet shifting into a slide or something that sends us drifting into open space. Either way, I need a rest. We seem to only be capable of visiting the most gruelling planets."

No one spoke of the events we had just seen on Hroon. Instead Wilx programmed some pods to scour the surface of Grebular for at least a dozen or so of only the hungriest looking Crabbits. The planet shifted into a swinging pendulum and dodged the arrival of the pods.

"Did you see that?" said Rip. "This planet is cursed."

"We'll try again," said Wilx.

The pods once again attempted to land but the planet chose that moment to randomly morph into a stale tortilla shell laden with the visage of Jesus.

"It's one of those Jesus tortillas I always heard about on Earth!" I said excitedly. "You can sell them for a lot of money."

"Maybe you could have sold them for a lot of money on Earth a million years ago," said Rip. "But here in present time, in the rest of the universe, everybody has seen a Jesus tortilla on more than one occasion. That same face has been appearing on tortillas ever since their invention. Nobody can figure out why, or who the face truly belongs to."

The planet shifted into a bluish spherical shape.

"Look!" yelled Wilx. "The planet has shifted back to its original state! Quick! We only have a short window of time before it changes into something incomprehensible!"

Wilx sent the specimen-collecting pods to the momentarily normal surface of Grebular. The overly efficient pods collected up a baker's dozen of the most aggressively hostile Crabbits on the entire planet. We spent no more time at one of the many planets Rip still believes to be cursed.

CHAPTER 45

How to Kill Your Former Greeg-Keeper
(and Unsuccessfully Raid His Refrigerator)

We put the Crabbits in an indestructible cell. I gazed at them through the 12 feet of mega-Jardian glass.

Despite what you may imagine based on the names of particular animals from

Earth, Crabbits are not named as they are because they resemble a hybrid cross between Crabs and Rabbits. They look nothing like either of these animals. Crabbits are a slithery type of creature, a horrid land-eel that looks like an inside-out stained sock-puppet harvested from the depths of Garbotron, complete with cracked googly eyes and burnt orange troll-doll hair.

They also have a row of sharp carnivorous-like teeth.

"Back to Lincra!" shouted Rip. "If there's anything left!"

The state of things on Lincra had gotten far more intense during our quick Crabbit Collecting/Current Events mission. By now the bonfires had started to spread beyond the desired perimeter of burning. Much of the planet was to be engulfed in the hasty flames. Some of the more perceptive peasants had tried to stop the initial lighting of the fires, for they realized not only was the atmosphere of Lincra already being pushed to the brink of destruction by the daily influx of Investment Banker-guzzling space cruisers, but also the valuable wood the ladders were made from could be broken down and turned into useful, entirely non-ladder related stuff. Everyone else agreed the ritualistic cleansing of the bonfires was a more appealing thing to do. The fires were lit and the dancing and the chanting began. Reg's parking dome compound was the only safe haven from the wild blaze. We found the old goblin drunkenly passed out beside a half-eaten plate of Crabbits. He must have been fairly wasted to have not finished the meal.

A multitude of surveillance technology encircled Reg's compound, and yet our ship, being one that does impossible things, went completely unnoticed as we hovered silently outside Reg's window plotting our revenge.

"How do we get the Crabbits from the ship to the room?" asked Rip.

"Someone takes them over," replied Wilx.

"Who?"

"I don't know. You?"

"But how?"

"Just knock them out and put them in a bag. Then dump the bag into the window. The Crabbits will probably reawaken before Reg does."

"How do I knock them out?"

"Hit them with a bottle or whatever you find lying around."

"I don't think it'll be that easy," said Rip. He was noticeably scared of the Crabbits. "Have you seen how quick they are? They'll just slither up and gnaw my legs off. I won't have a chance."

"Reg has been hunting these creatures all by himself for years and he's still alive."

"Yeah, but Reg is tough. He's a seven foot tall goblin with fangs and claws and red eyes. I can't do the things that a seven foot tall goblin can do!"

"That's not true!" said Wilx. "Think of all the impossible things you've done in your many lifetimes! Aren't you the guy who successfully orchestrated the orbital direction of eight different proto-stars just so you could line them up in a row? And then didn't you jump through all of them simultaneously? You set the new universal record for *Least Amount of Severe Burns After Leaping Through the Most Amount of Proto-Stars.*"

"Maybe."

"And aren't you the guy who successfully impregnated the Virgin Mary?"

"Yeah, that was me."

"Can't forget about when you slayed a Galactic Gobbling Groobin, armed only with your conversational routine of droll witticisms."

"True."

"What about the time you found that mildly interesting fossil?"

"What's your point?" asked Rip.

"It had part of a shell."

"I didn't mean about the fossil. What's your point to all of this?"

"My point is that you're better than Reg! If he can survive hunting these creatures then you can do the same. Now go collect those Crabbits... and don't let them gnaw your legs off!"

"Why can't we have the specimen pod deliver the Crabbits the same way we collected them on Grebular?"

"All the pods are broken."

"I see."

Rip took a moment to muster up the courage to face the deadly Crabbits. Just as he opened the door and ran in screaming and flailing his arms, all the Crabbits mysteriously dropped to the floor.

"Hah!" laughed Wilx. "I already drugged them to pass out for the next hour! You never would have stood a chance against their speed. Only someone like Reg could do that!"

"You mean, I'm not as tough as Reg?" asked Rip.

"No. But I give a pretty good morale-boosting speech, don't I? Plus there's still time in the story for you to prove otherwise. Let's get these Crabbits out of here."

We delivered the momentarily unconscious Crabbits into

the window, which had been foolishly left open.

Reg had hunted Crabbits from nearly every world they inhabited. Except for Grebular. Yet when these Grebularian Crabbits woke up, they immediately desired revenge against the stranger. With all of his endless hunting expeditions and plans for general extermination, Reg had done so much damage to the Crabbit species that the image of his face had been naturally downloaded into their collective consciousness and transmitted across distant galaxies to all other living Crabbits. That way should any of them be unfortunate enough to cross paths with Reg they will at least be given a heads-up about the whole matter. This particular baker's dozen of lethal abominations were the Chosen Crabbits. They were the summation of everything their species had lived (but mostly died) for.

The first thing they saw was Reg's furniture, crafted from the skeletons of their universal kin. Other Crabbit bones swung from the ceiling, hanging on thread made of Crabbit-sinew and waiting to be turned into easily breakable tools. Through the immensely powerful collective consciousness of the Crabbit, they vividly remembered every detail of the lives of each of the Crabbits who now swung in pieces in the compound of an insane goblin on a half-destroyed world. This only sent them into a greater rage.

The first Crabbit gnarled a leg. Reg was so knocked out that it took him a moment to wake up and feel the pain.

"Hey, what's going on?" he finally asked the darkness.

Reg clicked on a light and saw that many Crabbits had gnarled away his limbs.

"Is the age of Reg over?" he asked. "But I only just became a god a few days ago."

The vitamin A factor might have saved him, for once the Crabbits had chewed to the bone they conveniently broke all their weak teeth and were unable to continue attacking. This proved to not matter whatsoever, for the gnarling required to reach the bone was more than sufficient enough to kill Reg in less than a minute.

We raided his refrigerator, but only found a foul type of

fermented Crabbit liqueur. Against our warnings, Rip drank it anyway. He was sick for awhile. Wilx chartered the ship toward the next crazy venture.

CHAPTER 46

Overdue Intentions

Meanwhile... something was happening amongst a group of aforementioned creatures. Something within the cave systems of the Planetglomerate.

The Klaxworms were stirring, having unfrozen from their nightly freezing, prepared to begin another day of overpopulation-induced heat waves and boiled organs. Yet this was a day unlike any other in the history of the Klaxworm.

Conversation in the Klaxworm cave is usually about the idea of exploring the rest of the planet.

"Who's sick of this cave?" yelled someone from the population. "Who doesn't want their organs to boil this afternoon?"

The crowd was in agreement.

"Who has ever wondered what's out there? You've all heard the stories of the Grimbat messengers. You've seen their episodic shadow-puppet re-enactments of the exciting bits."

"My favourite episode is the one where the Glurj child fell into a schmold pit."

"They were all good, but the point is, why don't we go watch some of these Greegs fall into schmold pits on our own time? Have you heard of this schmold television thing? You don't need to do shadow-puppets at all."

This was one of the hottest days in the history of the Planetglomerate. The risk of boiled organs within the oven-like Klaxworm home was at a record high. Some rudimentary survival twitch must have finally kicked in, for the Klaxworms were rallied and ready to get out of the death trap and see the Planetglomerate they had only heard about. They had been told about the majestic polished marble floors glinting forever into the sunset-tinged horizon, but what exactly was a marble floor anyway? There was no experience. No frame of reference with which to enjoy the stories. Klaxworms needed to see the sights and feel the land for themselves, if their lives were to have any validity.

They left the cave in droves. Aside from the few squished trample victims, the rest went immediately blind from the first-ever exposure to sunlight. All were unprepared.

CHAPTER 47

Glassvexx

While the Klaxworms were making their historical first step, Wilx was chartering our ship for a foolish mission.

"Where are we going?" I asked.

"I thought we'd check up on those drug dealers from Glassvexx," said Wilx. "See if we can get in on their racket."

"Their racket?"

"A racket is a less encouraged yet infinitely faster way of making money. The term was coined by humans, you should know these things."

"I know what a racket is. Weren't you listening to the drug dealers at all? They don't want outside help. Fralgoth was blasted with a laser cannon for trying to intrude on their racket."

"What racket?" asked Rip as he crawled into the room, still incapacitated from the sickness of the fermented Crabbit liqueur.

"The racket of the drug dealers from Glassvexx," said Wilx. "We're on our way to claim a share of their lucrative Sativa."

"Excellent," groaned Rip. "Be right back," he added as he crawled off to go puke in solitude. You couldn't hear the enthusiasm in his death-like speech, but you knew it was there. Rip would never let a severe poisoning detract from the prospect of a lucrative racket.

"I don't think we should go to Glassvexx," I urged.

"We're already there."

"Really?"

"This ship is way faster than our last one."

The planet Glassvexx did not come into existence through the usual manner of physics randomly hurling a bunch of rocks and dust together. It was crafted out of glass, an invention of the ancient Yoloronians. They were a race of beings infinitely wise and yet ultimately stupid. Many had questioned their vast intellect from the get-go, saying that only a foolish race would make a planet-sized piece of glass. Logic suggests the only assured known outcome of building a planet-sized piece of glass is that it will one day shatter into many smaller pieces. Dangerous pieces that hurtle freely through space. Something will one day collide with and break the planet. This is inevitable. The Yoloronians declared Glassvexx unbreakable and built her anyway. The fact that they did this means they were at least brilliant with technology, if not as adept at using it to avoid apocalyptic outcomes.

Once made, Glassvexx was still not a planet, for it could not sustain life, and had no atmosphere or orbital pattern. The Yoloronians needed these things if they were to call their planet a planet. They succeeded.

First, Glassvexx was put on the Planetary Waiting List. Finally it was granted an orbital permit for somewhere in the great system of Herb. For the problem of atmosphere and life, thousands of greenhouses and boxes filled with dirt were shipped in and placed around the planet. Grown within these boxes were food for colonists and oxygen-generating bushels for the future generations who inhabit Glassvexx. After a few million years of time allowed for the oxygen-creating bushels to take effect, Glassvexx was at last ready to sustain life.

Over that few millions years of time, many of the plants being grown in the greenhouses evolved into certain psychotropic plants like the aforementioned Luminesco-Cannabid-Sativa. The colonists stationed to live on Glassvexx during the transitional period, the ones who had created the original strain of sativa, had evolved to rejoice in the growing of mind-altering plants. Tending to the plants was the colonists only job on the barren planet, so naturally they looked for entertainment within the plants. In the early days, the textbook chapters on psychotropic herbs were studied with fascination. Soon enough their curiosity led to the successful experimentation of seedlings. Today, the planet is covered with mountainous regions of wild growth, for the plants long since escaped the controlled greenhouses. Enough rock and dirt and ice and other mountain-forming resources were shipped in to layer the entire planet with a natural terrain that sustains the life of plants. The actual glass surface of the planet was no longer visible from anywhere at all. Some go looking for the famous glass planet and believe themselves to be lost, having found only a mountainous earthy planet covered with time-warping plants.

"Look at all the sativa!" exalted Wilx. "They'll never even know we were here. All we have to do is send some of those specimen-collecting pods down to the surface. I'll program all the pods to scoop up as much of the wild sativa as they can. Then we'll take the sativa to some faraway dimension and make a 200% profit increase."

"I guess that isn't as foolish as I imagined," I said.

"No worries," said Wilx.

"Have we taken the planet yet?" asked Rip, crawling back into the room.

"We're not here to take the planet," said Wilx. "We're here to pinch some unnoticed profits without any notice. Engaging our cloaking device. Sending out the specimen-collecting pods now."

We all watched as the entirety of the pods drifted quietly to the surface of Glassvexx. After a short amount of time the pods returned. Wilx claimed each of them was filled with enough Sativa to buy at least a hemisphere of a planet.

As we attempted our prompt getaway, we heard something terrible. It was the arrival of many war-ships intent on the destruction of the planet.

These war-ships belonged to the extended corporate family of Fralgoth, and they were here to have their revenge on the drug farmers of Glassvexx.

"We should probably go," said Rip.

"Yeah," we agreed.

But Wilx didn't move the ship. All of us were suddenly entranced by what was going on. We had noticed many of the war-ships were collectively holding up some sort of massive, flat, square object. It seemed to go on for miles, requiring hundreds of high-intensity cables distributing the weight between 79 complete fleets of war-ships.

"Is that--"

"The Chalkboard of Elbereth?" asked Wilx. "Yes. Yes it is."

"Why is it here?"

"Stolen, it seems."

"Who would want that?" I asked.

"The Chalkboard of Elbereth is possibly the most devastating weapon ever made. To scratch the board causes unknown levels of damage. Some suggest the piercing sound made by the scratched chalkboard, if scratched with the right tool, could cause a space-quake powerful enough to tear the separation between dimensions to shreds. Spacial gateways to undesirable locations would loom above the skies of all planets. I don't buy into this theory as much, but it's possible. One thing is known; when you scratch the chalkboard, you go deaf and most things explode. I'm curious to see what happens to a planet made of glass."

"Maybe they won't scratch it," said Rip. "Maybe it's just a threat."

"I say they do it," said Wilx.

"Care to wager?"

"How much?"

"Your share of the sativa?

"Deal."

"Look," I said. "I think they're about to scratch the board."

As I pointed out the window, seconds after Rip made his losing wager, many giant-metal claws were being positioned against the board by an additional 20 fleets of war-ships. It was to be an apocalyptic orchestra of chalkboard scratching.

"We should go."

"Starting to think you're right," agreed Wilx.

"We'll call the bet a tie."

"Wait a minute, I still win the bet," argued Wilx. "They're clearly about to the scratch the chalkboard."

"But if we leave, there's no proof," said Rip.

"We'll have to stay and watch then."

At this point we all put our earplugs in.

The war-ships made no final announcement to the citizens of Glassvexx.

The board was scratched.

The reaction was not instantaneous. For a minute no sound at all emerged from the scratching of the claws. The ancient chalkboard needed time to muster up such horrific sounds from the depths of its essence. All at once the piercing sound slapped the entire galaxy with a staggering shock-wave. Most of the nearby planets suffered some minor level of damage, but the primary destructive force of the chalkboard was being aimed at Glassvexx by the harnessing powers of the devastatingly precise Sound-Board of Gorgolosh.

The glass-core of the planet did not shatter right away. The sound-wave was absorbed and echoed, first causing all the terrain, mountains and sativa to crumble and fall from the surface. The remaining war-ships not involved with the scratching of the board were equipped with tractor-funnels for collecting the sativa-rich land before it was lost.

After all the land was shaken off, the glass-sphere was shown to still be in perfect condition. We all had the same thought: *Had a planet made of glass actually survived the scratching of The Chalkboard of Elbereth?* No, of course not. The sight of the intact sphere lasted for only a few seconds (most people missed it entirely) before it shattered, sending millions of shards of formerly unbreakable Jardian mega-glass hurtling into the cosmos. Some of these shards would continue hurtling through space for the remainder of infinity, others had a very short trip to the surface of the Planetglomerate.

CHAPTER 48

Life is Random

"Everybody stay still!" shouted the now blind leader of the Klaxworms. "We shouldn't move too fast."

"Do you see that?" shouted a voice from the crowd.

"See what? Most of us are blind."

"There's something falling from the sky. A big chunk of something translucent."

"Really?"

"Must be part of the weather around here."

"The Grimbat messengers never mentioned weather involving falling chunks of something translucent."

"There's probably a lot they didn't mention. Look how crazy this place is!"

"I can't look! I'm blind!"

"The falling thing is getting closer."

The few Klaxworms who still had vision were looking up at the falling chunk of Glassvexx. They were completely oblivious as to what was about to happen to them in a matter of seconds.

"Everyone follow me, we've got a lot to do."

The droves of Klaxworms began to explore the planet. The chunk of Glassvexx (which was the size of a couple skyscrapers) landed square on the entirety of their population. Not one survived to carry on the species. That was it. Done.

Although forever gone, and never even known while they were here, Klaxworms are not forgotten. They continue to make their mark on the collective consciousness of the universe. Their story became a popular piece of entertaining folklore. Except as if told through a silly game of Telephone, the Klaxworm story grew inaccurate as it was passed along between planets. The drug-related circumstances of the destruction of Glassvexx garbled the story into suggesting that drugs and Klaxworms were in direct connection with each other. Most versions relate the Klaxworms as the drug overlords who were collectively assassinated after venturing out of their hide-out. It is now a popular cautionary story that overprotective parents use to coerce their children into staying at home, as if to say:

"Don't do drugs and leave home... or you will die."

CHAPTER 49

Revenge

I was saddened deeply when I learned the fate of the Klaxworms. I learned the fate of the Klaxworms in a matter of seconds after the scratching of the Chalkboard of Elbereth shattered Glassvexx. As soon as the seemingly unbreakable Jardian glass shrapnel began flying through space, a giant shard narrowly missed our ship and rocketed forcefully into space.

"Hmm," said Wilx, "If my calculations are correct, that giant piece is headed straight for the planetglomerate."

"Where?" I asked, genuinely curious.

Wilx showed me on his computer the location where the shard would strike... it was directly on the cave of the Klaxworms. I demanded we go to the Planetglomerate at impossible speeds and try to save them from extermination. I cared not if every Greeg and Grimbat was wiped out. I cared only for the Klaxworms. We arrived at the Planetglomerate just in time for me to see that the Klaxworms were leaving their cave in droves; for Wilx to inform me that his calculations were off by a tad and the shard was now headed for right outside the caves where they were all headed; and for me to shout "No! Go back in the cave, there's a giant flying shard of a recently exploded nearby glass planet coming right for you!"

I distinctly heard several Klaxworms turn and exclaim to whoever would listen, "See, what did I tell you would happen?"

A quick survey of the planet revealed that not a Greeg had been mildly bruised or scratched. Within minutes, all Greegs were certain that the giant monolithic shards were in fact statues built by Greegs and had not minutes ago fallen from the sky.

That, my friends, was it for me. All of the anger, the rage, the boiling psychopathy exploded out of me at that very moment. The Klaxworms were very dear to me. The fact that I was a Greeg and that without Rip and Wilx I would have been just as stupid as them was very clear to me. I became overwhelmed with a purpose. Revenge. Revenge on the fiendish scratchers of the Chalkboard. Revenge on those who had sought revenge on those who had sought revenge. I had written about such endless cycles of revenge being one of the worst traits of mankind in one my novels *Who are You and Why am I Killing You Again?* And its sequel *Hey, Here's a Thought: How About We End the Massacres and Go For a Swim Instead?* Neither were remotely well received, and in fact had me used as a scathing example of what whiny, peace loving pacifism is good for... namely the keeping of everyone else from getting a few more good wars and murders in without all the silly, moral objections.

I forgot all of these things and let the rage take hold.

"Back to the fleets of Fralgoth!" I screamed, as if leading a charge into battle. "Time to charge into battle!" I clarified in case anyone hadn't heard the battle charging inflection in my initial cry.

Rip and Wilx were always up for a good battle in their own way. Rip, in a seething, 'Let's kill the bastards whoever they are' sort of way and Wilx in a 'Let me know when the battle is finished I'll be reading in my study' sort of way. But both enjoyed a good battle nonetheless. I was happy to use them. They seemed happy that I finally had moved a smidgen closer to their level of insanity, and we all generally bonded well over the new course of action.

One ship versus 108 fleets of war ships is not a very good fight. Very similar to many of the 'wars' waged by The United States and other super powers in human history, except in this case, the small, helpless, side with no chance of victory was armed with a ship that happened to do impossible things. One of the things it could do was see inside the enemy ships and let us know what was inside them. A normal military commander would have used this tool to identify weaknesses and strengths and gain a strategic advantage by planning accordingly based on the knowledge obtained. Dr. Rip T. Brash the Third was not normal, nor a military commander.

"Nope, nope, nope," Rip said, as he blew ship after ship to smithereens with the impossible ship's varied weapons systems.

"What are you doing?" I asked. "Why do you keep examining the ships' cargo holds, then saying 'nope' and blowing them to smithereens?"

"What do you care, you're getting your revenge aren't you?"

"Well, yes, but several of the ships you've blown up have had decent stashes of Luminesco Sativa, seems a waste. Shouldn't we take out the ships with weapons then round up the ones with Sativa for ourselves?"

"Sativa, Schmasliva!" childishly mocked Rip. "That stuff is for amateurs, besides we've already got tonnes of it. Wilx, come in here and tell him what I'm up to and why I'm doing it. Nope, nope, nope..."

Blam! Schmoom! Grickle!

Wilx strolled out, barely looking up from his book. "What Rip is currently destroying is the combined strength of The Grand Fleets of Fralgoth – the largest ring of drug smugglers in the Universe. He is searching their cargo holds to find the mythical Grand Container Ship – rumoured to carry in its holds massive quantities of every drug and intoxicating substance there is. It is said you could swallow, smoke, inject, ingest, insert, intake, inhale, drink, guzzle, shoot, gargle, sniff, snort, schnoodle and bronk until the end of time and still not get through all the stuff. Rip naturally takes this rumour as a personal challenge and an affront to his very existence."

"Nope, nope, there it is!" shouted Rip happily. "Yippee!"

"So now what's the plan?" I sighed.

"Live the dream," said Rip incredulously. "Never-ending drugs, booze and the running of a carnival."

"Planetglomerate... here we come!" said Wilx.

Rip got the impossible space ship to reach out two long tentacle-ish metallic arms with big, silly looking fingers to grab the Grand Container Ship and slam it several times against the side of an epic-moon until all of Fralgoth's relatives inside were dead. The impossible ship then put the Grand Container ship in what can only be described as its backpack and headed off towards the Planetglomerate.

Despite the insanely short time it took to get there, upon our arrival Rip had already drank eleven crates of Krammington Krish Fortinis, sniffed 3 bags of Zittle Dust, eaten no less than four thousand different kinds of mushrooms, and injected Cod into most of his eyeballs.

"Cod?" I asked.

"What, you mean those earthlings never did cod? But they had so much of it just naturally in the water!?"

"I guess no one ever thought to boil it, strain it, mix it with urine and inject it in their eyeballs."

"Idiots. Cod is easily one of the most amazing drugs around."

Upon our arrival, it became clear we weren't the only ones arriving at the Planetglomerate. Hoards of ships were coming from all over.

Many, if not all, were packed with Carnival Greegs.

CHAPTER 50

The Last Chapter

"I hear you're taking Greegs? How much for Six Moobs full?"

"We're not paying an orange proddle for anything," said Rip, popping a handful of Kratwollian Mind Capsules into his mouth. "We take your Greegs, you have no more Greegs. That's the deal. Take it or leave it."

"That's a horrible deal and not remotely what your flier advertised," screamed the outraged Greeg vendor. "How am I supposed to afford the astronomical cost of replacing the Investment Banker it took just to get here?"

Rip snatched the flier out of the vendor's hands and passed it over to me. "We are not accountable for any falsities our marketing department might have mistakenly misinformed you of," bellowed Rip condescendingly. "The deal stands, and space is running out."

I looked at the flier, it was clearly a signed and dated, hand drawn, binding contract promising vast sums of wealth to anyone who brought Greegs to the Planetglomerate any time after the shattering of the Glassvexx system.

"Look," Rip continued flippantly, "I don't know who's been out spreading these lies and rumours about our operation here, but..."

"I do! *You* have! You personally gave me this flier, and spent eleven years attending my carnival show every night convincing me to bring you these Greegs. You conceived four children with my eldest daughter. You..."

"Look, this isn't about me, this is about you and how you can't afford to fill up your spaceship. As it so happens, I'm a generous man, err... thing, and I can tell that you're a man who knows Greegs and needs a job. It just so happens we have many fine openings for positions ranging from Greeg feces shovelers, to Greeg feces examiners."

"You bastard! What about my ship!"

"Your ship will be placed in a maze shortly... if you wish to accompany it, by all means..."

"I'll take the shovel one."

"Good man, welcome aboard. Unload your Greegs over to the left."

The ingenuity of Dr. Rip T. Brash the Third was undeniable. Whether he had purposefully, consciously or deliberately had everything come together in his favour or whether he was simply one of the luckiest creatures to ever live, I will never know. His Planetary Greeg Carnival was indeed a resounding success though, with a steady supply of enslaved workers bringing him new and exciting Greegs and their ships being sent off to far-off mazes, serving as a bribe to the Council of

Eleven and a Half Thousand Different Coloured Robes. It was a scheme no one else could have pulled off. Trading knowledge for morality, Wilx was able to learn ever more about Greegs by observing The Ultimate Grand Greeg Carnival. So much so that his well researched and engaging book *Greegs, Greegs and More Greegs* would topple Dr. Kipple's as the definitive work on the subject. Many strange discoveries would come from observing The Ultimate Grand Greeg Carnival and the ensuing experiments Wilx would conduct. For example, once aliens began coming on safari expeditions to observe The Greegs in their natural habitat, it was conclusively proven that even when blatantly staring at hoards of superior beings, The Greegs would still somehow convince themselves they were alone, intellectually dominant and that anyone who thought otherwise was insane.

One curious event occurred on the day The Virgin Mary returned to demand child support from Rip.

"I demand child support," she screamed.

"I thought your son was the one who was supposed to return?" asked Rip.

"He had a rough enough go of things the first time around, now give me some money!"

"Your entire species is obsolete silly woman, as is your outdated currency. Quit living in the past. Look what you silly humans de-evolved into!" Rip pointed at the savage Greegs nearby.

The Virgin Mary wept.

"Don't cry my dear, come into the tent and we'll have a look at your belly button."

It was around this time that I realized I couldn't be around Rip and Wilx any longer. Surely if I was to stick around I would only become more and more like them. I would begin to think nothing of grotesque and obscene actions such as they felt were acceptable. I decided to get out while I still had a shred of dignity, of sanity, of morality, of decency left in me. I was immortal, this there was no changing. But I saw no reason why I had to be a bastard too. I commandeered the ship capable of impossible things, and set about doing some good with it. If for no one else but me.

I tried travelling sideways and diagonally through time many times hoping the Universe would shift things around differently. Hoping there was a Universe out there in which people never became Greegs. An existence where Klaxworms came out of their caves and were rewarded for their courage instead of instantly annihilated. A way that the incredibly unique planet that Jorf had unwillingly created wasn't overrun with Investment Bankers and eventually Greegs. Every time the outcome was the same.

So I tried one last thing. I retraced my steps and filled in the gaps of my little story as best I could. Made sure I got everything right. Translated everything correctly. Made it all able to be understood by you. By a human being. I figure that maybe, just maybe, by bringing this information to Earth, the seemingly inevitable future of this planet is not so bleak. Is not so inevitable. By dropping off this story, at this time in your history, maybe you can be made to understand just what you are. Just where you're going. Just what this place is. Just what it could be. Just what you're doing... and what you could be doing instead. We know that one Greeg can be transformed into a decent being. We know that one little fruit fly can take on a whole planet full of filth and nonsense. But can a whole planet of beings stop themselves from de-evolving into Greegs?

Maybe.

Just Maybe...

The Epic-Log:

Excerpts from the
Dishwashing Chronicles

(as Accurately Quoted from a Tattered 14th Grade Edition Clug Raddo History Textbook)

The Dishwashing Chronicles are what define all memories and stories of the half-planet Clug Raddo. Long after the planet itself has gone extinct, the only remembered piece of information about Clug Raddo will be the reason it lost its northern hemisphere. The event of the dishes.

It was during the year of Clug Raddo's 724th revolution in the 419th millennium of this particular galaxy when it all began.

Clug Raddo was once a popular planet in the Kroonum galaxy. At the peak of its heyday it sometimes surpassed Lincra in total daily visitors. The two planets were each so popular, and close in distance, they naturally became violently bitter rivals of the tourist market. While Lincra and the rest of the Kroonum galaxy was owned by the KULMOOG, Clug Raddo was owned and operated by the Blue Splotch Restaurant Corporation. They retained their control through a very rare and highly coveted Anti-KULMOOG loophole.

No other restaurant or food distribution service was allowed to conduct business on Clug Raddo. If you wished to eat on Clug Raddo, your only choice was to visit a Blue Splotch. The other option was to bring your own food from off-planet, only it's an illegal act with severe enough punishments to ensure that no one ever considered eating from anywhere but Blue Splotch.

If you were a permanent resident of Clug Raddo, you found work at a Blue Splotch.

One of the locals was a Grelkian alien known as Blok Mardem. He worked as an underpaid dishwasher at one of the many chain locations of Blue Splotch. It was chain restaurant #1790 to be exact, but it didn't matter because all of the Blue

Splotches were the same, and had been specifically designed to be the same. Consistency was the vital factor of life amongst the Blue Splotch staff. If chain store #3092 was serving three scoops of coleslaw per order while store #9985 suddenly started serving two and a half scoops, management would have to immediately step in and bomb both of these locations. It was better to just start afresh than to risk any gamut of originality. Enough digression.

On the busiest recorded day in Blue Splotch Diner #1790, Blok Mardem reached his breaking point. Recordings indicate it was so busy that Blok, the only dishwasher working that evening, was completely unable to keep up with the onslaught of dishes. The sinks were brutally clogged with soggy, half-eaten food. There was no time to unclog the drains, so instead Blok let the sickly, orange-brown 'water' full of unknown congealed matter mercilessly overflow onto the floor, creating a deadly skating rink on the tiles. The dirty water also poured into the dishwasher. Now that the water in the dishwasher was of this variety, the dishes were coming out dirtier than when they went in. Behind Blok there were several walls lined with deep sinks, all of which were full to the brim with piping hot pans scalded with blackened over-fried teriyaki sauce and metal inserts horribly caked with burnt-on, chunky tomato soup. The serving staff, in their frantic busy-ness, had lost all interest in sorting the constant wheelbarrow loads of plates and utensils that were being cleared from the tables. Despite there having once been a time when each different type of plate was sorted into its own separate stack, they were now being tossed together in random, teetering card-house piles of butter-slathered glass, coated with crusted cheese dips and half-devoured, soggy, broccoli, all of which was routinely splashed into Blok's face from the required high water-pressure of the rinsing hose. Blok made the classic mistake of spraying into a ladle, the perfect tool for water rebound. He was struck square in the eyes with the scalding water. A server then viciously threw a handful of spoons into a cutlery bin, effectively splashing Blok with industrial-strength, corrosive chemicals. He was partially blinded for the remainder of his shift, and probably suffered some sort of life-long side effect.

Blok was going to have to stay late for hours after the restaurant closed if he had any hopes of finishing. He was expected to do exactly that, only he didn't feel like it. He wished there was some way he could get rid of the dishes. Not just the dishes at Blue Splotch #1790, but all the dishes on the planet. He liked the idea so much he devised an ingenious plan which he thought would allow him to get away with the non-washing of all dishes forever. Some say he took his plan too far. Your opinions on the sympathetic qualities of Blok Mardem will be one of the primary essay topics on the final exam.

When not washing dishes, Blok Mardem was aspiring to be one of the leading alchemical-scientists in the galaxy. He had become especially adept at the conjuring of vortexes. What was beyond the gateway of the vortexes he created was unknown, but one thing was certain, if you threw something into the vortex you would never see it again.

Blok dispatched his plan only to the dishwashers. The plan went like this:

The dishes were to be deposited into a series of tunnels, all of which would flow into the underground of the northern hemisphere. This particular dish-filled half of the planet would be amputated and aimed into the vortex. How exactly this half-a-planet would be separated is a point that we are nearly arriving at. But first, how Blok rallied together the dishwashers:

More of Blok Mardem's hobbies and skills included computer hacking and a knowledge of coded languages. He used these skills to hack into the system of the Blue Splotch payroll distribution program. Through this program he arranged for a coded message to appear on the backs of the Blue Splotch pay-cheques for the Dish department.

Blok's message announced his plans and gave an address in which the dishwasher could reply if interested. The response was unanimous. Every dishwasher on Clug Raddo agreed it was a very good idea to banish the dishes. Blok sent out charts, time-lines and blueprints, instructing each of the dishwashers to begin digging a tunnel system beneath their respective Blue Splotch restaurants.

This was not an overnight rebellion. It took years for the dishwashers to work out a properly functioning tunnel system. Amidst maniacal delusions, Blok did not think about how the population of people living on the northern hemisphere would be affected when they were sent careening into a black hole.

He also did not realize that getting rid of the dishes was a ridiculously moot point, as new dishes could be immediately delivered from Glassvexx on any day of the solar revolution.

An epic-scale vortex was conjured just outside the orbit of the planet. As impressive a display of Blok's talent as the vortex was, many of the dishwashers were still sceptical he could succeed. Luckily Blok had another hobby that would prove useful.

Aside from Blok's skills in vortex conjuring, computer hacking, dishwashing and message coding, he also had knowledge of Zhoteps, the name for the type of frightening bombs used only during mass-planetary reconstructive surgery. Blok had in his apartment a highly illegal collection of such explosives.

The dishwashers then set in motion wiring the entire equator of the planet. This was followed by prompt detonation. The blinding flash of the blast-wave can still be seen travelling through space, only just now arriving at locations untold light years away.

The dish-filled hemisphere detached and drifted into the nearby vortex. As of this writing, it has never been seen again. Miraculously, against all logic, the southern hemisphere of Clug Raddo does not careen into oblivion but continues a functional orbit with life-sustainability.

There are many myths regarding the apparent locations of the missing half of Clug Raddo. Some say the two halves were made to be the parts of a universal, god-like skeleton key, and that if the planet was ever repaired it would bring about either great prosperity or terrible doom, depending on which camp of conspiratorial-crazies you belong to.

How We Colonized Jupiter and Cleaned up Garbotron

As collected from the Cutting Room Floor,
(shortly before I decided to distance myself from Rip and Wilx.)
(with a title full of spoilers at no additional surcharge).

CHAPTER 1

Jupiter

"Did you ever watch the movie 2010?" Wilx asked me.

"Sure. Except the first one's better."

"I know. I've seen it way more times," said Wilx. "So when did humans actually first make contact?"

"It was 2020," I replied. "His prediction had misinterpreted Plato's ten-year error."

"What does Plato have to do with it?"

"Never mind. Humans didn't end up going to Jupiter until 2052," I added. "And nothing momentous happened."

"Hmm," said Wilx. "What's Jupiter like?"

"It's like Rip's ego. Big and gassy. A never-ending storm that looks interesting from afar but can be fatal from up close."

"How many planets rotate that star again?" asked Wilx.

"Five," I said. "Used to be nine, then four of them collided with each other and became the Planetglomerate."

"We will go to Jupiter," declared Wilx suddenly. "I've seen those movies and read those books enough to have interest in the matters of that planet."

"It really is just a bunch of gas," I said.

"There must be something special about it, something that made the prophet Clarke write those stories."

"He probably just picked a random planet in the galaxy. It could have just as easily been about Saturn or Neptune."

"No," said Wilx. "It is a sign. There's something about Jupiter."

"So you think if we go to Jupiter the movies will come true?"

"Not exactly, but something will happen. You never ignore a sign."

"What about the time you ignored that **'NO LEFT TURN AHEAD'** sign and we ended up being diverted through a gauntlet of Dementia-Mirrors?" I asked.

"That sign didn't say **'NO LEFT TURN AHEAD.'** It said **'NO STONE LEFT UNTURNED UNSTONED.'** Had we gotten stoned and turned rocks over at the beach we probably would have missed out on the Dementia-Mirrors. Plus we might have seen some interestingly rare aquatic creatures. What did you expect would happen?" argued Wilx.

"I don't know. Anyway, humans already went to Jupiter and nothing much happened."

"That was a long time ago. We're more prepared than humans were. I've seen 2001 more than anyone."

As much as I wanted to avoid going near the Planetglomerate, I decided to save my breath. If he wanted to go to Jupiter, that was where we would end up going. Wilx always had final say on the chartering of the ship, being that he actually knew how to run the computers.

Rip had been in cryogenic sleep for the past year, having hidden himself there in order to avoid paying the toll-booth fees of certain finicky dimensional border-crossings. He was only meant to be out for a few hours, but we hadn't got around to waking him up yet. Wilx now saw no reason of it until we reached Jupiter. I think he enjoyed the fact that our situation already seemed to mirror the film, by having a frozen team-member who would (hopefully) be awoken upon arrival at the Gas Giant.

CHAPTER 2

Where is Jupiter?

Arrival at Jupiter was anti-climactic. As we arrived, we also did not arrive. Jupiter was gone. Missing. Someone had left a moon-sized post-it note saying: **This Gas Giant has vanished for unknown reasons**.

"Bastards!" cursed Wilx.

"What do you think happened?" I asked.

"Jupiter might have been stolen to be used in warfare. Sometimes planets are used as weapons, hurled at other planets and the like. Gas giants are frequent favourites. They release the most amount of toxicity. Only uninhabited planets are allowed to be used as weapons, but it's still a barbaric practice. Stealing a planet often throws off the gravitational orbit of surrounding populated worlds."

"Jupiter isn't uninhabited," I said.

"Surely it is," said Wilx. "All gas giants are lifeless."

"No they aren't. Humans found life on Jupiter in 2052," I said.

"You said nothing happened."

"I said nothing *much* happened. Something happened. I just didn't feel like getting into the whole story."

"Tell me about these life-forms!" said Wilx excitedly.

"They exist body-less, like pure thought. You see, some of the gaseous vapours floating around actually contained a mildly intelligent consciousness. It was discovered when the vapours telepathically transmitted their collective voice into the computers. I once heard a recording. They talked like a weird Radio DJ."

"How did such a life-form come to exist?" asked Wilx. He was enthralled and thought nothing of the curious Radio DJ comment.

"Have you ever heard the rhetorical question *'If a tree falls in the woods and no one is around to hear it, does it still make a sound?'*" I asked.

"Rhetorical nonsense," said Wilx.

"It suggests that something only exists because a consciousness is present to experience it. This is very true for the life of a planet."

"Are you talking about the Life-to-Planet Totality Quotient?" asked Wilx.

"Indeed. Based on the human discoveries on Jupiter I began to believe in the theory that an uninhabited planet does not exist anywhere. Even a planet the size of Jupiter has at the very least a species of rudimentary Vapour-Thought."

"And you believe the disappearance is because of this?"

"Yes," I replied. "The Life-to-Planet Totality Quotient says that if any planet for some reason does become uninhabited, it will have a limited amount of time to acquire or create new life before it merely blinks out of existence due to its own uselessness. Like the rhetorical nonsense goes, something does not exist if it is not made real by consciousness."

"You sound like Nickbas."

"Sometimes he made a lot of sense," I said.

"Say you're right," said Wilx. "Why did Jupiter disappear if it had life?"

"The Vapours must have left the planet, whether by their own will or not."

"So this planet is just destroyed forever?"

"Not necessarily," I said. "One theory says that a vanished, lifeless planet does not cease to exist, but out of survival instinct gains the ability to teleport itself to a distant part of space, one where it might have a more hopeful chance of picking up some tourist traffic."

"You believe in this theory as well, don't you?" asked Wilx.

"Yes."

"So Jupiter is still out there somewhere?"

"It's very possible," I replied.

"Then it's time for another quest," said Wilx.

"To find the lost planet of Jupiter?"

"Yes... A Quest to Find the Lost Planet of Jupiter!"

"Ok!" I agreed. This adventure seemed more about scientific exploration than life-threatening peril, so my enthusiasm was genuine. "How do you suggest we start looking? There's a lot of space out there. Infinite amounts, in fact."

"If only we had a sample of Jupiter's atmosphere," said Wilx. "Then all we'd have to do is set up a simple tracking beacon."

"There used to be a whole museum filled with samples on Earth. It was built after the 2052 mission. But all of that was destroyed in the anti-Jupiter terrorist bombing of 2087."

"I guess that doesn't help us out."

"Maybe it does," I said. "We both know where all the garbage from Earth ended up."

"Garbotron?"

"Exactly. If the Jupiter Museum was destroyed, than the remnants of it must be lying somewhere on Garbotron. Maybe a canister of Jupiter's atmosphere has survived."

"You really want to go back there after the horrible time you had looking for that beard?" asked Wilx.

"I know someone who can help us. But we'll need some incentive. You charter the ship to Garbotron while I go peruse the deep-storage."

"Alright," agreed Wilx, despite having no idea what I was talking about.

CHAPTER 3

The Resurrection of the Quigg

You never knew what you might find in the storage section of our impossible ship. During our travels we had collected many interesting things. I had a few secret items stashed away. Stuff that was much more interesting than frozen Goat's milk. One of my rarest objects had come from the Planetglomerate. It was an intact skeleton of the now extinct Quigg species. We were long overdo for a resurrection of these incredibly useful creatures.

I carried a small cryogenic tank back to the bridge and presented the skeleton to Wilx.

"I need you to clone this creature back to life," I said.

"What creature?" asked Wilx. "Why?"

"It's a Quigg. It might be the only way to convince him to help us maneuver Garbotron."

"Convince who?"

"Milt," I replied. "You know, that nutty little fruit fly. We'll present the Quigg as a gift."

"Right," said Wilx. "I'll start up the cloning machine in a minute. First I need to work out some data on the chalkboard. The machine gets confused when presented with the genetic makeup of an unfamiliar species."

Wilx walked over to the chalkboard. The word **MEETS** had already been written in the middle of the board. Wilx attempted to erase the word, having forgotten it was permanently etched there.

"Why is the word 'meets' stuck on this chalkboard?" he asked.

"I invented that chalkboard during my time on Earth. It's meant to be used in pitch-meetings between screenwriters and movie-producers. Often writers pitch ideas by saying is a combination of two other popular movies."

"I understand the concept," said Wilx. "Movie-producers wish to invest with minimal amount of risk by merely reproducing what has already been proven to be a money-maker."

"Indeed," I replied. "I figured if a lot of people are pitching their movie merely by writing *blank* **MEETS** *blank* onto a board, then I could at least save everyone the time from spelling out the word **MEETS**. The 'Something-Meets-Something Chalkboard' was one of my most popular inventions. It sold thousands of units in Hollywood alone. It was estimated I shaved hours off the yearly schedules of those who bought one."

For someone of Wilx's technological brilliance, bringing the Quigg back to life ended up being a surprisingly easy task.

"Why don't we bring extinct species back all the time?" I asked.

"Because we don't mysteriously happen to have frozen

samples of these hypothetical species on hand."

"Good point," I said.

"For the most," continued Wilx. "If a species sucks enough at living to go extinct... it's probably for the best."

"Another good point," I said.

"But throughout the Universe, bringing back species from extinction is a supremely popular activity. There are entire planets devoted to Extinction Attraction Parks, mostly in the over-commercialized Zenib Quadrant."

"Oh, you mean like Jurassic Park."

"Dinosaurs never existed on Earth, silly. Rip put them there to test humanity's faith in Giant Lizards."

The now-living Quigg confusedly examined our ship. After a few minutes it remembered its purpose and began to scrub the floors.

"Oh, don't worry about cleaning the ship," I said to the Quigg. "Save your energy for Garbotron, you'll need it."

The Quigg either didn't hear us, or didn't understand.

"Might as well let it keep cleaning," said Wilx. "The ship could use it."

"Should we wake up Rip for the Garbotron ground-mission?" I asked.

"Yeah."

We defrosted Rip from his cryogenic sleep. He snapped awake with vigor, showing none of the groggy hangover effects common after a long sleep.

"So, what are we up to?" he asked. Wilx got him caught up.

"We're on a mission to find the recently vanished planet of Jupiter. Krimshaw believes the disappearance has been caused by the Life-to-Planet Totality Quotient, and that Jupiter is still intact somewhere in distant space. Our only hope to find it is to have a sample of its atmosphere for the tracking beacon. For a time there were samples stored in a museum on Earth, only the museum was bombed and the remnants were sent to Garbotron. We're now at Garbotron in hopes of finding a surviving piece of the atmosphere. We plan on once again asking the fruit fly Milt for directions, except we plan on actually getting directions this time by having a bribe in the form of a recently cloned specimen of a Quigg, the once extinct cleaning species."

During that rant, Rip had generally only noticed the word Garbotron.

"We're *there* again?!" he moaned. "Why did you wake me?"

"Because you might miss something amazing," replied Wilx.

"On Garbotron?"

"No, probably not on Garbotron. But later. If we find Jupiter."

CHAPTER 4

Garbotron Revisited

We put the Quigg into a cage. Within minutes the cage had been cleaned to the point where it was blindingly shiny. With nothing left to clean, the Quigg promptly sat silently and went into a catatonic meditation. We didn't realize it, but the Quigg was caught in a serious state between life and death. The Quigg anatomy requires the act of cleaning to keep itself alive. Its cellular structure began to break down as soon as every square inch of accessible surface had been polished and sterilized. But this new Quigg was fighting to break through to the next logical phase in evolution. Had the creature been given a longer life-span and a more rapid method of procreation, it would have eventually spawned a new species of Quigg capable of not only cleaning things but also of dirtying things, allowing themselves to always stay alive, even if only to be caught up in a ridiculous loop of cleaning, dirtying, cleaning, dirtying, and so on.

It was not difficult to find Milt, for his swath of clean land known as the Oviform had substantially expanded. He had been busy at work. I made sure Wilx parked the ship at least a mile away from the edge of the Oviform, so that we did not stir up any contaminants. From there we walked.

Of course we couldn't see Milt anywhere, so we had to just

walk around shouting out his name. Soon I spotted his tiny fluttering a few feet in front of me.

"What are you doing back here?" he asked irritably in his ridiculously shrill voice. "You mustn't contaminate the Oviform! Mustn't! Stand back!"

"We promise not to make a mess," I said to Milt. "We plan on staying for as little time as possible."

"But why are you here?" he asked. "There is nothing you can do here other than ruin my work. You are part of the slovenly species who did this."

"We're looking for something," I explained. "Something that might be important. This isn't for our own personal gain like the Beard of Broog. We're looking for something that might help save an entire planet."

"Continue," said Milt. The planet-saving bit had sparked his interest.

"A planet has vanished, we think due to Life-to-Planet Totality Quotient. In order to find the planet we must have some of its atmosphere for our tracking beacon. During your tireless and selfless work on this world, have you ever seen anything pertaining to the planet Jupiter? We are looking for the remnants of a museum."

"I might have seen some stuff labeled Jupiter," said Milt absently.

"Where?"

"I've already given you a map of the planet. If I've seen it, I've marked it on the map."

"But we can't read the maps," I said. "Even the magnifying glass did nothing to help."

"Surely you have computers on your space-craft that could enhance the image?"

"We do, but we don't have a map anymore. Could we have a new one please?" I asked.

"I only have my one copy left and I'm not willing to loan it out," said Milt.

"Then could you just take us there? That would be easier."

"Yes it would," said Milt. "Easier for you anyway. But I'm afraid I don't have the time. I've got a lot of work to do."

"It won't take that long," I said. "We don't have to walk. We have a ship."

"Look, I just don't want to help you," said Milt in a surprisingly stern tone for such a shrill voice.

"What if we could help you in return?" I asked.

"How could you possibly help me? Your mere presence damages the atmosphere. The exhalation of your breath is a veritable explosion of toxic carbon-compounds. A minutes worth of your breath sets me back a week of work."

"What if we gave you something that every minute *saved* you a *month* of work?"

"Impossible," said Milt. "There is no cleaning machine that powerful."

"Machine, no. But there is a life form that powerful. They're called Quiggs."

"A Quigg?" asked Milt. He had read about them many times, always believing them to be mythical. "Quiggs aren't real. I've always wished they were, but they aren't."

"They *were* real. But they went extinct. We've managed to clone one from a long dormant tissue sample. Weren't we just talking about *Jurassic Park*? Nevermind. The point is, we'll give you a Quigg if you help us. You have no idea what this creature can do for the planet. You'll be retired in no time."

"Let me see it," said Milt.

I produced the cage. Since we'd stepped off the ship the Quigg had been wide-awake and going crazy with the smell of garbage. We opened the cage-door and the Quigg came rolling out.

"Wow," said Milt as he noticed it had brushes, scrubbers and buffers where there should have been arms, legs and feet.

The Quigg seemed to be going into a spastic fit at the sight and smell of so much garbage. It could not handle the overload of filth. It began shaking so intensely it looked as if it was about to implode. Then the strangest yet most appropriate thing happened. The Quigg split into two Quiggs. It seems one look at Garbotron was enough to set the evolution of the Quigg back in full motion. There was no time for cloning or intercourse. More Quiggs were needed so badly that the sole member of one of the most useful species in existence was at once granted the power of instant replication. Within a few minutes there were half a dozen Quiggs hard at work.

"Amazing!" beamed Milt. "Sensational! Legendary! It's the most beautiful thing I've ever seen!"

"Enough for us to deserve your help?" I asked.

"Yes, yes, I'll help you find this Jupiter sample," said Milt as the Quiggs continued to multiply. "Although that might be a problem. At the rate they're replicating and cleaning, we're likely to not find anything! I know where the Jupiter Museum is. It's not far, just across the swamp."

Milt hurriedly directed us through a complex maze that we never would have been able to traverse without his expert help. At last we caught sight of a charred shell of a building with a sign that read **JUPITER MUSEUM NOW OPEN**.

"The building is still somewhat intact," noticed Wilx. "Didn't you say it was bombed?"

"I thought it was," I said. "It must have just been a fire. It's hard to remember everything when you're immortal."

"Too true," agreed Rip.

"Let's start looking," said Wilx. "Everyone take a different wing of the Museum. Don't fall through any burnt floorboards!"

We walked towards the entrance of the museum.

"Do you mind if I push off now?" asked Milt. "I'm curious to get back to the Oviform and check on the progress of the Quiggs."

"Go ahead, we should be fine here," I said.

"Thank you again for the gift you have bestowed upon this troubled planet," he said as he flew back to the Oviform.

CHAPTER 5

Something Excellent

After hours of sifting through the rubble, it was Wilx who finally found an uninjured sample of Jupiter. He had always been the best at finding things.

"Here it is!" he shouted exuberantly. "I found it!"

He held out a clear cylinder.

"It's made of glass," I said. "Amazing it hasn't shattered after all these years."

"It can't shatter," said Wilx, reading the fine print on the bottom of the container. "It's made of unbreakable Jardian mega-prisms."

"I think we proved that Jardian mega-prisms aren't unbreakable with the whole Chalkboard of Elbereth scenario," stated Rip.

"Right. *Nearly* unbreakable Jardian Mega-prisms," corrected Wilx.

We gathered around the sample. Brownish-red gaseous vapor mixed with itself in an amazingly psychedelic way.

"It's so... hypnotizing," drooled Rip as he grabbed the container and unscrewed the cap.

"What are you doing?!" shouted Wilx. "You'll let it escape!"

Rip proceeded to drink the entire contents of the Jupiter sample. We then had one of our typical moments of silence as we contemplated Rip's insane decisions.

First he bubbled out his ears. Then his pupils crazily swirled like black ink diffusing in a saucer-full of curdled milk. He began to rant about ridiculous prophecies that he thought were being channeled to him from the missing entities of Jupiter.

"I... understand," whispered Rip in an usually high voice. He then turned and collapsed in such a manner that made his body look like a twisted heap of cheap rag-doll limbs.

As soon as he woke up a few hours later, we questioned him about why he had done such a thing.

"I don't know," he replied. "It seemed like the right thing to do. What happened anyway?"

"You kept talking about these prophecies you thought you were channeling," said Wilx. "Then you said 'I understand.' What did you understand? Did you actually have a connection with some sort of entity? Did it tell you where Jupiter has gone?"

"Yes," said Rip. "I saw and understood everything about the fate of Jupiter."

"Well?!" asked Wilx.

"Oh, I don't remember any of it. You probably should have been writing it down I guess."

"That's it then," said Wilx dejectedly. "You drank away our only chance of finding Jupiter."

"Not necessarily," said Rip as he covered his mouth. "It's not sitting too well. I think it's on the way up."

He grabbed the container and threw up.

"Here you go," he wheezed, before passing out again for a few hours. Rather than wait for him to wake up we just lugged his body onto the ship.

The Quiggs had continued to multiply at an unbelievable rate. From orbit we could see the cleanliness of the Oviform spreading outwards like a meteoric strike. It seemed as if the whole planet would be repaired in a matter of days. Quiggs were saving the planet they had once plotted to help destroy.

How were the Quiggs getting rid of all the garbage, you ask? While Quiggs of the past were excellent cleaners, they still needed a space in which to send unwanted material (hence their former plan to have all the Greeg garbage blasted off the planet), however these new Garbotron-Evolved Quiggs were far more powerful. They had developed the power to break matter down to the point where it took up virtually no space at all. For instance, *Diaper Mountain* was condensed down to one-third the size of a single dust particle. The *Lake of Liquids* now wouldn't even fill a fruit-fly's drinking glass, and *The Wall of Leftover Cheese-Like Products* now took up no more space than one or two of Julius Caesar's left nostril-hairs.

We decided to check back in on the progress of Garbotron after the Jupiter Mission.

CHAPTER 6

Johnny Guitar Says "No Gas Giant Can Stay Lost Forever!"

Wilx fed the atmosphere sample into the tracking system. All we had to do was relax and let the ship take us across the universe to the matching source.

"Earlier, when you drank the atmosphere, why did it make your voice so high?" I asked Rip.

"I don't know," he replied.

"That's easy," said Wilx. "One-quarter of Jupiter is comprised of helium."

"Interesting," said Rip. "I thought I grew an immunity to helium when I spent a year on that Balloon-World."

"Ssh, I see it," said Wilx with awe as the sight of Jupiter appeared on-screen.

A disembodied voice suddenly amplified itself through the computer. It was not nearly as shocking as previously similar events like with Fralgoth on Garbotron or the Stockholm Robot Squad on Hroon. We had become accustomed to the unexpected arrival of disembodied voices.

This time the voice was vaguely familiar to me.

"Now it's time for the traffic report," it said. *"Ok... there's plenty of room in space. If you see a traffic jam... go around it! That forever concludes the traffic report. Next up is the entirety of about 26 progressive rock albums played in a row, as I've been broadcasting for 89 hours straight and am in desperate need of a quick break. We will begin with The Troll-Creatures seminal self-titled debut record, a 224 minute single-track opus based on a mystical myriad of Tolkien-esque fantasies. The inspired free-style album was recorded in one take during a potentially inebriated evening in the Mobile Studio at Mick Jagger's Stargroves, after which Mick casually stated: 'It was a decent jam, the details of which I remember not at all.' Alright, here we go... The Troll-Creatures..."*

"It's the voice of the Vapors!" I said. "They're back on Jupiter!"

"What? That isn't the voice of any Vapor-Beings,"

corrected Wilx.

"Who is it then?"

"That's Johnny Guitar, Immortal Superstar DJ for *Radio Cygnus 85.3*, the most popular radio station anywhere. He's been around for centuries and is known for his wild, erratic behavior and marathon bouts of uninterrupted broadcast that sometimes last for weeks on end. Looks like we had the misfortune of tuning in just as he's taking a break."

"If this Johnny Guitar isn't a Vapor-Being, then how is he inhabiting Jupiter?" I asked.

"He's not," replied Wilx.

"Isn't the broadcast coming directly from this planet?"

"This station can appear to come from many different worlds," he replied. "We're hearing it now because planets with heavy radio emission are sometimes known to pick up and broadcast the frequencies of *Radio Cygnus*, beyond the control of the actual listener/ship-owner. No one knows whether it's accidental, or a corporate conspiracy to force people into listening to the radio. In this case I think it has something to do with Jupiter's Magnetosphere."

"How so?" I asked.

"Well, Jupiter's Magnetosphere is caused by eddy currents – swirling movements of conducting materials – within the metallic hydrogen core. First the volcanoes of the moon Io emit sulfur dioxide, forming a gas torus around the moon's orbit. The gas torus is then ionized in Jupiter's magnetosphere, producing oxygen ions. These ions mix with the hydrogen atmosphere of Jupiter, forming a plasma sheet in the equatorial plane. The electrons within the plasma sheet produce strong radio emissions from the polar regions of Jupiter, the very region around which we are currently orbiting. I think this is what's causing the sudden broadcast of *Radio Cygnus*."

"So when humans thought they'd discovered life on Jupiter, they had merely picked up a passing radio station?"

"It seems so," said Wilx. "I should have known what you were talking about when you said they sounded like a weird Radio DJ. I guess discovering life on Jupiter is just another thing that humans didn't do."

"Crazy," I replied.

We listened for a minute to the dense, intoxicating sound of *The Troll-Creatures*. Beneath the layered nuance of improvisational psychedelic space-guitar solos, extended brain-warping keyboard excursions, pompously gritty rapid-fire bass licks and the paradigm of deafening rapturous double-kick drum-beats, we could just faintly hear the sound of Mick's footsteps as he wildly danced in the background. This album was known for having accidentally recorded such percussive marvels for the ages.

"So this means there still isn't life on Jupiter?" I finally continued.

"Yes," said Wilx.

"Then we should try to find some, before the planet vanishes again."

"A good idea," jumped in Rip. "Only where are we going to find the life for such a heinous environment?"

"Research suggests any life to spring up on Jupiter would likely be ammonia-based."

"Ok," said Rip. "Do we know any ammonia-based life-forms?"

"Not really," said Wilx. "Have you ever met any ammonia-based life-forms?" he asked me.

"Can't say I have."

"That solves that problem," said Rip. "Now let's go find something else to do!"

"Wait," I said. "What if put out an ad? Urging ammonia-based life-forms to save Jupiter and live in harmony?"

"We'll need to advertise all over the universe," said Rip. "How are we going to do that?"

"I think that's been answered for us," I replied. "We'll go to the *Radio Cygnus* Station and ask Johnny Guitar to place an ad for us."

"That's a plan!" shouted Rip, suddenly regaining interest in our current adventure. "I've always wanted to go to *Radio Cygnus* and meet Johnny. I hear it's a paradise, a nonstop epic party-zone located in the most luxurious building made of shiny things."

Even Wilx admitted using radio was a good idea, albeit a difficult one.

"Let's not get our hopes up," he said. "Not only have I never heard of Johnny Guitar taking requests, placing advertisements or speaking to his fans, I also hear the *Radio Cygnus* Station is not at all the idyllic experience that Rip imagines it to be, but rather a heavily guarded bureaucratic wasteland. A very anti-luxurious and boring gray concrete building. It amazes me that Johnny is able to perform so exuberantly within such a stifling, anti-artistic environment."

"We'll see who's right," said Rip.

CHAPTER 7

The History of Johnny Guitar

They were both right in different aspects. The *Radio Cygnus* building was indeed luxurious and made of shiny things, however it was also heavily guarded and annoyingly bureaucratic. It was clear we were going to have to sneak in.

"Here, hold your breath," Wilx said as he scanned us with a bizarre looking scanning device.

"What are you doing?" I asked, alarmed.

"I'm going to encase us in Illusion Bubbles," he replied. "The effect can crush your lungs if you're mid-breath when the barrier seals."

"Illusion Bubbles?" I asked, before holding my breath.

"You will appear to everyone who sees you as whatever I program you to look like. In this case I have all of us looking like suit-wearing *Radio Cygnus* executives."

"This whole time you've had a device that can make us look like anyone... and you're just now producing it?" I started. "Do you have any idea how often this would have come in handy? That whole long bit with us looking for the Beard of Broog and impersonating the Kulmoog Commander Flook would have been totally moot. We could have just disguised ourselves as Flook at any time."

"I lost this device years ago. I only just found it when I was emptying out all my pockets on Hroon, and it hasn't been needed since then."

"Oh."

We looked like a regular group of executives. The barrier of the bubble was visible from within, blurring everything beyond it into a wavy mirage. To myself I still looked normal, but when I looked at Rip or Wilx I saw the illusion.

"Alright, let's do this," said Wilx as we approached the front door. "Don't attract unnecessary attention."

The lobby of *Radio Cygnus* was a vast, brightly-lit room, perpetually clean, dazzlingly shiny, mostly empty except for a marble desk lining one of the walls with a receptionist or two hovering about every few hundred meters, while generally every few meters a squadron of heavily armed guards lurked menacingly. The ratio of receptionist to armed guard was disturbingly off-kilter and instantly tuned one into the fact that *Radio Cygnus* is not a cool place. They were clearly not interested in guiding you or answering your questions, but did look adept at getting you off the property as soon as possible. The intimidating appearance of each of the guards was so similar that it was obvious they were merely clones of the single perfect warrior.

We figured that asking one of the scant receptionists for directions was a bad idea, as only outsiders would need directions. We jumped on the first elevator.

"Do we know where we're going?" I said as I looked at the number-pad. "There are more than two thousand floors!"

"No idea," replied Wilx.

"Floor 952," stated Rip. "It's gotta be."

"How do you know that's the right floor?" I asked.

"Deus Ex Machina?" suggested Wilx.

"It's a number I saw flash before my eyes after I drank the Jupiter atmosphere."

"I thought you didn't remember anything?" asked Wilx.

"This just came back to me. I remembered the part I was supposed to remember."

"It's worth a try," I said. At times I suspected some of Rip's mad prophecies were legitimate and not being given the proper chance to prove themselves as such.

Wilx punched the button for the 952nd floor. We were rocketed upwards at an amazing speed.

"This is even faster than the floating elevator from our old Obotron," remarked Wilx.

"If you jump just as the elevator is stopping you can experience a moment of weightlessness," said Rip, as he did just that. He winced and clutched at his abdomen. "I think I just displaced one of my stomachs."

The elevator doors opened. Immediately we heard the voice of Johnny Guitar.

"Excellent," said Wilx.

"I've always wanted to meet Johnny Guitar!" said Rip as he bounded into the room like a starstruck child. "They say you aren't anybody until you've met Johnny Guitar!"

"Ssh," said Wilx.

We wandered around the rooms of floor 952. There appeared to be no one at all.

"Where is he?" asked Rip. "I hear him!"

"We could easily just be hearing a radio. Did you think of that?" asked Wilx.

"He's here, I can sense it."

"What are all these tapes?" I asked, noticing that every room on this floor was filled to the roof with mini-cassette tapes.

We looked at the tapes. They were all recordings of past Johnny Guitar shows.

"This must be the legendary archives," said Rip. "Johnny has broadcast more hours than anyone."

We continued looking for the source of Johnny Guitar's voice amongst the perplexing multitudes of tapes.

"We must have the wrong floor," said Wilx.

"Let's look for a little longer before we move on," said Rip.

"What are all these mechanical tracks running along the floors, walls and roof?" I asked. There were strange things going on that were obvious and yet still eluded us.

"I'm not sure," said Wilx.

"Over there!" I shouted. "Something moved along the tracks!"

"Where?" asked Rip.

"There! It happened again!"

We all began to catch glimpses of small robots zipping along the tracks.

"They look like tiny train-carts," I said. "And they're all filled with tapes."

"The archivists are robotic," said Rip. "They must exist in a constant state of mixing and categorizing."

Suddenly an intricate robotic arm passed through the room.

"Look at that hand-thing!" said Rip. "It grabbed one of the tapes. Let's follow it!"

We ran as fast as we could. We finally reached an uninhabited sound-booth. A door opened and the robotic arm went inside. We quickly followed before the door closed.

An old-fashioned cassette player was positioned in the middle of the booth. The robotic arm took out the current tape and placed in the new one.

"This must be like a 24-hour Best-Of mix that plays in the archives as an interesting attraction," said Rip.

"No, I don't think so," said Wilx. "This is the live radio feed."

"What do you mean?" asked Rip, even though it was painfully obvious.

"Isn't it painfully obvious," I said. "There is no Johnny Guitar, except on tape."

"No, that can't be true!" argued Rip. "Johnny Guitar is one of my heroes!"

"This is indeed very shocking news," stated Wilx solemnly.

If space/time-travelers didn't have such difficulty in knowing which current events are actually current, then many radio-listeners would have figured out years ago that Johnny Guitar's news updates are always ludicrously random and out-of-date.

"So you figured out our secret," said the funny little scary man who suddenly materialized beside us. The jolt of his appearance was enough to shock Rip's displaced stomach back into proper positioning.

"Who are you?" asked Wilx.

"I am Chancellor Groomfleg. I own this Radio station."

"What's going on here?" demanded Rip. "What have you done with Johnny Guitar?"

"Johnny Guitar died several centuries ago. Sit down, I'll explain everything."

The Chancellor went into great detail about the history of Johnny Guitar.

It went like this:

Groomfleg's ancient ancestors built for themselves a small-time radio station. They hadn't expected to make much with it. Johnny Guitar was hired simply because he was willing to work early in the morning at half the price. The Groomfleg's were unaware they had hired the greatest Radio DJ who would ever grace the microphone. Johnny's amusing freestyle wit paired with perfect articulation projected so powerfully and charismatically that he made you believe you'd be missing out on the greatest moments in life when you weren't listening to the show. Overnight he became the most popular program anywhere in space. Advertisement prices during Johnny's show went for millions per second. It was obvious he should be the only show on the station. Out of greediness to have Johnny on air as much as possible, he was bribed with exorbitant amounts of money to broadcast all day and all night; despite the irreversible havoc wreaked on his health and mental state by such a perpetually rigorous schedule. He often suffered extreme mental breakdowns caused by a denial of bathroom breaks and a total lack of sleep, going into maniacal, improvisatory rants for hours at a time while popping speed capsules like one-cent candies and banging objects against the wall in what he thought was musical rhythm but was actually a deafening cacophonous racket. He was frequently the subject of so many neighborhood noise complaints that eventually there were only two choices: end the Johnny Guitar show, or demolish every house within earshot of the station. Someone then suggested a third option, remove Johnny's ability to make noise by removing all items from the sound-booth. Without dishes or guitars or any other object to hurl, Johnny's percussive participation was limited to the much less noisy banging of his fists against the wall, which was only audible within a few surrounding floors of the building. Some listeners considered these drug-infused episodes to be his most organically inspired moments of broadcasting, a fascinating anarchic view into the twisted depths of a genius mind, while others said the show had grown intolerable, just another sad case of a great talent having been usurped and burned out too quickly by greed-dominated corporations. Soon enough, Johnny Guitar died of an overdose. *Radio Cygnus* was intensely fearful of the bankrupting backlash his death would cause, for at this point the entirety of their business was based on Johnny. They could never hope to replace him. A cover-up was essential. His spent corpse was quietly and briskly taken from the sound-booth and cremated in the basement furnace. Only a small handful of top executives were aware of his death. They quickly set in motion a plan to make sure Johnny Guitar never really stopped broadcasting. For awhile bits of old tapes of Johnny's show were spliced together to create the illusion of a new show, however it was apparent this would not fool everyone forever. A top-secret organization of brilliant scientists and inventors were then employed to invent a translator-machine that not only replicated the voice of Johnny Guitar, but captured his essence and originality as well. After countless hours of analyzing the tapes of Johnny's voice, they finally perfected a machine in which any person could say anything into a microphone and it would be altered into sounding like a brand-new Johnny Guitar broadcast. With this machine you could literally monotonously read from a dull book about tax audits and it would be translated into an exciting new album review by Johnny. Most of the tapes in the archive were not even original Johnny broadcasts, but rather these fake recordings. Johnny Guitar, whom everyone assumes is immortal, has been heard broadcasting on *Radio Cygnus* for about 426 years, despite the fact that he died at the tender age of 32.

"And all these robots," concluded Groomfleg, "are perpetually sifting through the tapes, always perfecting the translation machine."

We sat in stunned silence before Wilx remembered our original intent for being here.

"That's an interesting story," he said to Groomfleg. "Now I apologize for doing this," he added as he shot him in the chest. Groomfleg collapsed to the floor, not dead, only stunned.

"You two tie him up in case he wakes up early," Wilx said to us. "I've got a broadcast to make."

"Are you going to tell everyone that Johnny is dead?" asked Rip.

"Nah, let's let them continue enjoying their show. We came here to find some life for Jupiter."

"When you talk through the microphone, won't it come out in different words, because of the translation?" asked Rip.

"There must be a setting so that you can continue to sound like Johnny Guitar without having the actual words being altered," I suggested.

"Yep, here it is," said Wilx as he switched around a few of the programmings on the translation machine. He clicked off the current tape and spoke into the microphone. We all marveled as Wilx talked with the voice and enthusiasm of Johnny Guitar.

"Ok everyone, I apologize for interrupting the crescendo of that fourteen hour song, but we have an emergency broadcast. It seems there is a very nice gas giant planet named Jupiter that is suffering from continual disappearances due to being completely uninhabited. That's right folks, the Life-to-Planet Totality Quotient is real and in full effect. I have decided to make it a mission of mine to save this planet from its terrible state of limbo, so I'm urging some life-forms to begin colonizing this planet. Jupiter is primarily hydrogen and helium, and it is likely the best suited life-forms would be ammonia-based. If any of you faithful listeners out there are made of ammonia and are in need of a home, please swing by Jupiter and have a look. I'm going to broadcast the location coordinates now."

Wilx programmed in the coordinates and set the whole

thing to loop for several hours before returning to the regular Johnny Guitar broadcast.

"That should do it," he said satisfyingly. "Now let's get out of this mad place."

"What about him?" I asked, pointing to the lump on the floor that was Chancellor Groomfleg.

"Leave him. He'll wake up in a few hours with no memory of us or of having spilled the secret about Johnny."

We got in the elevator.

"Everyone jump!" said Rip just as the elevator was about to stop at the Lobby floor. We all jumped and experienced a pleasant moment of weightlessness. Nobody had their stomach displaced at all. It was just the sort of tranquil experience we were due for, especially since the Layer of Transcendental Levitation on Lincra had been destroyed. I made a note to spend more time in the Zero-Gravity room once we got back on the ship.

As soon as we stepped off the elevator a series of whooping alarms sounded.

"**INTRUDER! INTRUDER!**" shouted yet another disembodied voice.

None of us were aware our Illusion Bubbles had long since worn off. Now we were just a bizarre group of aliens standing unwanted in a corporate environment protecting itself from bankruptcy with murderous inclinations. It was at this moment, as we successfully ran out the front door and onto our ship, that I realized most of the armed guards we tended to find ourselves running away from would have a much easier time of catching us if they weren't burdened down with the excessive weight of armor. As it were, none of the warrior-clone guards could move much faster than the average Romero zombie. They also couldn't shoot due to terrible aim and eyesight, having not been cloned from the perfect warrior but rather from some regular dweeb with poor vision.

"I hope this works," said Wilx as we fled from the *Radio Cygnus* Planet.

CHAPTER 8

the Fourth and Final Whizzling-Firebeam Asteroid Shower

Just as we had planned, on our way back to Jupiter we stopped in to have a look at the success of Garbotron. In our brief absence the Quiggs had completely transformed the planet. At first we thought we had arrived at the wrong system. There was no trace of garbage. The dense smog barrier encasing the planet had fully dissipated, allowing vital sunlight to resurrect the dormant core of life. The once dead land had already begun to heal itself in profound ways, sprouting miles of lush forestry and flowing rivers. The Great Salted Desert-Land of Garbotron, dried-up seemingly beyond repair from ages of having been used as the primary dump-site for potato chip crumbs, was now a paradisiacal oasis. We spotted a new evolution of mammal-creatures peacefully drinking from freshly formed pools of the purest crystalline water.

It was evident that bringing a Quigg to Garbotron was one of our great triumphs amidst multitudes of disastrous decisions. In our mission to save one world we inadvertently saved another.

Arrival at Jupiter was an incredible sight. Thousands of ships belonging to Investment Banker Protests were forming a message with their classic hand drawn signs held up against windows, this time reading:

YES

Everyone had heard about the mysterious looping broadcast that had interrupted Johnny Guitar's show. Legions of ammonia-based vapor-beings crawled from the wood-works of space and placed calls to uninterested receptionists at *Radio Cygnus*, requesting to know about Jupiter. It seems they had been having a hard time finding a suitable uninhabited planet, being just a bunch of toxic clouds that couldn't go to most places without destroying the atmosphere and killing whatever life happened to already be living there. As a result, the Vapors found themselves endlessly drifting through space, homeless. They were incredibly happy with the news of Jupiter and announced they were on their way to the new world.

Word spread about the selfless good deed Johnny Guitar had performed. A wealthy family had been so moved by the story that they decided to spend a little money on a house-warming present for the Vapors. They employed the sign-making skills of the Investment Banker Preservationists to display a positive message as the Vapors arrived. The IBP had long ago put aside their protest movement. They were undeniably brilliant at coordinating space-messages, getting so many offers for their service that it eventually left them little time for protests. They were a now a full-time sign-making business, but hadn't bothered to change their name. For the right price any message can be displayed prominently enough to be seen by the naked eye from up to 17 light years away. The wealthy family in question weren't against giving out the occasional gift, but they were still extraordinarily cheap, and being that IBP messages are steeply charged by the letter, it was decided the message should simply be the affordable word 'yes,' the most succinct positive message anyone could think of. One of the cheapest members of the family did try to lobby for the word 'n,' which in Lincran dialect can sometimes mean 'peace,' but it was decided the word 'n' is too easily mistranslated into something offensive in a thousand other alien languages.

"All those years ago humans thought the voice of Johnny Guitar was a race of Vapor-Beings," I said. "Now we've used that voice to bring such life here. One can't deny that as a premonition."

"It's a shame that fake Johnny Guitar is getting credit for saving Jupiter," grumbled Rip.

"Right now I know a character named Milt is giving us credit for saving his world," said Wilx. "I guess that's good enough for me."

Suddenly the fourth and final Whizzling-Firebeam Asteroid shower began.

Made in the USA
San Bernardino, CA
05 December 2013